WICKED UNION

JILLIAN FROST

WICKED UNION

JILLIAN FROST

Also by Jillian Frost

Princes of Devil's Creek

Cruel Princes

Vicious Queen

Savage Knights

Battle King

Boardwalk Mafia

Boardwalk Kings

Boardwalk Queen

Boardwalk Reign

Devil's Creek Standalone Novels

Wicked Union

For a complete list of books, visit JillianFrost.com.

WICKED UNION

JILLIAN FROST

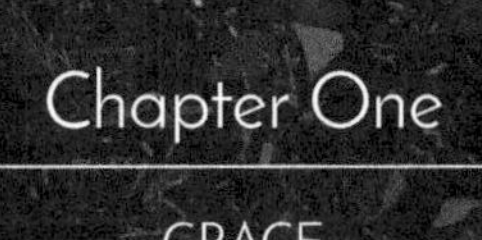

Chapter One

GRACE

Ten years ago, I died, replaced by someone else. Katarina was a distant memory of the past. A girl who laughed and loved life. Someone who didn't know the real monsters of the world were wealthy men in suits.

"These people know who I *really* am," I told my grandfather as the limousine journeyed up the steep hill. "Does that mean I can go back to being Katarina?"

The founders of Devil's Creek and their children were aware of my situation. They understood why my grandfather changed my name to Grace and sent me to live with Colonel John Hale. I'd been using my new name for ten years. But sometimes, I wanted to return to the girl I was before my life went to shit.

"You're never to use the name Katarina Adams Romanov," my grandfather said in a firm tone as we headed down Founders Way. "She's dead."

"I don't want to pretend anymore."

I knew better than to speak out of turn with my grandfather. So when he slapped me across the face, I expected it.

"Don't you dare talk back. If not for me, you would have been in the foster care system."

If only I were that lucky…

I rubbed my sore cheek and sighed.

His jaw clenched as he studied my face. "I showed you mercy by sending you to live with the Colonel."

My grandfather was the wealthiest man in the world. He owned banks, tech and oil companies, and a list of other businesses he probably strong-armed the owners into selling.

Despite growing up with so much wealth, I never had anything. For the three years that I lived with him, he imprisoned me in his mansion and home-schooled me. I never had friends or left the confines of his house. We lived on the beach, but he never let me go beyond the front gate.

After my mother's murder, my grandfather sent my father to a prison on the sea. But when I was eleven, he escaped and had been looking for me since. If the rumors were true, my father was an evil man.

A terrorist.

So I became Grace Hale.

With each day I lived with my grandfather, my heart slowly blackened, the anger and rage bubbling inside me. I even wondered if I was like my biological father.

Then, a stranger saved me. The Colonel became my dad.

I had a family again.

So I soaked up my freedom with my adoptive father. He gave me everything I never had with my grandfather. We got to travel the world and live on military bases.

My dad was like a brother to a man named Mark Marshall. He lived in Devil's Creek, a small town on the coast of Connecticut. The residents were my grandfather's allies and loyal to him.

We could trust them.

The Colonel was away for the summer on a training mission for the Marine Corps. While he was gone, I would live with Mark Marshall and his family. Only five families lived on Founders Way. They were rich, powerful, and connected, and I feared they would be cruel and hateful like my grandfather.

My heart clambered in my chest as the limousine stopped

at the guarded gate. I could see why they called this place Fort
Marshall. The estate looked like an old fortress on the sea,
with armed men dressed in black camouflage clutching
machine guns.

You couldn't see much beyond the high brick walls. The
home was set so far back on the property I could only make
out a pointed tower that reminded me of architecture from
another century.

We parked in front of the three-story mansion with dozens
of windows and painted shutters.

This wasn't a home.

It was a compound.

Aside from the main house, there were five other buildings
on the property that I could see. They had three garages with
several exotic cars parked out front.

My grandfather's home took up half a block but always
felt small. Probably because I stared at the same four walls for
years. I even ate most of my meals in that room.

"I better not hear anything but praise from the Marshalls."
My grandfather's haunting eyes locked on me. "They have
three boys. One is your age. You are your mother's daughter.
Don't get any ideas."

Like what?

He often made backhanded comments about my parents.
I didn't bother to ask questions. My cheek still stung from his
hand, and I didn't want to anger him. It was best to follow his
rules.

I learned the hard way that Fitzgerald Archibald Adams
IV always got what he wanted. And as he often reminded me,
some *silly girl* would not get in his way.

"The boys are not to touch you," he said when the driver
opened the door. "They are under strict orders to keep their
filthy hands to themselves. And I expect you to act like a lady."

I almost laughed in his face but bit my tongue. He never
gave a damn about me. So why would he care if a boy
touched me?

"Do you understand me, Grace?" Grandfather said when I didn't confirm.

"Yes."

The Marshalls came from old money and had connections from here to the White House.

"The Colonel will pick you up at the end of the summer," my grandfather added. "If you try to run, I will drag you back to my estate and chain you to the basement floor." He pointed a long, bony finger at me. "And this time, you won't leave my house."

A shiver rushed down my arms at his threat. It wouldn't have been the first time he did that to me. I was eight when I lost my parents. Eleven when I finally left my grandfather's estate. Until then, I didn't know there were sick, demented people in the world. I had no idea someone could be so heartless.

I strolled into the mansion beside my grandfather, dressed in a baby blue sundress. He had insisted I wear this and even hired a woman to coat my face in makeup.

I looked like a doll.

Pink cheeks and long, blonde hair that spilled down my back in thick barrel curls. The woman applied several layers of eyeshadow that made my blue eyes appear as if they were jumping off my face.

I didn't look like me.

We followed the butler into the great room. It was ten times the size of my current living room and had a dozen windows. The ceiling was at least twenty feet high, decorated with wood planks.

My grandfather's house was equally impressive but looked more like a museum than a home. Cold and uninviting like him.

A tall man with black hair stood beside a beautiful blonde woman. Three boys clung to her side, the oldest of the group blond like her and taller than his dad. The other two boys were identical twins and had their father's black hair.

The man and his wife closed the distance between us, the oldest boy a few steps behind. I couldn't take my eyes off him.

"Fitzy," the black-haired man said with his hand extended. "Welcome back to Fort Marshall. How was your drive to Devil's Creek?"

Grandfather preferred the nickname Fitzy. No one ever called him Fitzgerald, per his request. It was strange that the uptight bastard would let anyone call him something so informal. But no one challenged him.

"Tiring," Grandfather grumbled. "Let's get on with it."

He hated pleasantries and small talk. Most people didn't bother to speak unless he asked a question.

The dark-haired man offered his hand. "I'm Mark Marshall. And you must be Grace."

I forced a smile. "Nice to meet you. Thank you for letting me stay at your home. It's beautiful."

The words sounded rehearsed as they left my mouth. My grandfather went through the script on our drive from The Hamptons to Devil's Creek.

The blonde woman was close to my height and wrapped her arms around me. "Hi, Grace," she said in a sweet tone. She had kind blue eyes and a warm smile. "I'm Willow Marshall. It's so nice to meet you, sweetheart."

She held me in her arms like we had known each other forever. I instantly lowered my guard in her presence. Willow reminded me of my mom.

The oldest boy moved in front of her. He was probably around my age, early twenties at most. "I'm Colton." He offered his hand for me to shake. "But everyone calls me Cole."

Cole Marshall was the cutest boy I had ever met. I shook his hand and avoided his gaze to still the nerves coursing through my body.

The twins didn't speak as they stared at my breasts. Willow said their names were Sloan and Knox, but I couldn't tell them apart.

"Cole." Mark tapped his son on the back. "Why don't you show Grace the movie theater? I have business to discuss with Fitzy."

His eyes met mine, so big and blue, the color of the ocean. "Do you like Marvel movies?"

I pressed my lips together and nodded.

Cole dragged me out of the room and led me down a long hallway with the shiniest white marble floor. I could see my reflection in the tile.

He slipped his fingers between mine, and as we walked through the house, my hand trembled.

"You don't have to fear me. I won't hurt you."

Everyone in my life hurt me at some point. The Colonel was the only person who kept his promise. He taught me how to survive and how to fight. I wasn't the same scared girl anymore because of him.

We entered a room at the back of the house with movie theater seating and a concession stand. My grandfather had a similar space in his home, but I couldn't use it. I entered without his permission once, and he locked me in the basement.

Cole slid behind the counter and grabbed the box of kernels. After he prepared the popcorn, we sat in the back row, eating and watching the first Captain America movie. His eyes didn't leave the screen, though I caught him looking at me a few times.

Midway through the movie, Cole moved his hand to the space between us, tapping his long fingers on the leather chair. I felt a strange connection to him and inched my fingers closer. We didn't touch, but I could feel the heat radiating off his skin.

I leaned over and whispered, "Can I tell you a secret?"

He angled his body to look at me. "You can tell me anything."

"My name isn't Grace."

I had been dying to tell someone.

A frown tugged at his mouth. "I know."

"It's been years, and my grandfather won't let me use my name."

Cole took a deep breath, shoving his fingers through his white-blond hair. "You're in danger. Bad people are looking for you. But you don't have to worry." He gave my hand a reassuring squeeze. "The Knights will protect you."

The Devil's Knights. One of many secret societies overseen by my grandfather. He had his hand in everything.

"So you follow my grandfather's orders, too?"

He nodded. "Fitzy is a very powerful man who controls our futures." A hint of sadness crossed his handsome face. "We all have to answer to someone. And that someone is your grandfather."

We were the same.

Not completely free.

Our lips almost touched when he leaned closer. "I meant what I said, Grace. I will always protect you. You never have to be afraid again."

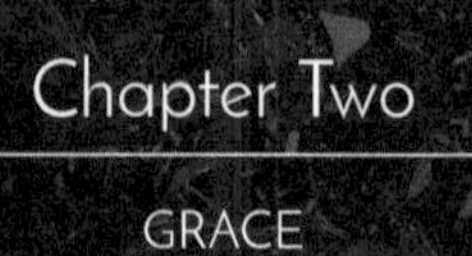

Chapter Two

GRACE

I studied every inch of the house as we left the theater, still not over the fact the Marshalls had a bowling alley. When I asked Cole about it, he said, "We only have eight lanes."

The horror.

I assumed since he lived in a house the size of a small city and it had a name like Fort Marshall, what seemed like great accommodations to me were nothing to Cole. He was used to a lifestyle my grandfather never afforded me.

Cole gave me a house tour, showing me one wing at a time. We started in the East Wing at the theater, making our way to the bowling alley before we landed in the solarium.

"It's a sunroom," I said as we entered the glass room with a vast terrace.

"Yeah." Cole laughed. "Solarium is just a fancy name for it."

The solarium was bigger than any house I lived in with my dad. You could have built another house on the patio and still had room. This place was unreal, a dream come true.

We stopped at the library, which was two stories and had a domed ceiling and stained-glass windows. There were more books than I could ever read lining each wall. Ladders attached to the shelves went up to the top floor. I wasn't afraid of heights, but climbing that high for a book worried me.

"When I'm home, I spend most of my time here," Cole said. "Feel free to take any books you like. If there's something specific you want to read, and we don't have it, we'll order it."

I've died and gone to heaven.

I saw myself getting lost in the library, buried under thousands of books. Growing up, I didn't have much entertainment. My grandfather only let me read. That was the one pleasure he never denied me because he believed reading was a superpower. He said the world's smartest and wealthiest people read daily, and I would be wise to follow their lead.

So I did.

That was the reason I chose Library Science as my major. I hoped one day to be free from my family and use my college education to become a librarian.

"If there's ever a time you can't find me," I said on our way out of the library, "there's a good chance I'm trapped under an avalanche of books."

A grin tugged at the corners of his mouth. "At least we have one thing in common."

I let his words linger as we headed toward our next destination. Did we have other things in common?

I doubted it.

Cole had a normal life with friends and a real family. His father wasn't a terrorist, a painful fact that haunted me.

Am I like him?

Am I evil, too?

"I'll let you in on a secret," Cole said, returning my attention to him. "I'm usually one of two places—the library or the game room."

He pushed open the door to the game room. Like the other rooms, it was equally impressive and looked as if it had every game ever invented.

A sectional couch that could fit thirty people comfortably sat at the center of the room. They even had a bar with stools that took up half a wall. I didn't feel like I was in someone's home and wondered how often this stuff got used.

On our way to the West Wing, we passed the great room. I glanced at the spot my grandfather stood when I met the Marshalls. I was so relieved to be rid of him.

When my adoptive father left for his assignment, he hugged me and said, "It's only temporary, Gracie. You're a strong woman. You can survive a few months without me."

"But how do I survive *him*?" I tipped my head at my grandfather, who waited inside the limousine impatiently.

"He won't hurt you," he assured me. "There's a reason the old man has kept you around this long."

No one knew why, though. That was the billion-dollar question. My cousin Bastian was older than me and should have been in the line of succession. But for some reason, Fitzy chose me.

"Mark Marshall is my oldest friend," the Colonel added before we parted ways. "He will take care of you. You will always have a home with the Marshalls."

I snapped out of my thoughts as we approached the natatorium, an enclosed pool house larger than the one at my father's last duty station.

"When my friends come over," Cole said as he held the door open for me to see into the room, "we usually hang out here. Everyone in town wants an invite to Fort Marshall." He gave me a cocky smirk. "I'm known for having legendary parties."

I'd never been to a party or had friends. My family kept me sheltered from the outside world, fearful of my biological father finding me.

After leaving the natatorium, we stopped at the scullery, which Cole explained was a butler's kitchen. They also had an entire room dedicated to the pantry, hidden behind a paneled wall with enough food to feed an army.

"There are other kitchens in the house," Cole told me. "The chefs need room to work without us in the way."

"Because one kitchen isn't enough?" I laughed. "My last house had a galley kitchen that barely fit two people."

His smile stirred something strange inside me. Desire, maybe? I'd never been this close to a man who looked like Cole. My adoptive father made sure I had no dating life and no friends.

He was all I ever had.

All I ever needed.

"This place might seem like a maze at first, but you'll get used to it."

I peeked up at him. "I may need you to draw me a map."

He winked. "I'm an engineer. That I can do."

On our way through the house, Cole pushed on walls, twisted candlesticks, and even hit a button on a fireplace to show me the secret passages built into the house.

"My ancestors were paranoid," Cole said. "Evan Marshall built this house during Prohibition. He was a big whiskey drinker and refused to give up his vice. That's how my family got close to the Salvatores. They were alcohol smugglers back then with ties to the Italian Mafia. My grandfather never went without his whiskey because of Angelo Salvatore."

The Salvatores adopted my cousin Bastian. Like me, he'd lost his parents at a young age and temporarily lived with my grandfather before escaping his wrath. Tragedy seemed to follow the Adams family. We were cursed, despite having so much wealth.

Cole guided me to the left, and we ascended the stairs. "There are five founding families of Devil's Creek."

"What's the difference between The Founders Society and the founders of Devil's Creek?"

I knew the basics about each secret society but not everything, only what the Colonel wanted to share.

"With the exception of the Salvatores, the founding families of Devil's Creek are also descendants of the Founding Fathers of the United States. You must prove your lineage to become a member of The Founders Society. The Salvatores were the first to settle in Devil's Creek and start building here. And they founded The Devil's Knights, which helped to get their foot in the door with The Founders Society."

I could relate to the Salvatores. For the first eleven years of my life, I was an Adams. But I never felt part of this world, like an outsider looking through a window.

"Are you friends with the other Founders?"

"Yes." He gripped my bicep and steered me to the left. "Drake Battle is my cousin on my mother's side of the family. He lives at the end of Founders Way. Sonny Cormac lives next to him. His family owns Mac Corp. I'm sure you've heard of their shipping company. Like the other Founders, their wealth grew exponentially during Prohibition."

"So all of your families are linked because of Prohibition?"

He bobbed his head. "Drake started Battle Industries to improve on his grandfather's weapons manufacturing company. The Battles provided The Founders with weapons back then. Still do."

"And the Salvatores were smugglers? So what do they do now?"

"They own Salvatore Global and have made billions providing security services. But off the books, they help wealthy men do illegal shit. Their connections to crime families are useful to The Knights."

"And the fifth family?" I asked as we entered my new bedroom on the second floor.

The space was the size of a sitting room. I had a king-size bed with tons of comfy pillows and bedding so soft it felt like silk.

"The Wellingtons," he said with a curt nod. "Carl Wellington is the third wealthiest man in the world. He owns Wellington Pharmaceuticals and a ton of other companies."

My lips parted in shock. "I use their lotion and shampoo."

Wellington Pharmaceuticals made everything from hand lotion and makeup to vaccines.

Cole opened the double doors to the walk-in closet. I imagined myself sitting on the bench at the center of the room, getting lost in a pile of expensive clothes. Hangers, drawers, shelves, and racks were filled with clothing that didn't belong to me. I couldn't even count all the shoes—everything from jeweled flip-flops to heels.

"My mother went a little overboard when she heard you were coming to live with us," Cole said with a light shrug. "She always wanted a daughter but got three boys."

"I can see that." My cheeks hurt from smiling so hard. "Remind me to thank her."

My last bedroom was smaller than the closet and had a twin bed and a dresser. Military housing had no frills, and my dad kept things simple. The Colonel believed in only bringing what you need.

We exited the closet, and he opened the French doors to the patio overlooking the bay. The salty air floated into my nostrils, along with a cool breeze that rustled my hair.

"I'm right down the hall if you need me." Cole pointed his finger. "Last door on the left."

He was five balconies from mine.

"We're not the type of family that eats every meal together when we're home," Cole said as we entered the bedroom, closing the doors behind him. "My mom is usually busy with charity work. The twins rarely are home during the summer. And my dad tends to hole up in his office, drinking and trying to find ways to take over the universe."

I couldn't tell if he was kidding about the last part, but I laughed.

He nodded at the desk with an intercom. "If you get hungry, dial one for the kitchen."

"What can I order?"

"Anything." Cole slid his hands to his hips, a blank expression on his face, so I couldn't tell if he was serious until he said, "We have chefs on-site who can make any dish you want to eat. It doesn't matter what time of day. Someone is always working."

"Wow," I mouthed and let my gaze fall over the room fit for a queen.

"I'll let you get settled in before dinner." Cole flashed a killer grin that made the dimple on his right cheek pop. "Welcome to Fort Marshall, Grace. I hope you like your stay here."

Chapter Three

GRACE

My first few weeks at Fort Marshall were a lot of the same routine. Breakfast in the dining room with Cole. Sometimes, his brothers got out of bed to join us. But it was usually just the two of us.

Most days, we had lunch by the pool under the cabana. Today, we ate a burger and fries before I dipped my feet into the infinity pool. Living with the Marshalls was a dream, like something from a movie.

I would have grown up like Cole if my grandfather had been decent. The life I had before Fitzy was charmed from what I remembered. We lived in a big house with a dozen bedrooms. My parents had money and spoiled me.

Life was good once.

I leaned back against the pavers and soaked up the sun. The water was warm and felt amazing. This was the best summer vacation I'd ever had. Maybe even the best weeks of my life. I couldn't recall when I felt happier than I did at that moment.

Cole spotted me staring and closed his book, dropping it onto the chair as he rose to his full height. With a cute smile, he strolled toward me, his perfect body teasing me with each step. He was thick in the chest, with chiseled abs and broad shoulders holding up his big biceps.

Cole waded through the water, grabbed two floats, and passed one to me. "We can't stay in much longer. Maybe another thirty minutes."

As I attempted to hop onto the float, it glided across the pool, slamming into the wall. Cole moved behind me, his long fingers digging into my hips, setting my skin on fire. And when his hand cupped my ass to help me onto the float, I gasped.

I plopped onto my backside, breathing hard as our eyes met. His chest rose and fell faster, and I could tell I had the same effect on him. Cole's eyes lowered to my cleavage for a second, which spilled out from the red bikini top. I didn't have big boobs, about a handful, but enough for him to notice.

My foot brushed against his inner thigh, and I felt how hard he was for me. Biting my lip, I stared into his eyes, hoping he would make a move. So when he didn't, I leaned forward and let our lips brush. He breathed harder but wouldn't open his mouth for me.

As if it were too painful to continue looking at me, he stepped back and slapped the water. 'Those fucking bikinis," he mumbled under his breath, not thinking I could hear him as he turned his back to me and effortlessly climbed onto the float.

Cole covered his raging boner with his hand and drifted away, gazing at the sky. It was as if nothing happened. Like we weren't about to kiss.

"The boys are not to touch you," my grandfather had said on our way to Fort Marshall. "They are under strict orders to keep their filthy hands to themselves. And I expect you to act like a lady."

To spite him, I wanted to get my first kiss and ditch my virginity by the end of the summer. But it was clear Cole wasn't going to break the rules.

He walked away or turned his head whenever he stared at me for too long. Then things got awkward between us.

Like now.

I floated in the shallow water while Cole was already in the deep end, lounging on the raft like a spoiled prince. His muscles flexed when he moved, water rippling off them. Even from a distance, I could make out every detail of his body.

I liked Cole.

A lot.

Apart from the Colonel, no one had ever said they would protect me. No one had ever made me feel safe. I could see a lot of my dad in Cole. They were both raised by the military and were good at following orders. And if they were as alike as I thought, Cole would never touch me. Not in the way I wanted him to.

A fter changing out of my bathing suit and showering, I searched for Cole. He was supposed to stop by my room but still hadn't shown up. We were going to dinner at a cafe in town.

Cole's bedroom door was half open, so I stepped inside. His bed was made, every inch of the space clean and decluttered. He'd grown up at York Military Academy, and it showed.

A laptop and a computer monitor sat on his desk beside a stack of books. I halted by the bathroom door, which was open, steam billowing out from the room. From behind the glass shower, I spotted Cole with his hand on the wall, the other wrapped around his dick.

Oh my God.

Cole's body was a work of art sculpted to perfection. Water ran down his forehead, dotting the rugged ridges of his eight-pack. But that wasn't what I focused on most.

He jerked his shaft hard, eyes closed, and grunted. As if he could read my thoughts, his eyes snapped open. He didn't look away, and neither did I. To my surprise, Cole continued to jerk off, staring at me as if I were the object of his obsession.

My skin pebbled with tiny bumps of arousal. A deep ache settled into my core. Transfixed by Cole and the sounds he made, I bit my lip, wondering if he was getting off to me.

"I'm so sorry," I muttered after my brain started working again.

I could have sworn Cole said, "I'm not," as I shut the door.

Chapter Four

COLE

I was about to come when I caught a whiff of *her* sweet perfume. My eyes snapped open to Grace standing in the entryway to the bathroom as if I had manifested her.

I should have stopped jerking off or at least asked her to leave so that I could finish. But after weeks of staring at her killer body in those tiny bikinis, I needed a release.

I needed *her*.

And since I couldn't have her, I had to settle for the next best thing. Her grandfather would destroy my family if I touched a single hair on her head. The Knights were threatened and forced to swear an oath to The Founders Society.

It was our job to ensure her safety, not fuck her. Not think about her every waking moment. I knew it was wrong to want anything from Grace. The strange emotions I felt for her would eventually pass.

Through the glass, I watched Grace lick her lips. She was just as interested in me as I was in her. Her nipples were so hard they poked through her dress. Even her tanned skin had little bumps from her arousal.

As steam billowed out from the room, it clouded around her. I pretended she was a mirage, something I conjured to help me come faster.

With my hand on the wall, I stroked myself with the other, keeping my movements quick and precise. Everything was about efficiency for me. I said I would come to her room at five, but she was early.

Her eyes wandered up and down my body with desire. She often turned her head whenever we got too close. But within the confines of my bedroom, no one could see us. With each tug on my cock, I raced to the finish line, imagining I was coming inside the girl of my literal dreams. I thought about her each night, wishing I could have one taste.

Just once.

But I needed order and control, two things I wouldn't have if I crossed the line with Fitzy's granddaughter.

I was so close, seconds from coming, when Grace said, "I'm so sorry."

"I'm not," I grunted as she ran out of the room, coming into my hand seconds later.

This was bad.

A girl like Grace was probably already promised to another man. Her grandfather likely had someone in mind for her to marry. My dad had been toying with a few options for me, but I told him to get lost. Unless it was essential, I didn't want to get married until I was closer to thirty.

My life as a Knight was dangerous. And with how much heat we had been under lately, I couldn't bring a woman into this situation. Having Grace at Fort Marshall was bad enough. The Russians had infiltrated Devil's Creek only a few weeks before Grace arrived. We'd lost a few Knights over the past year because of The Lucaya Group.

Grace made my job harder.

She was too tempting, far too distracting. I was afraid I would slip up once and fail her. That couldn't happen, not on my watch.

Friends.

That was all we could ever be.

After I dressed in a button-down shirt and slacks, I headed

to Grace's room. She sat on the bed, hands clasped on her lap and staring at the floor.

I knocked. "Ready to eat?"

Her head lifted a few inches. Then, she nodded, using some of her hair to shield her eyes. She was so quiet. Some days, I barely heard her voice. And when I did, I couldn't get the beautiful sound out of my head for hours.

I offered my hand to Grace. "C'mon, we have a reservation." She slipped her fingers between mine, and I led her out of the bedroom and down the hall. "You'll love this place. They have the best seafood on the coast."

We had a reservation at Cafe Lacroix, a restaurant in town on the water. It overlooked Devil's Creek and Beacon Bay. The two towns were practically on top of each other. Except there was a significant difference in wealth among the residents.

Devil's Creek had more billionaires than any city in the country. Beacon Bay had some millionaires but not many. Most of their residents worked menial jobs that catered to tourists. Each summer, people visited the area to see what it was like to live like kings.

But most people didn't discover Devil's Creek was gated until after they arrived. We didn't have hotels or any rental properties. The Founders didn't allow anyone to rent their home for security reasons.

After I helped Grace into my Ferrari, my cell phone beeped with a new text message from Drake. I stopped outside the driver's side door and sighed at my cousin's message.

Chapter Five

GRACE

Never in a million years did I think I would be eating dinner at a fancy restaurant with a gorgeous man at my side. I had envisioned a lot of things, even hoped for them. But I never thought I would have this kind of freedom.

We sat on the outdoor patio at Café Lacroix, where by the looks of it, half the town dined. And I could understand why. The food was incredible, some of the best I'd ever eaten.

A few people said hello in passing as the waitress guided them to a table. Cole seemed to know everyone, even the girl who glared at me like I stole her boyfriend.

"Did you date that girl?" I asked Cole in a hushed tone.

He lifted an eyebrow, confused, and followed my gaze to the table on our left. "Not exactly." Cole laughed. "Cynthia has had a crush on me since we were kids. She was my girlfriend in first grade. But that was just stupid kid shit. Our parents thought it was cute and pushed us together."

"So that's it? You never dated her after that?"

He shook his head, chewing the rest of his steak before he said, "No, she's not my type."

"What is your type?" I blurted out and instantly regretted it.

To occupy my stupid mouth, I took a bite of my gourmet

burger that didn't have cheese on it because the chef refused and said it would ruin the meat. So I slathered it with a pound of ketchup, which slid down my chin as I bit into the thick burger.

"I don't know if I have a type. But Cynthia is not it." Cole shrugged. "I've never dated anyone for more than a few weeks. Maintaining a relationship was hard when I spent nine months every year at the academy." He leaned back in his chair, tapping his fingers on the table. "I guess I'd have to keep someone around long enough to know what I like."

Cole graduated in June from York Military Academy with a degree in aerospace engineering. At the end of the summer, he was going to work at Battle Industries with his cousin.

I wiped my mouth and dabbed at the ketchup on my lip. "So you only dated when you were home from the academy?"

He smirked. "I wouldn't call it dating."

"Oh," I mouthed, and my cheeks grew hotter, feeling a little foolish. I was so out of my depth with a guy like Cole that I asked all the wrong questions.

Cole downed the last of his drink, his eyes on me. "As I said earlier, being curious is okay, Grace. Anything you want to know, you can ask me. All of this is new to you."

Although thankful for his openness, I frowned, mostly because I felt stupid. Like I was some science experiment created in a lab and just learned how to be human. Cole was my age and didn't need to have the world explained to him.

"Am I that weird?" I said and wished I had more of a filter around Cole.

Why did I keep embarrassing myself? I wanted to hide under the table and disappear into another world.

"No," he said without hesitation, putting his hand on the table, his fingers inches from mine. "I didn't mean to offend you."

"I'm not. It's just… I feel like such a freak. I've never had a friend. I didn't have a childhood boyfriend and never dated anyone. I don't even know what it's like to go to a party, drink a beer, or have my first kiss. I missed out on everything. And when you talk about your life, I feel so behind. I missed years of my life."

Cole studied my face as if trying to extract the thoughts from my brain. We would have been greeted with awkward silence if not for the people talking around us.

He opened his mouth and then stopped himself, considering his following words carefully before saying, "I can help with that if you want." Cole scooted his chair so close our elbows almost touched. "We can throw a party at my house. And I'll drink your first beer with you. Whatever you want to do, we'll do it."

Everything but the kissing part. God forbid he broke my grandfather's rules.

I smiled. "Thank you, Cole."

He patted my hand, and when his hand lingered for too long, he pulled away. Unfortunately, that happened more often than I would have liked.

The waitress removed our empty plates from the table and asked if we wanted dessert. I was stuffed, but Cole insisted we get the best banana split in the state and ordered one to share.

The sundae was the size of a fish bowl and came with two long spoons almost the length of my forearm.

Cole dug in first, with a big-ass smile plastered on his lips. "You've traveled the world with your dad," he said between bites. "What was your favorite place?"

I chewed the banana and licked my lips clean of whipped cream, which drew Cole's attention to my mouth. A beat passed between us, where he stared, and I couldn't breathe until he pulled his eyes away from mine.

"Um," I said as I thought over his question. "I guess my favorite place was Germany. We lived there for a year before he got reassigned to another duty station."

"You missed out on some things, but that must have been fun traveling all the time, living someplace new."

I rolled my shoulders against the chair. "I guess. We didn't stay in one place as long as other military families because of me."

"The Colonel's a pilot," Cole cut in. "So that gave him some flexibility. The Founders made sure he always had somewhere else to go."

I nodded. "He taught me how to fly a plane when I turned eighteen."

Cole gave me a shocked but impressed look. "What else did you learn from the Colonel?"

"We've never had a normal father-daughter relationship." I licked my spoon clean and dropped it onto the cloth napkin so he could eat the rest of the sundae. "He showed me how to hunt, fight, shoot, and many other skills. I also went to a survival camp for a few weeks every summer. It was in the middle of nowhere and run by his friend from the Marine Corps."

"That sounds like fun," Cole said with a genuine smile as he scooped the last of the ice cream onto his spoon.

"Yeah, I guess. But I missed out on all the normal kid stuff. I wasn't allowed to have friends outside the classroom. That meant no school dances, no movie nights, no parties, and not having any social media accounts. We couldn't risk my face popping up online, especially not with the artificial intelligence software they have now."

"It's too risky," Cole confirmed. "The Colonel did the right thing. He kept you safe all this time because he's smart."

"I miss him," I confessed. "We've never been apart for this long. But I also enjoy having some freedom. This is the first time in my life that no one expects anything from me. I can hang out by the pool and stay up late watching movies with you. It's nice." A grin split my face in half. "This is the best summer I've ever had. Thank you, Cole."

He returned my expression. "How about we get out of here, so you can drink your first beer?"

Chapter Six

COLE

As I approached the Battle Fortress, the front doors swung open for me. "Welcome back, Mr. Marshall," Lovelace said, her voice soft and without much of an accent. "Your heart rate is slightly elevated. Are you upset?"

You didn't need to touch anything in the house. Everything was digital, motion or voice activated. Lovelace could tell by my footsteps alone it was me. She knew everything about me. Drake had encoded all of The Knights' traits into the system, so she would sense us immediately and be able to communicate effectively.

"No," I told Lovelace. "I'm just worried about something. That's all."

I always worried about Grace. She was my number one priority.

Tate Maxwell pushed off the wall and greeted me with a firm handshake. "Hey, Cole. I hope you can talk some sense into your cousin. He hasn't come up from the basement since last night. We're worried about him."

Tate and his younger sister Olivia worked for Drake. Olivia was his assistant, and Tate was the head of security. They were foster kids, starving and desperate for a place to live when Drake found them in high school. His mom often joked that he liked to bring home strays. But they became family, especially after his dad passed away.

Drake emerged from the basement, his clothes wrinkled and dark hair a mess, longer than usual and hanging in his eyes. My cousin was a big comic book nerd. He usually wore a Marvel or DC Comics T-shirt under his suit. Today, I could see a black Spider-Man shirt through his white oxford.

"He's alive," Tate joked, smacking Drake on the back. "I can't effectively do my job if you use Lovelace to keep me away from you."

"No one can reach me that far underground," Drake said with a forced smile. "The Battle Cave is the safest place on the property."

"Not the point," Tate said in a clipped tone. "Liv has been fussing about you all day. She's even prepared your favorite meal. So you better eat with us. No excuses."

"Okay." Drake gave him a look of defeat. "I need ten minutes alone with Cole, and then we'll catch up. Promise." He steered me down the hallway by my shoulder. "Thanks for coming. We need to talk."

"What's going on?"

"Lovelace, initiate lockdown sequence," Drake said on his way to the elevator.

"Yes, Master Battle," she responded. "Initiating sequence in five, four, three, two, one."

The front doors locked, and I could hear glass and metal shifting behind me, sealing off the entry from intruders. Someone with Drake's money and influence could never be too careful.

"I think The Lucaya Group wants more than Grace and Alex." Drake tapped the button on the wall. "I've been monitoring the Dark Web, and there's a lot of talk about me."

We got into the elevator.

I cocked a concerned eyebrow at him, and he added, "My board put me in a dangerous position when they asked me to demo Lovelace. Only a handful of people were supposed to see the presentation. But it's on the Dark Web, and the wrong people are talking about it."

The elevator stopped several floors beneath the home, depositing us into Drake's version of the Batcave. There were monitors and screens on every wall. Some even hung from the ceiling.

Drake led me to the bar on the right side of the room. "Lovelace can do a lot more than I told the board. No one knows her true capabilities. I've been working on Lovelace for the past ten years in secret. She's optimized over time." He grabbed a bottle of scotch, hesitating for a moment. "I never foresaw her becoming so powerful."

"What are you saying?"

Looking down, he poured two glasses of scotch and slid one to me, breathing hard through his nose. "In the wrong hands, Lovelace is a weapon of mass destruction."

My eyes widened at his confession. "What are you going to do?"

Before he could respond, Lovelace interrupted us to define a weapon of mass destruction.

Drake took a sip from the glass and sighed. "Lovelace, Night Mode."

"Goodnight, Master Battle," she replied before going to sleep.

"What can I do?" Drake said to me. "I have no choice but to shut her down."

"But," I protested, following him to the sectional couch large enough to seat twenty people. "She's like your child. You don't have to do that. Tell the board she's too unstable to go public and keep her for yourself."

I could see it was killing Drake even to consider turning her off. She ran every aspect of his personal life and business. The AI was like another family member to Drake.

"I tried." He scrubbed a hand through his dark hair. "Except there's one small problem. The board has already accepted bids from outside investors. The United States government expects to use Lovelace next year for military operations. And they're not the only countries interested."

"What does this have to do with Alex and Grace?"

Drake leaned his head back on the cushion and tipped the glass to his lips, downing the contents in one gulp. He rested the empty glass on his knee and glanced over at me. "I think they're using Alex and Grace to distract us. I'm not looking at the real target if I'm busy keeping them safe."

"I'm sure you're just being paranoid. Grace's father is the leader of The Lucaya Group. She's his target. And Alex is the granddaughter of a Founder. Viktor Romanov would kill to get his hands on the Wellington Black Book."

Viktor was Grace's biological father and an ex-KGB officer.

"Maybe we should consider getting Grace and Alex out of Devil's Creek," I suggested since it seemed like the only move we had left. "It will give us time to regroup and devise a new plan."

Drake shook his head, and brown hair flopped onto his forehead. "That's not an option."

In a matter of days, he looked as if he'd aged a few years. Dark circles ringed his eyes, and his hair was all over the place, sticking up in different directions as if he'd been tugging on it. He wasn't built for so much stress and hadn't been sleeping much. Alcohol and sleeping pills could only get him so far.

The Knights were under a lot of pressure. We'd been on high alert for months without getting much of a break. Even before Colonel Hale left for his mission, Grace was in danger.

Fitzy wouldn't have left her in my family's care if he wasn't worried. The old man couldn't bear to lose his heir, even though he hated Grace. Her cousin Bastian should have been the heir to the Adams fortune. So there must have been a reason Fitzy kept her around. My guess was it had something to do with money.

"Drake Battle," a female voice boomed through a speaker.

"If you don't get your brilliant behind upstairs in the next five minutes, I'm calling your mom."

I laughed, and so did Drake.

"All the women in my life are so controlling." Drake tapped the cushion between us. "You should get back to Fort Marshall and look after Grace. I'll probably spend my night getting a lecture from Liv." He smiled. "That woman drives me crazy."

I bobbed my head. "I know the feeling."

Drake had been in love with Olivia for years but made a deal with Tate not to touch her. I knew how much it sucked to want someone I couldn't have. It was the worst pain imaginable.

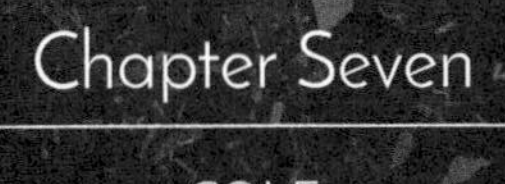

Chapter Seven

COLE

Grace was a test from God, a temptation added to my life to see if I could control myself. I liked to think of myself as a person with more self-control than most, but with my greatest sin sleeping down the hall, it was nearly impossible not to think about giving in to my desires.

But I couldn't.

I wouldn't.

Grace was off-limits.

I poked my head into her bedroom. The moon's light cast a golden hue on the room, and with the balcony doors open, a soft breeze blew the curtains.

She purred like a sleeping kitten. I could have stood there all night watching her sleep, studying her delicate features. I'd never met a girl like Grace.

She wasn't like the women I knew who took off their panties and stuffed them into my pocket as an invitation for sex. Grace was shy and quiet, and when she spoke—which was rare—my heart skipped a few beats.

I could tell she had been badly hurt as a child and that her past had shaped her into the woman she was today. Each time I looked at her for the past week, she blushed and turned her head. It was as if she couldn't stand the attention. But what man wouldn't want to stare at her?

How could I not?

Pretty and perfect, she had rosy pink cheeks like a porcelain doll. Long blonde hair brushed the tops of her breasts, which only drew my attention to her body, especially when she wore those skimpy bikinis to the pool.

I closed the door after a few minutes, not wanting to wake her, and entered the code to lock her inside. The security door was an extra precaution. While she slept, the door remained locked. Grace had a bathroom and a mini fridge, so she didn't need to leave her room at night.

She looked too peaceful when she slept to disturb her. Besides, I didn't want her to know I'd been doing this every night since she arrived. I couldn't sleep without knowing she was okay.

That she was safe.

As a member of The Devil's Knights, my duty was to protect her. She was the only granddaughter of the Grand Master of The Founders Society, and since The Knights answered to The Founders, I had to follow orders. But Grace was more than a job to me.

I crept downstairs and headed toward the back of the house. The hallways were dark, lit only by the wall sconces that provided very little light.

"Where are you going?" Dad asked as I walked past his office.

Despite spending the last ten years together at York Military Academy, we didn't have the best relationship. Because he was the commandant, it only complicated matters. Instead of having a dad, I had a commanding officer.

I popped my head into his office. "I'm meeting The Knights at the temple."

"To discuss Grace?"

I nodded. "And Alex. She's still listed for sale on the Il Circo auction site."

Alexandrea Wellington was the soon-to-be Queen of The Devil's Knights. She was the first and only queen we would ever have. It was the only way Carl Wellington, her grandfather, would allow Alex to marry one of The Salvatore brothers, the leaders of The Devil's Knights.

Instead of choosing one brother, she was dating all four, including Grace's cousin, Bastian. I wouldn't have agreed to an arrangement like that with my brothers, but whatever worked for them.

"Drake will find a way to get Alex off the site," Dad said confidently.

Someone added Alex to a site on the Dark Web where men from the depths of the criminal underworld could bid on anything.

Only the person who added her to the auction could remove the listing. Even with our money and resources, we couldn't track down the person responsible. No one knew who ran the auction.

Dad scrubbed a hand over the dark stubble on his jaw and sighed. "Drake will have to get over his issues before he can see the only way out is *through*."

I narrowed my eyes at him. "What issues does Drake have?"

My cousin was three years older than me and one of the youngest CEOs in history. He owned Battle Industries, the world's largest manufacturer of technology-based weapons. I'd never met anyone more intelligent than Drake. He graduated from MIT when he was nineteen and made the cover of *WIRED* by twenty.

I planned to work for him at the end of the summer because I loved how his mind worked and had admired him since I was a kid. I could learn more from him in one month than I did in four years of college.

"He has a deadly weapon in his possession and refuses to use it," my father said with disdain in his tone. "He could easily solve our problems with The Lucaya Group."

We suspected but couldn't confirm that Grace's biological father was the leader of The Lucaya Group. For that reason, The Devil's Knights had to protect her.

Fitzy hid her when she was eight. Her name change became essential at eleven when her father escaped imprisonment on Skull Island, where The Devil's Knights locked up the worst offenders.

That day, she became Grace Hale, and Katarina Adams Romanov died. If you were to do a Google search—or any search for that matter—you wouldn't find a trace of Grace's former identity. It was as if she were never born.

"Drake isn't like you," I told my dad. "Or like the other Knights."

My cousin had a kind heart and genuinely wanted to change the world. Maybe he could, but his personal beliefs contradicted our current situation.

"No, he's not," Dad agreed. "But one day, he will change his mind, and when he does, it will be too late."

If anyone could take down The Lucaya Group, it was him. But he let his conscience guide him. My dad and I hadn't told any of The Knights about some of Drake's developments. Because we knew if the Salvatore brothers found out about it, they would force him to use his work for evil.

Drake believed the only way out was to find a backdoor. He thought like a hacker, not like my dad and The Founders. So, for now, his secret stayed within the family. No one but us would ever know he could stop this war.

And that meant I had to pay extra special attention to Grace. Until her adoptive father returned from his assignment, I wouldn't let her out of sight—only on the rare occasions when I met with The Knights.

"Can you check on her if our meeting goes longer than expected?" I asked him.

He nodded. "Grace is safe under our roof. Nothing will happen to her, Cole."

I wanted to believe that.

If there's a will, there's a way, my grandfather used to say. Ten years of relentless searching proved that Viktor Romanov would never give up on his daughter, no matter the obstacles.

I turned to leave, and my dad added, "I know you have feelings for her, son. But getting in Fitzy's way will hurt our family."

"I understand what's at stake for us."

But my dick doesn't.

"Good." He raised a tumbler of scotch to his mouth and drank. "I have seen first-hand what happens to Knights who disobey The Founders, and it would not end well for us."

"I have to go," I said, hating that I could only ever look at Grace and never touch her. "The Knights are waiting for me. You know how Luca gets when we're late."

I stopped in the library, removed a few books from the shelves, and set them on the table. Then, I reached into the open space on the center shelf and pulled on the lever. All the founding families of Devil's Creek had a similar passageway in their homes. You only had to remove the correct books to find the secret door, which swung open for me.

In every house, the lever was behind *The Count of Monte Cristo* by Alexandre Dumas. Choosing a classic novel about a man tunneling his way out of prison only seemed fitting. Our ancestors had an interesting sense of humor. But it would take forever to discover this door in a library of this size, with a thirty-foot ceiling and wall-to-wall books.

I closed the door behind me and hit the button on the wall to illuminate the narrow channel. Then, taking the stairs two at a time, I headed into the catacombs beneath Devil's Creek and followed the familiar path.

The cramped passage smelled like mildew, salt water, and earth. And this far below ground, the air was dense and harder to breathe. Iron lanterns cast a soft glow on the stone walls with symbols etched into them.

Some images depicted skulls with knives driven into the bone. My favorite was a knight wearing a helmet with the eyes of a demon. Beside that one, a knight in full armor held the Scales of Justice, but the weight was unbalanced. It dipped to one side from a giant serpent holding it down, slithering up the arm of the knight.

Most of the wall had deranged and borderline satanic markings. The Knights were like other secret societies, but we killed people. We did horrible things for a good cause, to protect the citizens of this country from the scumbags of the world. But we also did some of those things for personal gain.

After a few minutes of walking, I entered a massive room with two thrones sitting on top of a dais. There was a ceremonial table laden with red silk sheets to my right. On my left, several Knights grabbed their hooded robes from hooks.

Luca Salvatore waited for us on the throne, already dressed in his robe and wearing an irritated scowl. He was about to take over for his father as the Grand Master of The Devil's Knights. Arlo had been transitioning his duties to his son for the past few months.

The Salvatores had ties to the Italian Mafia, ruling without fear for nearly a century. They weren't descendants of the Founding Fathers of the United States but had earned their place among us.

Without a word, I crossed the room, dressed in my robe, and took my place beside my brothers. The Knights were not my blood, but we were a family. Only those who lived locally were in attendance—the four Salvatore brothers, the three Cormac brothers, Drake, and me. We had several hundred members spread out across the country.

"The auction is approaching," Luca said with a bitter edge to his tone. "And we're no closer to shutting down the Il Circo website."

"I'm getting closer," Drake told him. "But whenever I hack into their site, they shut it down and lock me out. I'm doing everything I can."

"You're best isn't good enough, Battle," Luca snapped, his top lip curved upward like a pit bull ready to attack. "Try harder. Your future Queen's life is on the line."

I didn't think Luca cared about anyone until Alex came into his life. He was cold and cruel, one of the most ruthless men I had ever met. You would never know he was only a few years older than me because he never showed his age. Wise beyond his years, Luca was a good leader and never did anything without a plan.

"I'll find a backdoor," Drake assured him, though his voice lacked his usual confidence. "Give me more time. They have teams of hackers running that site. The Knights only have me."

Luca rested his elbow on the arm of the throne, looking like a gilded god holding court. He blew out a deep breath as he studied each of our faces. "Now that Alex and Grace are in Devil's Creek, we have even more of a target on our backs. We don't have time. Get her off that fucking site and do it quickly!"

Luca always had the appearance of rage simmering beneath the surface but rarely lost his cool. The thought of losing Alex must have set him over the edge. I could relate now that I had Grace to think about. Until she walked through my front door, I had no real purpose within the organization.

She gave me one.

"Luca," Marcello interjected in his usual calm voice, the peacekeeper of the Salvatore brothers. "Drake is doing everything he can to get Alex off the Il Circo site. Yelling at him isn't going to change a thing."

Luca shot up from the throne and was in front of Marcello instantly. "Don't tell me how to rule, little brother."

Marcello sighed. "Luca, we love her, too. We get it. Taking out your frustration on Drake isn't helping."

"Marcello's right," Bastian Salvatore chimed. "Let Drake do his job, and we'll do ours. Alex is at home sleeping. No one is going to touch a hair on her pretty head."

Bastian wasn't always a Salvatore. Before his parents were killed in a plane crash, he was Bastian Kincaid and lived with Fitzy before getting adopted by Arlo Salvatore. His childhood best friend Damian Townsend was also part of the deal and was now a Salvatore, too. Though, you would never know the Salvatore brothers were not blood-related. Only Marcello and Luca.

Grace met her cousin when she was younger. But they never had much contact, and Fitzy wanted it that way. Probably because he feared them conspiring against him. Maybe one day they could have a real relationship.

A ringing sound pierced the silence in the room. With a groan, Luca reached under his robe and removed his cell phone from his pocket.

"Time to go," he said to his brothers. "Alex is awake and looking for us."

Luca was a psychopath. He probably had a tracking device on her ankle.

"What about Grace?" I asked him before he adjourned the meeting.

He yanked off the robe and flung it onto the throne. "What about her? Do you think I give a damn about the terrorist's daughter? The Lucaya Group can have her."

"But you swore to The Founders," I shot back. "We all did. Are you seriously okay with them hurting Grace?"

"Do your job, Marshall." Luca stepped off the dais and leveled me with a cold stare. "Until my family gets admitted into The Founders Society, we will keep her alive."

"And after that?"

He shrugged. "I don't care what happens to her."

"Well, I do," Bastian cut in. "Grace is my only relative who isn't a piece of shit." He shoved a hand through his brown hair, glaring at Luca. "If anything happens to her, we'll have a fucking problem, *brother*."

Luca rolled his eyes. "Don't let her die, Marshall. That's your only order." He waved his hand at the group. "All of you are dismissed."

Chapter Eight

GRACE

The summer disappeared in a blink. Before I came to Fort Marshall, most days passed at a snail's pace. Because until the start of the summer, I didn't have a life. I had nothing to look forward to.

Now, I had a friend who would do anything for me. Even kill my enemies. And tonight, he pulled out all the stops by transforming the game room into a blanket fort.

We collected every available pillow and blanket in the house, stringing sheets up from the ceiling to create a small town. A place only inhabited by us. Our tent was the size of my bedroom, the floor carpeted with comforters and pillows. Before dimming the lights, Cole even hung fairy lights to create the perfect ambiance.

Cole dropped to the floor beside me on the blanket with a notepad and pen in hand. He donned a mischievous smile that made me instantly suspicious. "So, I was thinking…"

"Oh, don't go doing that," I quipped. "You wouldn't want to hurt yourself."

He curled his arm around me and laughed, rubbing his knuckles on my head. "She's got jokes, ladies and gentlemen. Since when did my shy girl get so cocky?"

My shy girl?

My heart fluttered with him this close. We spent every day together, but whenever Cole felt the spark of attraction blossoming between us, he always pulled away.

"I'm not *that* shy," I said in my defense. "It's taking me a little longer to crawl out of my shell."

"I like this side of you, Grace. You shouldn't be afraid of who you are." Cole slid the notepad in front of me. "So I was thinking about everything you haven't done yet." He handed me the pen, smiling with his big, blue eyes that lit up his handsome face. "It's time for you to make a bucket list. Write down everything. We'll cross off the things we've already done and work on checking off new experiences. This way, when you return home with the Colonel, you'll be reminded of this summer."

My heart ached at his last statement. I missed my dad but would miss the late nights watching movies with Cole, drinking by the pool, and Friday game night. I would cherish those moments.

I took the pen from his hand, tears stinging my bottom lids, forcing me to turn my head. "I don't want this summer to end."

"Me neither, Grace. But we only have a month left. So let's try to enjoy the time we got." He tipped his head at the paper. "Write down everything that comes to mind."

I thought about everything we'd done and scribbled them onto the pad.

~~Drink my first beer~~

After our dinner at Café Lacroix, we scratched this one off. Cole set every craft beer in the state on the bar for me to taste. I burped so loudly after the fifth sampling that I ran away, so embarrassed I couldn't look at him until he convinced me to leave my room.

"I'm not sure if you can cross this one off." Cole laughed. "That grilled cheese and tomato sandwich you made me tasted like charcoal." He shook his head. "In a blind taste test, I wouldn't have been able to tell the difference between charcoal from my barbecue and that sandwich."

I slapped his arm and chuckled. "It wasn't that bad. Sorry my cooking isn't gourmet like your private chefs."

"It wasn't good. But I still ate it."

He rubbed against me, and I secretly wished he would pin me to the floor and kiss me. A few times, I thought we would kiss, only for him to walk away. He even mentioned my grandfather and his rules on occasion.

"From what I recall, your attempt at cooking was less than stellar, Mr. Marshall." I gave him a cheeky grin. "You're forgetting the risotto you made that tasted like soup."

"Hey, cooking wasn't on my bucket list," he said to defend the horrible meal I nearly vomited. "I was only in the kitchen to help you out."

"Well, I guess culinary school isn't in the cards for either of us."

I returned to checking off items on my list to stop myself from looking at Cole. But, once we locked eyes, I had trouble not staring, wondering what he was thinking. Deep down, I hoped he would lean over, close the distance, and kiss me.

~~*Learn how to dance*~~

Cole's friend, a Knight who lived in Devil's Creek, helped us with this. Braxton Cade's mom owned a dance studio. She showed me how to dance salsa before pairing me with Cole. It wasn't as intimate as I had hoped, mainly because Cole was too stiff and danced like he was trying to perform the motions from a script.

"I will admit," Cole said when his eyes landed on this item. "I sucked major ass at dancing. Not my forte."

"I guess you didn't have many dances at York Military Academy."

"None. Until last year, it was an all-male college."

We'd shared everything about ourselves over the past two months, so I didn't hold back my next question.

"'Did you date any of the girls?"

"No," he said without a second of hesitation. "But my friends did. You remember Brax, right? He was hooking up with this one girl in secret. He didn't think we knew, but how could we not? His girl was a screamer. And the walls are paper thin at the academy."

What I wouldn't have given to be screaming Cole's name. Every thought seemed to flick back to Cole and how much I wanted him to kiss me. Hold me in his strong arms. I wanted so badly to lose all of my firsts with Cole. Too bad he had no interest in doing that with me.

Needing a distraction from his disarming smile, I returned to the list.

~~Drive a race car~~

I smiled at the memory of Cole teaching me how to drive his Ferrari, which was a nightmare but also really fun. He was patient and didn't yell when I almost crashed into the garage.

"You know," Cole said, tapping his pointy elbow against mine, "when you said you could fly a plane, I was expecting you to know how to drive a car."

"I'm too short to push in the clutch properly." I shrugged. "It's not easy knowing how much pressure to apply. But I eventually got the hang of it."

"Yeah." He snorted. "Seconds before our lives flashed before our eyes."

I flicked my hair over my shoulder to shield my face from him. Sometimes, looking at Cole was too much for me to bear.

Jump off a cliff

~~*Build a fort*~~

~~*Watch a movie under the stars*~~

"That was a good night," Cole commented as his finger hovered over the last one. "I thought Drake would kill me when I asked him to come over and set that up for us, but it was well worth it."

I nodded, a smile on my lips. "There's nothing better than watching Marvel movies with 3D glasses while the waves crash on the beach."

A moment of silence washed over us. I wondered if Cole was thinking about how much he would miss this. We'd grown so close over the past eight weeks that I felt I had known him forever.

"What's next on your list?"

I scribbled the next bucket list item on the paper.

Attend a party

"It's about time I throw a party at Fort Marshall, don't you think?"

"That sounds perfect."

Going to a real party with people my age sent a ripple of excitement through my body. Even if it was only one night, I wanted to feel normal.

"Keep going," Cole instructed. "I might need time to plan."

I hesitated for a moment because the things I *really* wanted to do involved him. What came next was the actual bucket list. The other stuff was filler.

I hoped he wouldn't freak out or act weird. Our time together had been so perfect I didn't want to waste it. So I sucked down my nerves and added the most important items to my list.

Kiss a boy
Get asked out on a date
Lose my virginity
Fall in love

Cole's eyes didn't leave the paper. My heart clambered in my chest, beating so loudly I couldn't hear anything else.

What did I do?

He stayed silent for a minute, and I couldn't tell if he was breathing. His chest didn't rise and fall in its familiar pattern. Meanwhile, my heart wouldn't stop pounding, the adrenaline pumping through my veins.

Kneeling on the floor in front of him, I gripped his thick bicep. Our eyes met, so I took this as my cue to lean in and test the waters. I could tell Cole had been fighting his feelings for me all summer and needed a push.

I wet my lips with my tongue, and his eyes followed the simple movement. He sat there, barely breathing, and I couldn't take it anymore. I pressed my lips to his, tasting a hint of mint from his breath.

"Cole, please," I whispered when he didn't part his lips for me. "Just kiss me. I know you're trying to follow my grandfather's rules, but he's not here. And he will never know about us."

After a long pause, he sat back, avoiding my gaze. "There must be other things you want to check off your list."

What the fuck?

I shook my head. "Not as much as the last four."

"I can't help with these. I'm sorry, Grace."

After he left the tent, I buried my face in the blankets, feeling stupid and regretting everything.

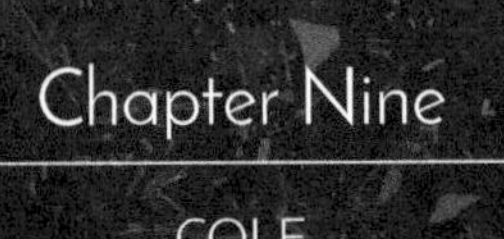

Chapter Nine

COLE

I was an asshole for walking out on Grace, but I didn't know what else to do. Following rules was coded into my DNA. And after seeing the last few items on her bucket list, it was impossible to be around her. Too hard not to think about giving Grace her first kiss or taking her virginity.

Fuck.

That.

List.

I regretted suggesting she make the damn list. If not for my stupid idea, everything would have stayed the same.

She didn't come downstairs for breakfast, and I couldn't blame her. At least she wasn't in the dining room when my dad dropped a bomb on me, hitting me like a punch to the kidney. It was better she wasn't here to see my reaction.

"Rhys Vanderbilt is staying with us for the rest of the summer," he announced as if it were something I wanted to hear this early in the morning. "The Knights need extra help protecting Grace and Alex. And he needs a place to stay until his parents are settled in California."

My heart nearly stopped at his confession. Of all The Devil's Knights, I hated Rhys the most. He was an unbearable, competitive piece of shit who thought the world revolved around him.

I dropped my fork onto the plate, fixing a stern glare at my dad. "Rhys is not staying here with Grace. We can't trust him."

My dad dismissed me with a head shake. "Rhys isn't a problem, Cole. I know you competed over everything at the academy, but it won't be that way while he's living here."

"Of course it will, *Commandant*," I shot back since I never called him Dad. He was my commanding officer at York Military Academy, but not my father for most of my life. "I had to deal with that asshole for nine months every year since I was twelve. He can find somewhere else to live for the next month."

It was always tit-for-tat with him.

Rhys hated to lose.

Grace would be a shiny new toy for him to play with. It was like dangling a banana before a monkey and not expecting it to take a bite. Even though all Knights swore not to touch Grace, Rhys would make it his mission to defy Fitzy's rules.

His family was on the verge of losing their standing with The Founders Society, so I didn't understand why my dad would want to be associated with the Vanderbilts.

"Get over your hatred, put aside your differences, and welcome Rhys into our home." Dad bit a slice of toast and chewed before adding, "He's a Knight. Same as us. And he needs a place to live. We can't turn him away when he needs help."

I shoved the plate across the table, sick to my stomach. "Well, maybe if his dad weren't such a shit human being, the Vanderbilts wouldn't be broke. We shouldn't even associate ourselves with people like them."

My dad frowned. "That's beside the point, Cole. Rhys is living here. End of story." He lifted the newspaper from the table and avoided my gaze. "My decision is final."

I shot up from the dining chair as if it were on fire. "If he does anything to hurt Grace, I will kill him."

"As usual, you're overreacting," he said without looking away from the paper. "Grace will be better protected with you and Rhys working together."

He didn't know Rhys the way I did. That sneaky fuck would do anything to win, anything to get what he wanted. Anyone could see I had feelings for Grace. And I couldn't let her be his next target.

Chapter Ten

COLE

R hys Vanderbilt arrived at Fort Marshall. Everyone except the twins was here to greet the person I hated most. Ten years of competing with Rhys at York Military Academy created a lot of hatred between us.

My mom fussed over every detail of his stay. Rhys could have slept on the cold floor for all I cared. After some of the shady shit he'd pulled our final semester at the academy, he was dead to me.

My mom left the great room to coordinate with the staff, ensuring Rhys's bedroom was ready. That gave him a second to set his sights on Grace. She smiled at him with a giddy expression on her face.

Sometimes, she looked at me like that. But after last night, I could tell she was trying hard not to stare in my direction.

"And who is this lovely creature?" Rhys said to Grace, offering his hand.

She placed her hand in his and laughed as he kissed her skin. "I'm Grace Hale."

"Fitzy's granddaughter?" He cocked an eyebrow at me. "How lucky for me?"

I heard the excitement in his voice, and when he said the

words, they were aimed at me. A new challenge. He enjoyed games because they could be won.

Rhys patted my back. "Miss me, Marshall?"

I sneered at him. "About as much as I'd miss hemorrhoids."

My father cleared his throat, interrupting our staring contest. "I spoke to Remington this morning. You can stay as long as you like."

"Thank you, Commandant." Rhys flashed a set of straight, white teeth. "We won't forget your generosity."

Like the Vanderbilts had anything to offer in return. They had enough money to last them until the end of the year if they were lucky.

Remington had sold every property on the East Coast to pay off his debts and moved their family to Bel Air temporarily. He would eventually sell that house. Who knew where they would end up after that?

Penniless.

Homeless.

The Founders hadn't decided what to do with them. Rhys was still one of us until they were down to their last dollar. Knights took an oath to put each other above all else. It was a brotherhood, a lifelong commitment.

The summer before we started college, Rhys and a few of my friends from the academy went through Initiation together. We endured months of hell to become members of The Devil's Knights. But even after all the challenges we faced, Rhys still hadn't taken his oath seriously. He broke the rules as he saw fit and didn't give a shit about anyone but himself.

Rhys cuddled up beside Grace, finding ways to touch her. I wanted to rip off his fingers and shove them down his throat one digit at a time. He whispered something in her ear, and she playfully slapped his arm.

"Oh, my God, Rhys," Grace lilted. "You're so bad."

I'm going to kill him.

"Vanderbilt." I tipped my head when he glanced at me. "A word, please?"

Rhys brushed his thumb across Grace's cheek and gave her a lopsided grin. "I'll be right back, princess."

Her face lit up like a Christmas tree, a blush spreading from her cheeks to her chest. I could see Grace had already fallen under his spell. Most women liked Rhys. He could charm a nun out of her chastity belt.

He followed me to the left side of the room, propping his hip against the wall. "What do you want, Marshall? I'm kinda busy."

"Look how fast you drop the nice guy act." I shook my head. "You're not fooling anyone. I know you're up to something."

"I'm just being nice to our Grand Master's granddaughter," he said in a clipped tone. "And from the look of it, you two aren't speaking. Don't think I've missed how she looks away from you like a wounded puppy." He scratched the corner of his jaw and grinned. "What have you been up to, Marshall? Did you fuck her to stick it to the old man?"

"No, of course not," I shot back. "Unlike you, I follow the rules."

His hand came down on my shoulder. "I hate to break it to you, but rules are meant to be broken."

"If you hurt Grace, you'll leave me no choice."

He leaned against the wall, arms crossed, pushing out his chest. We were solid muscle and close in height, but he was leaner.

"After the shit the old man put my family through, I'm done following his orders."

"You're still a Knight," I reminded him.

Rhys closed the distance between us. "Here's what you don't seem to understand, Marshall. I have nothing left to lose. You can try to stop me, but I wouldn't recommend it."

"What are you planning to do?"

He smirked. "A gentleman never kisses and tells."

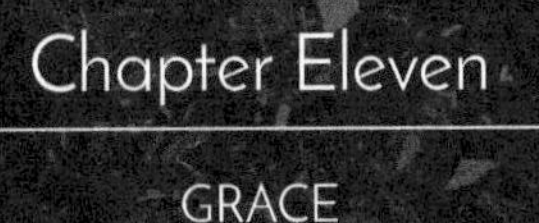

Chapter Eleven

GRACE

A new guest arrived at Fort Marshall at the end of the summer. Like Cole, Rhys Vanderbilt was from a wealthy family. Dark-haired and charming, he was the complete opposite of Cole.

While Cole was controlled and calculated, Rhys was like a storm rolling through the ocean. He was chaos and adventure, not a rule follower like his friend.

Cole rejected me several days ago, and we still hadn't spoken about that night. I doubted we ever would. He made it clear that he didn't return my feelings. But, for some stupid reason, it only made me want him more.

With Rhys here, I didn't have to be alone. He was a good distraction from Cole, and I could already tell he was the perfect person to help me scratch off the last four items on my bucket list.

Kiss a boy

Get asked out on a date

Lose my virginity

Fall in love

We didn't have much time until my dad would be home from his assignment to collect me before we moved to his next duty station. So I had to expedite my plans to check off at least three items.

I doubted I could fall in love that quickly, not even with Rhys and those killer smiles he flashed at me.

We sat by the pool under a cabana, sipping margaritas. I was a little tipsy from drinking for the past few hours and ready to nap by the time I finished my drink.

Rhys set his glass on the table and hopped up from the lounge chair, his hand extended. "Swim with me, princess."

I laughed the first time he called me that because it was far from the truth. If my life were a fairy tale, it would be one of the dark and twisted stories written by the Brothers Grimm.

Cole flipped up his sunglasses and groaned beside me, readjusting the book in his hand. "We just got out of the pool." He tipped his head at the chair. "Sit, Vanderbilt. Stop flirting with Grace."

They'd been friends for years and had attended York Military Academy since they were kids. But I could sense some hostility from Cole since Rhys's arrival. Whenever Rhys got too close to me, Cole treated me like his possession, which only drew me closer to Rhys.

He was fun and made me laugh. I didn't feel like another one of his responsibilities.

A part of me enjoyed watching Cole squirm whenever I let Rhys put his hands on me. I wanted him to feel my pain.

He made me feel stupid.

It was only fair Cole had to watch me with Rhys. There wasn't a damn thing he could do about it, even though he did his best to keep us apart.

Rhys wiggled his long fingers in front of me. "Don't listen to Marshall. He's no fun."

I took his hand, and he helped me up from the chair, scooping me into his arms. Rhys's muscled chest pressed against mine, which would have been okay if I weren't wearing a bikini that was a size too small.

His eyes dipped between my cleavage and then back to my face. Rhys licked his full lips.

I liked the way he looked at me. For the first time, I felt like someone saw *me*.

"You know the rules," Cole reminded Rhys, setting down the novel in his hand on the beach chair. "Grace is off-limits."

This was at least the tenth time Cole reminded Rhys this week. He was strict and what you would expect from a man raised by the military. In a lot of ways, he reminded me of my adoptive father, who was a Marine. But after feeling trapped for years, I wanted to be free.

I wanted to explore.

Rhys let me do that.

"Give it a break," Rhys snapped, yanking me away from the cabana. "Chill the fuck out and stop acting like we're at the academy."

Before he graduated, Cole was the platoon commander, which wasn't much of a surprise. He was the textbook cadet colonel, constantly issuing orders like he was in charge.

I followed Rhys toward the pool and squealed when he put his hand on my ass.

He grunted at my reaction, cupping my cheek with his palm. "You look good in this bikini."

"Vanderbilt," Cole warned from a distance.

Rhys waved his free hand in the air to dismiss him. "Save it."

Cole was at his side within seconds, ripping his hand from my body. "Don't fucking touch her."

Getting into Cole's face, Rhys folded his arms over his chest and smirked. "Fitzy isn't here. And he never said *I* couldn't touch her. Only *you*."

Cole shoved his palms into Rhys's chest, knocking him off balance. "The rules apply to every Knight. You're not an exception."

I didn't know much about their secret society, apart from my grandfather having his hand in it. He controlled all of our lives. And despite that fact, Rhys acted like he was untouchable.

Rhys gave a light shrug of his broad shoulders. "What the old man doesn't know won't hurt him."

He clutched my shoulder and steered me toward the entrance to the infinity pool, which overlooked the bay. The entire property had a stunning view of endless water from almost every window.

"Cole, this summer has been the best of my life. Rhys is right. My grandfather isn't here, and we're just trying to have a good time. Join us." I wet my lips with my tongue, and that gained a strong reaction from him. "Please."

Cole scrubbed a hand across his cleanly-shaven jaw and sighed. "Only if Rhys keeps his hands to himself."

I loved that Cole was so protective over me. But he needed to calm down about Rhys. It was harmless, nothing more than innocent flirting.

Cole bumped his elbow into Rhys's arm. "Hands off. Got it?"

With a chuckle, Rhys raised his hands. "Yeah, sure. Whatever you say, Colonel. But we're not at school, and you don't make the rules."

"You're staying at my house. So yeah," Cole fired back, "you follow my rules. Or you can get the fuck out."

We got into the pool.

Lounging against the wall, Rhys propped his elbows on the pavers and watched me. A slow fire spread across my skin when he lifted his sunglasses and winked.

My lack of experience with boys, let alone men, showed. Because when Rhys made advances, I just blushed and looked away. Like a shy girl who didn't know how to handle male attention. I reacted similarly when Cole's eyes seared my skin like lasers.

Cole grabbed two floats from the deep end and passed one

to me. Moving between them, he gripped my hips and hoisted me onto the float. Every inch of my skin heated from his touch.

I liked both of them.

How could I not?

Rhys looked like Henry Cavill's younger twin, and Cole reminded me of Alex Pettyfer but with more muscle and almost white blond hair.

I was determined to get my first kiss by the end of the summer. Whatever my grandfather had said to Cole must have scared him but not Rhys.

It was ridiculous for a girl my age to have never been kissed. But with my upbringing, boys were the last thing on my mind. Intimacy wasn't something I understood well.

Cole hopped on the float beside me, tugging mine closer. He held the white cord attached to the plastic to keep me away from Rhys. Whenever the raft drifted toward him, Cole pulled harder on the string.

"Who wants to play a game?"

I glanced over at Rhys. "What do you have in mind?"

He waggled his black eyebrows. "Wet Truth or Dare."

I sat up on the float. "How do you play?"

"No," Cole said before Rhys could explain. "We're not playing that."

I snapped my head at him. "Why not?"

"Because Rhys plays dirty," he said through gritted teeth.

Undeterred, Rhys ignored Cole and waded across the pool, stopping at the end of my float. "It's like regular Truth or Dare but in the water."

He gripped the float and pulled me toward him, which started a tug-of-war with Cole. As Cole tightened his grip on the cord, Rhys claimed his dominance over me. They went back and forth, shaking me until I nearly fell into the water.

"Hey, would you two stop fighting over me? I'm not a toy."

Rhys let go of the float, and before I rolled into the water, he lifted me into his arms. "I got you now, princess." He hooked my legs around his back and carried me into the deeper end.

"Put her down!" Cole flopped off the float and swam to us in seconds. His fingers dug into Rhys's thick bicep. "I'm not fucking around anymore. If you don't stop it, I'm sending your ass back to California."

Rhys curled his arms around me. "Try it. Your dad won't let you."

I expected them to act like friends since they had gone to school together and were Knights. Instead, I got constant bickering about me that was getting old fast.

"Cole, it's okay," I assured him. "Rhys isn't hurting me."

"Not now," he hissed, his angry blue eyes aimed at Rhys. "But he will if given a chance. You're not the type of girl he dates."

His harsh words stung as if he'd stabbed me in the chest.

"Thanks a lot, Cole."

"C'mon, Grace," he groaned. "That's not how I meant it. Rhys dates easy girls. Not sweet girls like you. I didn't mean to hurt your feelings. I'm only trying to protect you from men like him."

"Maybe I'm not *that* sweet. And maybe I don't need your protection twenty-four-seven. I've never been free a day in my life. So stop yelling at Rhys and play the game with us. All of this fighting is getting on my nerves."

"Mine too," Rhys commented. "Get another drink, Marshall, and relax already. You're killing our vibe."

Cole's nostrils flared.

I couldn't see Rhys's expression, but judging by the look on Cole's face, it was another victorious smirk. Seconds later, Cole stormed out of the pool, splashing water in his wake. Then, he headed toward the house, flinging a beach towel over his shoulder.

"You're all mine," Rhys said with a villainous look in his pretty green eyes. "Still wanna play the game with me?"

My stomach twisted into knots now that I was alone with Rhys without Cole to intervene. I hadn't expected him to get that mad over nothing.

"Promise to go easy on me?"

A sinister grin pulled at his lips. "I play games to win. So I'm not making any promises."

Chapter Twelve

GRACE

After Cole stormed into the house, Rhys stalked toward me. I inched backward, hoping to create some space. But I had nowhere to run.

"Where are you going, princess?" One of his sexy smirks lit up his handsome face. "You said you wanted to play the game."

I swallowed hard, clearing the lump in my throat. We were alone, and I was barely dressed, with the eyes of a hunter gazing at my breasts.

"Sure, I'll play," I bit out. "But I'll probably suck at it."

"I'm sure you're good at sucking," he said, and it sounded way too sexual. "How about I start?"

Rhys took up the space on my right, his elbow propped up on the ledge. I couldn't make eye contact when I knew I would find his bright green eyes on my body.

He leaned in, his lips dangerously close to mine. "Truth or dare, princess?"

I cleared my throat and responded, "Truth."

Dare seemed too risky.

Is the truth any better?

Not with all my secrets.

Rhys invaded my space with his big, muscular body. He

lowered his head, and black hair flopped onto his tanned forehead. Designer sunglasses pushed some of the strands back to give his hair a messy style that looked sexy.

He was too close for my comfort and smelled good—a mixture of sweat, suntan lotion, and his spicy cologne.

"Do you want to kiss me?" Rhys placed his hands on each side of me, caging me against the wall with his chest pressed against mine.

Hell, yes.

I'd never wanted to kiss someone as much as Rhys. Well, maybe Cole. He would have been my first choice if he wasn't a buzzkill.

When I took too long to answer, Rhys asked me the question again. I couldn't say the words aloud. Speaking the thoughts in my head felt too personal. Too vulnerable.

"I'm switching to dare."

His hand slid beneath my chin, stealing my attention back to him. "I dare you to kiss me."

Oh, shit.

Biting my cheek, I looked up at Rhys. He was close to a foot taller than me. So I had to trail my hands up his chest, using the connection to stand on my tippy toes and get closer to his lips.

Rhys lifted my feet off the ground, wrapping my legs around his back as his lips brushed mine.

I kissed him.

My first real kiss.

I mentally scratched another item off my list.

~~Kiss a boy~~
Get asked out on a date
Lose my virginity
Fall in love

His tongue swept into my mouth, his hands wandering

down my arms, applying the right amount of pressure with his fingertips. Rhys kissed me like he wanted to suck my soul from my body. Clutching his wrist, I encouraged him to continue exploring my body. Rhys didn't need much instruction, only the green light to slip his hand into my bikini top.

He captured my moans with his mouth, twisting my nipple between his fingers. I felt like I would spontaneously combust from the pressure building inside me. My nipples hardened into peaks that he massaged with care. Rhys was so good with his hands and tongue.

When his other hand slid up and down my thigh, I wanted him to touch my core. I was so wet and needed to get off, humping him—anything to create friction.

"You're purring like a kitten," he growled against my lips. "Fuck, princess." He laid his forehead against mine, breathless. "I don't want to stop."

I didn't want him to either.

"Do you want me to stop?"

I shook my head.

Rhys put me down and dipped his hand beneath my bikini bottoms. "Relax, princess. This will feel good."

My eyes darted in each direction. Thankfully, no one was outside, not even the staff. We had complete privacy out here as long as no one was spying on us from the windows. They had dozens of them along the back of the house. The bedrooms also had balconies that were unoccupied at the moment.

"What if someone sees us?"

Rubbing his thumb over my clit in a circular motion, Rhys ignored my question, determined to give me an orgasm. His lips slammed into mine, and his tongue swept into my mouth. This time, he didn't go slow. His movements quickened, and so did his fingers that pumped in and out of me.

My chest heaved as the orgasm brewed inside me. Waves of pleasure pebbled my arms and thighs with tiny bumps. An intense flash of heat spread across my chest, up my neck, and flushed my cheeks.

"Rhys," I said between kisses, my skin on fire and ready to burst into flames.

"I've been dying to hear you scream my name," he grunted, sucking my bottom lip into his mouth. "Make a mess on my fingers, princess."

"Rhys," I panted. "I'm coming."

He concealed my moans with another kiss, fingering me to the finish line.

I heard footsteps to my right and then, "Are you fucking kidding me?"

Cole stood at the pool's edge, jaw clenched with his hands on his narrow hips.

Rhys removed his hand from my bikini bottoms. "You didn't want to play the game, Marshall. Maybe you should've stuck around." He licked the fingers he had inside me one at a time. "You missed out."

"Get out of the fucking pool," Cole snapped. "Both of you." When we didn't move or respond, he shouted, "Now!"

I went from the best ten minutes of my life to one of the worst.

"Chill out, Marshall." Rhys rolled his eyes. "You're so uptight. We were only fucking around."

"Why do you always think you're above the law when everyone else has to follow it?"

"Don't get mad at Rhys. I wanted to play the game."

Cole ran his fingers through his hair, fuming with anger. "Grace, I'm not mad at you. Rhys knew what he was doing. He intentionally put you in a bad position." His gaze drifted back to Rhys. "Get out of the pool, Vanderbilt. If I have to tell you again, I'll drag you out of it."

Rhys stepped out from between my thighs and glanced up at Cole. "We were playing a game. Grace chose dare. I kissed her. Deal with it."

"You're going back to California tonight," Cole threatened. "Pack your bags."

"Cole," I interjected, "I think you're taking this too far. It was only a kiss."

"Only a kiss? Not quite, Grace." A dark chuckle escaped his throat. "I could hear you moaning his name from the patio. I know what a woman looks and sounds like when she comes. So don't lie to me. You were doing more than kissing Rhys."

"Are you jealous?"

Rhys snickered. "He's green with envy."

"I'm done being the responsible one," he shot back, his tanned cheeks growing redder by the second. "Do whatever you want. I don't care anymore."

With that, Cole rushed back into the house, slamming the glass door so hard it rattled.

"We should apologize," I suggested. "This is his house. And you two have been at each other's throats since you arrived."

"Because of you." Rhys kissed my lips, a quick peck that left me wanting more. "Marshall wants you, too. But he won't take the stick out of his ass. So you're mine now, princess." Another kiss. "All mine."

Chapter Thirteen

COLE

All day, I couldn't shake the sight of Grace and Rhys in the pool. I'd hated him before he arrived at Fort Marshall. And now that he was getting too close to Grace, I hated him even more.

I tried to convince my dad to send Rhys back to his family in California. But my dad wouldn't cave and said I had to find a way to get along with him.

He didn't believe that Rhys broke Fitzy's rule and kissed Grace. They were doing much more than kissing from where I stood. His hand was down the front of her bikini bottoms, ripping a soft moan from her throat.

It was dangerous to want her the way I did.

Was I jealous?

Fuck, yeah.

I waited until Grace was asleep to confront Rhys. He was fucking with the status quo and needed a reminder of his goal to protect her.

"What do you want, Marshall?" Rhys finished typing an email at his desk and hit send. Then, he spun around to face me, one of his usual smirks plastered on his stupid face. "If you're here to lecture me again, get lost."

My body shook from the anger surging through my veins like hot lava, so I folded my arms over my chest to stop myself from punching him. "We all took the same oath. You're not the exception to the rule, Vanderbilt."

We never called each other by our first names. At the academy, it was last names only.

Rhys rose from the chair, standing around the same height as me. Except I had a lot more muscle. "I make my own rules. And if Fitzy has his way, I won't have to answer to The Founders anymore. So fuck off and get out of my room."

I got in his face, our chests pressed together. "Listen up because I won't repeat myself. Keep your hands off Grace. This isn't about Fitzy or us. Grace is in danger. You're a Knight. So fucking act like it."

"You're an idiot for doing anything Fitzy says. He doesn't give a shit about any of us."

As he gave me a shit-eating grin, I refrained from tackling him to the ground and beating his pretty boy face to a pulp. Rhys could turn on the charm and win anyone over. Of course, Grace liked him.

Most women did.

"You're still a Founder," I reminded him.

Rhys hated Grace's grandfather. Whatever game he was playing with Grace had nothing to do with her and everything about his hatred for Fitzy.

"You're too much of a pussy to touch her." He laughed in my face. "You really should let go, Marshall. Her pussy is so tight. It's all I've thought about today. Maybe I'll let you play with her if you're a good boy."

Slamming my palms into his chest, I pushed him across the room. "Stay the fuck away from her. I won't tell you again."

He plopped onto the king-size bed and leaned back on his elbows. "When will you learn that your threats don't scare me? They didn't work at the academy and won't work now. You know what I think?"

"I don't care what you think."

He kicked off his shoes and got comfortable on the bed. "I think you want her. But you're too scared to defy The Founders."

"Following orders got me to where I am."

He snickered. "Deny it all you want, but I see how you look at Grace. Don't come in here and jump down my throat because you're a coward. I wanted her, so I took her. It's that simple."

"She's not *yours*."

"I'm growing bored of this conversation." He raised his hand to his mouth and yawned, but it was fake. "It's late. Don't you have to be in bed by a certain time, *Colonel*? I wouldn't want you to mess up your routine."

I was ten minutes late for my bedtime ritual. Yeah, I was a bit of a control freak. After living at a military academy for the past ten years, I craved structure. I had terrible anxiety if I couldn't complete my daily routines.

Rhys wanted to get under my skin to see if I would snap. He was good at provoking me and knew all of my weaknesses. That was one of his hidden talents. I bet that was how he talked Grace into making out with him in the pool. She was so inexperienced that she didn't know any better. Someone like Rhys could easily manipulate a sweet girl like Grace.

So I had to protect her.

"If you don't stop pursuing Grace," I told him, "I'll go straight to Fitzy and tell him what you've done."

He sat up and swung his long legs off the side of the bed. "It was a kiss. Relax."

"That was more than a kiss. And for your sake, it better stay that way."

Before he could get in another retort, I left the room and didn't stop until I was in my bedroom. Rhys was right about a lot of things. I wanted her and was afraid to cross The Founders. But if anyone should have been worried about pissing off Fitzy, it should have been Rhys.

His family needed the lifeline. What game was he playing? And what did it have to do with Grace?

Chapter Fourteen

COLE

Five days into Rhys's stay, we were summoned by Luca Salvatore to a meeting with The Devil's Knights—a quick five-minute update on Drake's progress with the Il Circo auction site. Alex was still on it. There was recent activity from The Lucaya Group on the Dark Web, and no trace of Grace's biological father anywhere.

Viktor Romanov had popped up on our radar at the start of the summer. He was putting out feelers, trying to find Katarina Adams Romanov, but he was looking for the wrong person.

Katarina was dead.

For now, Grace was safe.

On our way through the catacombs, Rhys said, "I want the code to Grace's bedroom door."

"No," I snapped. "She doesn't need you spying on her."

"It's also my job to protect her. I can't effectively do that if you won't give me the code."

"Since when do you care about her safety?" I snarled at him as we made a beeline toward the secret entrance to the library. "You've done nothing but put her at risk."

"I'm just being friendly. Get off my ass, Marshall."

We climbed the stairs and entered the library through the

hidden door. I hit the lever and sealed it behind us. Rhys helped me put the books in the correct place, and I saved *The Count of Monte Cristo* for last. In one of the homes Rhys's parents sold, they would have had a library just like this one. We all had escape routes for emergencies.

I didn't speak to Rhys, power-walking through the house until I was in front of Grace's door. "Are you watching? Because this is the only time I will show you," I said before entering the numbers into the keypad on her door.

Rhys took this as an invitation to open her door and pop his head inside. I grabbed him by the shirt collar, and he shoved me. The room was dark, save for the light coming in through the glass panels on the patio doors.

I followed him into the room and whispered, "Don't wake her."

Some nights, Grace had nightmares about her past. She never spoke to me about them, but I'd heard her call out for her father. A few times for her mother, who died in front of her.

Rhys lifted a notepad from Grace's nightstand, scanned it briefly, and showed it to me. "What's this?"

Fuck.

The list.

~~Kiss a boy~~
Get asked out on a date
Lose my virginity
Fall in love

"Nothing," I lied and ripped it from his hand, setting it on the table before I pulled him out of the bedroom, closing the door behind me.

"Was that a bucket list?" Rhys asked once we were alone in the hallway. "Because it looked like one to me."

I narrowed my eyes at him. "Forget you saw it."

"Kiss a boy," he said, scratching the corner of his jaw. "I was her first kiss?"

I nodded.

A smirk tugged at his mouth. "You had two months with her and didn't kiss her once?" He chuckled as we walked down the corridor. "I knew you were a pussy, Marshall. But damn, not even a kiss." His laughter filled the silence in the house. "How could you resist her?"

"It's called self-control. Something you lack."

I walked past him and headed into my room, slamming the door in his face.

At breakfast, I had to watch Rhys flirt with Grace. She giggled as he brushed against her arm and whispered something into her ear. A different side of Grace came out with him.

I hated seeing them together but had to shut my mouth unless he stepped out of line. Grace was angry with me for getting involved. We'd barely spoken more than a few words since Rhys arrived at Fort Marshall.

The kitchen staff emerged from the scullery, lining the banquet table with plates of food. My younger brothers were awake at this hour and hanging out at the end of the table, staring at Knox's cell phone.

The twins were my father's spitting image. They had the same jaw, the same black, wavy hair, and almost the same height. But they were nothing like him. While I was the model cadet, they wasted time at the academy and didn't take anything seriously.

It seemed like I was the only person who gave a damn. Why did my father insist I followed the rules when no one else did? The twins would become Knights the following year. They would be as lazy as Rhys, not cut from the same cloth as me.

Rhys grabbed an apple from the bowl and bit into it, eyes on me. "Forbidden fruit tastes so much sweeter," he said low enough for me to hear. "Don't you think, Marshall?"

"I wouldn't know. I take my oaths seriously."

He snickered and wiped the juice from his chin. "Yeah, you do. And that's why this time, you're going to lose."

After breakfast, Rhys grabbed Grace's hand and pulled her aside, giving her one of his boyish smirks. I hated how she looked at him because she used to look at me like that.

Like I mattered to her.

Rhys leaned against the wall outside the dining room and held her hand. "So, I thought we could go out. On a date," he clarified when she didn't respond.

She cleared her throat, glancing at me when she heard my shoes on the tiled floor. A second of nonverbal communication passed between us. I told her with my eyes to say no. With every ounce of my being, I wanted to stop her.

But so far, my plan to keep her away from him wasn't working. By getting involved, I only pushed her toward him. We were growing apart, which was my fault. She deserved to be happy. I wished it was with anyone but Rhys.

Her blonde head snapped back to Rhys, a pretty smile gracing her full, pink lips. "Of course," she beamed with delight. "I'd love to go on a date with you."

She only had two items on her list to check off.

Fuck.

I wanted to claim all her firsts, but I had other people to consider. A higher calling other than myself. My family and The Knights expected me to follow through on my orders.

Rhys winked at me, then yanked on her hand to lead her in the opposite direction. "See ya later, Marshall. Don't wait up."

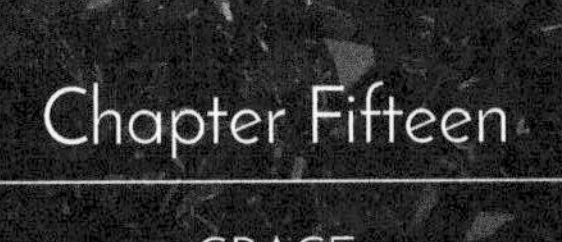

Chapter Fifteen

GRACE

I spent the entire day with Rhys without Cole hovering over me. Being out of the house and free from my warden was nice. Until Rhys arrived, Cole made it his mission to help me enjoy my summer. He was such a good friend, but I was dumb to think we could have more.

No matter what, I was determined to finish my bucket list by the summer's end.

~~Kiss a boy~~
~~Get asked out on a date~~
Lose my virginity
Fall in love

I didn't have time to check off the last one. But I felt something for Rhys. Even if it wasn't love, it was the beginning of what could be love. And that was enough for me.

Rhys took me for a walk on the beach. We swam in the bay and ate seafood at a restaurant in Beacon Bay. He kissed me at sunset, whispered sexy things into my ear, and promised to make me feel good when we were alone.

Cole wasn't around when we returned to Fort Marshall. I

wasn't sure if that was intentional or if he was lurking somewhere in the shadows.

I hooked my arms around Rhys's neck and kissed him the
second we were in my bedroom. He lifted my feet off the floor
and carefully laid me on the bed, moving between my thighs.

"You're so fucking sexy," he grunted between kisses.
"Fuck, princess, I want to devour every inch of your gorgeous
body."

I sat up, pulled my shirt over my head, and threw it onto
the floor. Breathing harder, Rhys gazed at my breasts, which
practically spilled out from the navy blue bikini top. He tugged
on the string around my neck with his teeth until it came
undone.

I giggled. "You're an animal, Rhys."

"You have no idea." He nibbled on my neck. "The things
I want to do to you."

"Show me."

Rhys loved a challenge, and his green eyes lit up with
excitement. After he discarded the bikini top, he flattened his
tongue over my breasts and licked, sucking the tiny bud into
his mouth.

I moaned when he tugged harder. "Rhys, oh my…"

The words died on the tip of my tongue, and as he moved
lower, my body trembled. He kissed my inner thigh before
lifting my leg over his shoulder. With his mouth near my
aching core, I panted like a dog in heat. I had been dreaming
of this moment for days, desperate to feel him everywhere.

He peeled away my shorts and bikini bottoms, no longer
taking his time. And I was thankful for that. Because when he
rolled his tongue over my clit, I said his name.

He peeked up at me, his lips glistening with my cum. "Feel
good?"

"Yes, yes, yes," I whimpered as he licked between my folds,
his tongue darting in and out of me.

A smirk tugged at his wet lips, and then he went back to
licking me. My fingers wove through his black hair, begging

him for more. He shoved two fingers inside me as if he could read my mind, filling me to the hilt.

"Rhys," I moaned.

His eyes held mine as a powerful sensation commanded control of my body. He growled against my pussy, loving the sight of me unraveling above him.

After the tremors left my body, I struggled to catch my breath.

Rhys wiped his mouth. "Damn, princess. You're a screamer. Fuck, that was hot."

He was still dressed, so I slid my hands to his chest and inched his shirt up his muscled abdomen. "Take this off."

Rhys stripped off his T-shirt and threw it onto the floor, climbing on top of me wearing only his board shorts.

"All of this is new to me," I told him. "I want to try everything I can before the end of the summer. We don't have a lot of time. Will you teach me what you like?"

He ran his fingers through his dark hair to keep it out of his eyes and smirked. "I thought you'd never ask, princess." Clutching my hips, he flipped us over so he was beneath me. "Get on your knees." He shoved his shorts down, fisting his hand around his big dick. "Wrap your lips around the tip."

I did as he instructed, and he hissed from the sudden contact.

He grabbed a chunk of my hair and moved it out of the way. "Good girl." His eyes closed as if he were trying to focus. "Now, suck me into your mouth."

It was a challenge to fit him, and my cheeks puffed out with each inch of him I took. I wasn't sure if I was doing this right, but he seemed to enjoy it. After a while, Rhys loosened his grip on my hair, watching me with his lips parted.

He grunted each time I felt him hit the top of my mouth. "Don't stop, princess. I'm so close."

I eventually found a solid rhythm, jerking his shaft as I sucked. This seemed to get even more of a reaction from him, and his legs started trembling. I felt a slow pulse moving down his length, and before I knew what was happening, he came into my mouth. His cum tasted salty, and I wasn't sure what to do, so I swallowed.

"That was some blow job." Rhys focused on my lips, his thumb caressing my cheek. "You didn't need me to teach you, princess."

A cell phone beeped with one message after another. I didn't own a phone. My dad only used burner phones and ditched them every month. He said we could never be too careful. Someone could trace us through the signal.

Rhys sat up and retrieved the phone from his pocket. He read the messages with his body angled away from me. But I could tell whatever the person sent upset him.

"Is everything okay?" I asked.

"Yeah." He shoved the phone back into his pocket and got dressed. "All good."

It sounded like a lie.

"It's getting late." He bent down and pulled me toward him. "You should get some rest. Willow Marshall is taking you to the salon bright and early." He glanced at the clock. "You won't get much sleep. Sorry about that."

I pressed my lips to his. "I would rather be doing this."

He kissed me back. "For once, I'm trying to do the right thing."

"That's why I like you, Rhys. You're a bad boy. You do whatever you want."

"Willow will tell my mom if I keep you up too late and you miss your appointment. I don't want to get on her bad side. That woman is a force to be reckoned with."

"She raised you, so she must be strong."

"I wish we'd met sooner." Rhys slid off the bed, staring down at me. "But I have a feeling you'll be in my life for a long time."

"Maybe." I gave him a sweet smile and covered my naked body with a sheet, suddenly feeling vulnerable with him fully clothed. "Who knows when we'll see each other again? I'm moving with my dad."

"Do you know where you're going?"

I shook my head. "I never do. My dad gives me a map and says to pick a place anywhere in the world. If I guess right, he'll buy me anything I want."

"Have you ever guessed correctly?"

"No, but that's what makes our game fun. It's kind of our thing."

"Do you remember anything about your bio dad?" He sat next to me on the bed. "Viktor."

Whenever someone said his name, I cringed.

Viktor Romanov.

My dad.

The terrorist.

"The scar on his right hand," I admitted with a sigh. "And a song he used to sing to me before bed. The man I knew wasn't bad. But I guess we don't really know people, do we?"

"Probably not. Most people hide their true selves because they fear being judged."

I leaned into his shoulder, meeting his gaze. "What about you?"

"I have nothing to hide." His words said one thing, but his face said another when he looked away. He kissed me once more and hopped up from the mattress. "Night, princess. Sweet dreams."

"Night," I murmured before he left in a hurry.

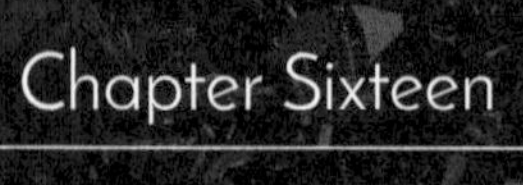

Chapter Sixteen

COLE

I hadn't spoken to Rhys or Grace since they left for their date. All night, I seethed about how much I wanted her. And how I couldn't let Rhys have her all to himself.

She was mine.

I felt a deep longing for Grace, unlike anything I had ever felt for another woman. But I valued my place among The Devil's Knights too much to risk it. If Fitzy were to find out about my feelings for her, he would use them to crush both of us.

So I left before they were awake and drove into the city to meet Drake. I would start working with him at Battle Industries at the end of the summer, and I needed to get the lay of the land.

I drove beneath the monstrous glass building with a giant satellite on the roof and gave my keys to the valet. Then I met with Drake's private security team and got a keycard, employee badge, and access codes.

Regular employees didn't have this kind of access. But given our relationship and The Lucaya Group breathing down Drake's neck, all this extra security was necessary.

I got into the elevator and inserted the special keycard into the slot on the wall. A panel opened and allowed me to enter the passcode that would take me to the hidden fifty-first floor. No one knew it existed, apart from Drake'a head of security and a handful of trusted people.

By the time the doors opened into a lobby, my ears popped again from the pressure.

"Drake," a woman said in a sultry tone. "My brother will kill you."

Her voice carried from the office at the end of the hall with the door open. Drake bent a brunette woman over his desk. It looked like Olivia Maxwell from this angle, but I couldn't see her face.

Tate would have killed Drake. After Tate caught them kissing, he made Drake promise not to touch her again. He didn't want his feelings for Olivia to ruin their friendship. And to my knowledge, Drake hadn't kissed her since.

His hand slid down her back and over her ass. "One night with you would be worth it."

Olivia giggled. "You only want me because you can't have me."

"Hmm." He cupped her ass with his hands. "Is that so, Miss Maxwell?"

Another laugh as she looked over her shoulder at him. "Are we back to formalities when you have your hands on my ass?"

Drake must have heard my shoes hit the tile because he dropped his hands from Olivia's body and glanced over his shoulder. "Oh, hey. I didn't hear you come up the elevator." He ran a hand through his dark hair to sweep it off his forehead. "I was a little busy."

I smirked as our eyes met. "Yeah, I heard."

He tugged on his tie and winked.

As I entered the office, Olivia turned around and fixed the red dress, pulling it down her legs. Drake liked bigger girls with thick thighs, curves, and big tits. My cousin had a type, and Olivia fit the bill.

"Liv, you remember Cole."

She pressed her lips together and nodded. "Nice to see you."

"You, too."

Olivia looked at Drake, sharing a moment that didn't need words. "I'll give you some space. If you need me, call my cell."

He stared at her ass until she disappeared into the elevator.

I closed the distance between us, one eyebrow raised in question. "Were you about to fuck her?"

Drake shook his head before sitting behind his desk. "No. Of course, not. I would never do that to Tate. But…" He scrubbed a hand through his dark brown hair and sighed. "I want to. Not a single day has gone by the past five years that I haven't wanted her."

I understood how he felt. Not having Grace was killing me.

"Then why did you hire Olivia to be your assistant?"

He leaned back in the leather chair. "She was already living in my house with Tate. And when she couldn't afford her student loans, I offered to pay them if she agreed to work for me for one year."

Olivia was fiercely independent and would never take money from Drake. When she applied to college, he said he would pay for her to attend any college of her choosing. But she wanted to do it on her own without his help. He had already done so much for her.

"That's a generous salary," I commented.

Olivia graduated from Kingston University over in Beacon Bay. It was one of the most prestigious colleges on the East Coast and came with a hefty price tag. One year of work in exchange for no student loan debt made Olivia the highest-paid assistant in history.

Drake held up his hands and shrugged. "It's Liv. I can't say no to her. She can be very persuasive."

Tate Maxwell was an associate of The Devil's Knights but

didn't come from money like us. He was Drake's head of security and his best friend.

Tate and Olivia left a lousy situation at their foster home when Drake found them wandering the streets. At first, Tate was a dick to him. But Drake was persistent and put them up in one of his apartment buildings. He fed them and made sure they got an education.

My cousin had a good heart. The Maxwells were like family to Drake. He was an only child and even lonelier after his father's death.

I sat in the leather chair across from him, resting my shiny dress shoe on my knee. "Does Tate know you're trying to fuck his sister again?"

"We haven't fucked. And we never will." He scrubbed a hand across his jaw. "She likes to torture me. And when she wears those goddamn dresses, I can't even concentrate." Drake groaned. "I think she likes giving me blue balls."

"I remember when she had braces and glasses and wore her hair in those stupid-looking clips. She's a knockout now."

He bobbed his head. "When she came home from college, I nearly had a fucking heart attack. Tate noticed my reaction to her and reminded me to keep my hands off his sister."

I laughed. "Looks like you've been doing a shit job keeping your promise."

He rolled his shoulders against the leather chair. "We were flirting."

"Uh-huh. Do you talk to all of your secretaries like that? Bend them over your desk, too?"

He snorted.

No.

My cousin was careful. He didn't fuck around or shit where he ate. Men like us had too much attention on us.

I surveyed the room, taking in the wall of glass windows that looked like mirrors.

Maybe they were mirrors.

It was hard to tell.

This level wasn't on any of the floor plans. Adding windows would have only made it more noticeable from the outside. So maybe the glass was to give the appearance of having a view.

He didn't have a receptionist or other support staff on this floor. Only his office and the lab where he kept his artificial intelligence software.

The Lucaya Group had been trying to steal it from him. So had other criminal organizations, corrupt governments, and even crime families. The threats against Drake had gotten so bad he took the AI offline and moved it to a secure room.

Drake shot up from the chair and cleared his throat. "Come with me. We need to do the retinal and hand scan. Just in case something happens to me."

"This place is better guarded than Fort Knox." I followed him out of the office and down the hall. "No one is getting into your building."

He turned left at the corner, his pace unwavering. "Someone made it into my office on the fiftieth floor last week. The guards subdued him before he could take anything." Drake bit his lip. "They're getting close, Cole. It's only a matter of time. The passcodes change every ten minutes. I'm doing everything I can to keep us on lockdown."

"How did he get into the building without security noticing?"

"Stole a badge from a guard."

Drake stopped at the door on our right and pressed his hand to the panel on the wall. "Good morning, boss," Lovelace said, and the door clicked open. "Have you remembered to take your vitamins today?"

"Not yet," he sighed.

"Would you like me to schedule a reminder?" Lovelace asked.

"No, I will remember."

We entered the room, and he nodded at the massive super-computer in front of us—endless rows of data storage devices with blinking lights. "This is Lovelace. Part of her, anyway. Some of the AI/DL data is on the cloud. The rest of the software is on data servers. So even if The Lucaya Group could breach this room, it wouldn't do them any good."

He shut the door behind us and locked it with his handprint. My eyes swept over the wall with dozens of flat-screen monitors. Numbers moved on them at an impressive pace, changing every second. None of this shit made sense to me. I was an aerospace engineer, not a systems or software engineer.

Drake wanted me to help him with a new aircraft he'd been trying to get off the ground. But that wasn't a fixed position. So whatever Drake needed, I would be there for him.

He steered me to a glass room with scanners that shone red lasers on the walls. "I can't trust anyone. Only family and The Knights. I have the media up my ass, the government breathing down my neck, and lunatics who think I'm trying to play God want me stopped."

"People are afraid of AI."

"They've been using it for years and don't even know it." He tipped his head back and laughed as we entered the glass room. "People are so fucking stupid."

Drake was a genius. He'd coded his first program before his tenth birthday and graduated from college when he was nineteen.

Drake led me to a computer with a monitor that took up the entire desk. "If anything happens to me, I will activate the Battle King protocol. Lovelace will lock down all of my company's buildings and homes. You're the only person, other than Tate, with access to override the system."

"What happens when you activate the Battle King protocol?"

"Whoever is in the building will be trapped temporarily. But it's for their safety."

"Can the police get inside?"

He shook his head. "No one in or out. So I need you to pay attention." Drake's fingers glided across the keyboard, his eyes on the giant monitor. "I'm going to take a retinal and hand scan. You will also need the deactivation codes."

I stuffed my hands into my pockets and moved beside him, attempting to read something from his face. But he gave away nothing. "What are you not telling me, Drake?"

His jaw clenched. "I'm preparing you for the worst-case scenario."

Chapter Seventeen

GRACE

My relationship with Cole had been strained over the past few days. I could tell he wasn't happy with me hanging out with Rhys alone. But he didn't protest when we went on another date.

I had a good time with Rhys. He made me laugh and smile. Whenever I was with him, I felt special. I liked both of them, which only complicated matters more. Eventually, I would leave with my father, and I wouldn't see them.

So this was temporary.

I had to remind myself daily that I couldn't fall in love, even if my heart didn't get the memo.

Still wearing a black bikini from earlier, I slipped into a spandex skirt and a pink tank top with chunky jeweled sandals. Willow Marshall had chosen everything in my closet, clothing that probably cost more than my dad made in a year.

I met Cole and Rhys in the great room. Cole stood with his hands shoved into his shorts pockets, glaring at Rhys. He wasn't thrilled about us hooking up. God forbid anyone broke my grandfather's rules.

"Am I in trouble?" I asked Cole.

He shook his head, slowly approaching me with his hand extended. "I'm taking you to the pier."

"*We're* taking you," Rhys added.

My eyes widened in shock. "Really?"

Cole nodded, the start of a smile ghosting his full lips as his fingers slipped between mine. "I thought you'd want to check this off your list."

I smiled so wide my face hurt as I stared up at him, wondering if the person I craved at the start of the summer had returned. "That sounds perfect."

Rhys grabbed my other hand. "I can think of few things we can do." He waggled his eyebrows. "If you want to check those off your list, too."

My cheeks flushed. "You know about the list?"

I hadn't told Rhys. Only Cole knew about it, and he hadn't said a word since he walked out of the game room and left me crying on the floor.

What the fuck?

I didn't want anyone else to know about the list. In fact, I regretted even making it. That stupid thing killed my friendship with Cole. But so far, my plan to make Cole jealous by using Rhys was working. I could tell our dates bothered him, and every time Rhys kissed me, I thought about Cole. I pretended his hands and tongue were on my body.

Rhys tightened his grip on my hand and flashed one of his signature smirks. "It's my job to know everything about you, princess."

"You sound like Cole when you say it like that."

Cole groaned beside me, yanking on my hand to guide the way out of the house. "I don't sound like that." He held open the Ferrari passenger door for me. "Get in the car."

I slipped into the car, and Cole shut the door.

"You always say I'm a job."

He rounded the car and pulled open the driver's side door. "I don't mean it like that, Grace."

Rhys hopped into the backseat. "Lighten up, Marshall. It wouldn't kill you to let go for once."

"Why do you think I let you talk me into going to the

pier?" Cole started the engine, his eyes on Rhys in the rearview mirror. "For the record, we're making a horrible mistake taking Grace out in public. It's too risky to let anyone see her."

I raised an eyebrow at Rhys. "You talked Cole into letting me leave the house?"

He winked. "Don't say I never did anything for you, princess."

"Thank you," I mouthed as we drove off the property.

Ten minutes later, we arrived at the pier in Beacon Bay, which had games, rides, and concession stands. We walked down the boardwalk, and I drank in the saltiness of the bay, taking in my surroundings.

Kids played games with their parents. Some people shot darts and basketballs, while others were engaged in water gun races. I'd never seen anything like it. Most of my childhood was spent indoors.

No games.

No fun.

I loved it here.

The fond memories of my time in Devil's Creek would stay with me forever. Memories I made with Cole and Rhys. Watching movies under the stars with the waves crashing on the beach. Our lazy days by the pool. Dirty Truth or Dare.

My first kiss.

Rhys must have asked me on a date because he knew about the list. He made my dreams come true and gave me what Cole denied me.

We stopped in front of a Ferris wheel that lit up the sky, the bright lights shining in the darkness. Dozens of people waited in line, but Cole cut ahead, bringing me with him.

He spoke to the man running the wheel in a hushed tone, patted him on the back, and stuffed money into his hand. We never waited for anything. When people in town saw Cole, doors opened for him. Being a Founder had its perks. People respected the Marshalls as much as they feared their power.

After the wheel spun again, a gondola stopped in front of us. People tumbled out from it, laughing. Cole tipped his head and gestured for me to follow. With Rhys on my tail, he grabbed my ass, never missing an opportunity to touch me.

Anyone looking at the three of us must have thought I was dating two men. I wasn't opposed to the idea. Rhys and Cole were both tempting. The kind of men I could see myself having a future with.

We got into a gondola that was large enough to fit four people on each side. I took the seat to my right, and surprisingly, Cole and Rhys sat beside each other. They kept their distance, hands on their spread thighs.

My gaze flicked between these delicious men who sparked a naughty desire in me. Silence hung between us as we made our way up to the top. Their eyes roamed my body until they settled on my face.

We hadn't moved from the top, not even an inch. I glanced over the side, my stomach knotting at the steep drop to the ground.

"Since we're stuck up here," Rhys said, "why don't we play a game?"

I wasn't afraid of heights, but we were so high I didn't want to look down again.

"No," Cole shot back, thick biceps crossed over his chest. "You don't play fair, Vanderbilt."

Rhys snickered. "It doesn't matter if you play dirty as long as you win. Didn't your old man teach you that?"

Cole turned away from Rhys, his top lip curled upward in disgust.

"What did you have in mind?" I asked, needing a distraction from the fact we were sitting at the top of the Ferris wheel without moving.

Rhys leaned forward, bracing his elbows on his thighs as he met my gaze. "How about another game of Truth or Dare?"

"No," Cole cut in.

His attitude was getting on my nerves. The first two months alone with Cole were perfect. But after the night I showed him the bucket list, he hadn't been the same. It was as if a light had switched off in his brain. Cole was moodier and distant, unlike the person I met before Rhys arrived.

"I want to play," I said with my eyes on Cole. "You should play, too. It will help us pass the time."

He scrubbed a hand over his jaw and groaned but didn't protest.

"I'll go first," Rhys announced, a little too enthusiastically, his pretty green eyes landing on me. "Truth or dare, princess?"

I learned last time that it didn't matter which one I chose. And at least with a dare, I got to check another item off my list.

I smiled at Rhys. "Dare."

Rhys held out his palm. "I dare you to take off your panties."

"Are you serious?"

He wiggled his fingers and nodded. "You chose dare."

I glanced across the dimly lit car at Rhys before looking to Cole for an objection. He wasn't thrilled about my choice to play the game, but he wasn't saying anything, either.

Did he like this dare?

I took this as a sign that Cole was okay with the game and that maybe he would play, too.

"I'm wearing a bikini," I told Rhys and spread my legs for him to see. "Not panties."

"Same thing," Rhys said with a wicked glint in his eyes. "Hand them over, princess."

Despite the nerves slithering down my spine, I pushed up my skirt, so they could get a good look as I untied one side of my bikini bottoms. Cole's jaw clenched, but he didn't look away, his chest rising and falling rapidly.

Rhys rubbed his thumb across his bottom lip, hunched forward to get a better look at me. "Spread your legs wider, princess." He licked his lips. "Don't be shy. Let us see your pretty pussy."

I tugged at the other string, letting the fabric fall onto the bench beneath me. Cole looked like he had stopped breathing, his eyes laser focused between my thighs.

Rhys cursed as I sat up, yanked the fabric from under me, and tossed the bikini bottoms at him. My bathing suit landed on Cole's thigh.

"Stay just like that," Rhys said when I attempted to close my legs. "Don't move."

I'd never felt so exposed while still mostly clothed. And with both of their eyes searing my skin, my insides practically turned molten lava.

"Fuck, princess," Rhys said, his voice deep and smooth. "Touch yourself."

Cole remained unusually still, keeping his opinions to himself. He wanted to play the game without complaining or telling Rhys to stop.

He liked seeing me.

I recalled when I found Cole jerking off in the shower and how far I had come since then and was ready to explore my sexuality.

"Cole," I said, keeping my legs wide for him to see me. "It's your turn. Truth or dare?"

"Don't be a pussy, Marshall." Rhys didn't even let him respond. "Choose dare."

Cole rolled his eyes. "Don't tell me what to do, Vanderbilt."

"We both know you'll punk out and take the safer route."

Cole's nostrils flared. "You don't know shit about me." Then he turned to look at me once more. "I choose dare."

Putting my hands on my thighs, I slid my tongue across my bottom lip. "Ever since I walked in on you in the shower, I've wondered if you were thinking about me. It was so steamy in the bathroom I didn't get a good look at you. I might as well be naked right now. It's only fair I get to see you, too."

Rhys put his elbow on the bench and got closer to Cole. "You let Grace watch you jerk off in the shower? Doesn't that go against your rules, golden boy?"

Cole sneered at him. "It wasn't like that."

"You didn't tell me to leave," I interjected. "You let me watch. I still think about that night, Cole." I inched my hand up my thigh, tapping my fingers on my skin to refocus his attention on my pussy. "When I'm alone in my room, I imagine you're touching me."

Rhys made a strangled sound. "Hear that, Marshall? She thinks about you when she plays with her pussy. You should hit that." He nudged him with his elbow. "Check another item off her list. If you don't, I will."

For some reason, Rhys intentionally pushed Cole's buttons. Cole didn't take the bait and ignored him.

"She wants to watch you jerk off again," Rhys said. "You chose dare, Marshall. Stop holding up the game."

"I want to watch you, too," I told Rhys.

"Oh, yeah?" His lips parted, eyes wide. "Then, I have a counter-dare. We'll let you watch us jerk off if you finger your pussy."

The gondola still hadn't moved, and we were stuck up here for the duration, so I said, "Deal."

"Grace," Cole groaned. "You don't have to do this."

I flipped my hair over my shoulder and flashed a sexy smile at Rhys. "I accept your counter-dare."

Was it wrong to want both of them? The sound of their voices and their muscles bulging beneath their fitted shirts had me dripping wet.

Rhys unzipped his shorts, whipping out his big dick. "Your turn, princess."

I shoved my skirt higher and dragged my finger up and down my wet slit. My experience with men was almost non-existent. But I knew what I liked and how to make myself feel good.

"Cole," I whimpered as I slid a finger inside me. "This is your dare. Don't leave me hanging."

A moment of hesitation ensued before he unzipped his shorts and stroked himself through the slit in his boxer briefs. He was big, around the same size as Rhys, but slightly thicker.

I could see why they acted like alpha males all the time. It was all the big dick energy.

"Fuck," Rhys grunted, stroking himself harder. "You're so wet for us."

Us.

He said it like they were a team when they had done nothing but argue with each other. But tonight, the three of us were a unit. No complaints from Cole, only the sounds he made as he jerked his shaft.

I added another finger, biting my lip to silence my moans.

"Are you going to come for us, princess?"

I nodded. But as I watched them, I felt the pressure build inside me. Those soft moans quickly turned to much louder screams of pleasure.

Rhys hopped up from his seat and covered my mouth with his hand. "Go ahead and scream."

He resumed playing with himself, breathing hard as we both raced toward the finish line. "Get over here and touch her, Marshall," Rhys ordered as the wheel moved downward. "We don't have much time to make her come."

I couldn't believe Cole did anything Rhys asked of him, shocked when he sat beside me and rubbed my clit.

"You smell so good," Cole hissed, knocking my hand away to finger me. "Fuck, you're tight." Burying his face in my neck, he sucked on my hot skin and pumped his fingers into me at the same pace he rubbed his dick. "I wish I could come inside you."

Cole was losing control.

He grunted in my ear.

So did Rhys.

Sandwiched between two sexy men, I lost all control with

them working as the perfect team. An inferno brewed inside me, heat licking my skin. I whimpered against Rhys's hand, my legs trembling as I came on Cole's fingers.

Seconds later, Rhys came on my right thigh. And not long after, Cole joined him. The wheel slowly approached the bottom. With my thighs wet with their warm cum, I let out a breath of relief that we were going up in the air again.

Rhys lowered his hand from my mouth, and my eyes found his green ones that were wild and filled with desire. "You surprise me every day, princess."

I glanced at Cole, who looked as if the devil possessed him. "I'm sorry, Grace." He pulled his T-shirt over his head, revealing his muscled chest, and wiped the cum from my legs. "I shouldn't have done that."

"Don't apologize, Marshall." Rhys laughed. "Look at how turned on she is right now. It's about time you let go. Rules fucking suck. Stop following them."

"Look at the mess *we* made," Cole shot back, cleaning my skin with the soft fabric. "She's covered in our cum, asshole."

"She likes it," Rhys challenged. "Don't you, baby?"

I nodded.

"Do you want to come again?"

Another nod.

Rhys slid off the bench, dropped to his knees, and moved between my thighs, pushing Cole away. "Put your legs over my shoulders."

I did as he instructed, and he rewarded me by kissing my pussy. His tongue slipped between my folds, his lips glistening with my juices.

He looked up at Cole before licking me straight down the center. "Forbidden fruit tastes so much sweeter. You should taste her, Marshall."

He gripped the backs of my thighs and lifted my ass off the bench, sucking my clit into his mouth. Cole tucked himself back into his shorts, staring at me with wonder. I could tell he had a hard time processing what we did. He fought his attraction to me for so long, only for Rhys and his games to push him outside his comfy bubble.

"Eyes on me, princess."

I looked down at the gorgeous man between my legs. But instead of following Rhys's order, I grabbed the collar of Cole's shirt and brought his lips to mine. "Kiss me."

He rested his forehead against mine. "Grace, what are you doing to me?"

"I won't tell anyone. This stays between the three of us."

"Kiss her, Marshall," Rhys said between licks.

I was shocked Rhys wasn't the jealous type. He was an alpha like Cole and didn't seem like someone who wanted to share a woman. But he didn't mind one bit. And I liked that I didn't have to choose between them.

I pressed my lips to Cole's as Rhys split me in half with his tongue.

I could die and be happy.

Cole's hand moved to the back of my head, deepening the kiss. My first kiss with Rhys was soft and gentle, becoming more aggressive with each flick of his tongue. But with Cole, it was like our tongues were dancing.

We were in sync, moving in harmony, melting into each other's arms. He captured each of my moans, helping Rhys get me to the finish line again.

And by the time our lips separated, I was panting. "I've wanted to do that for a long time."

He sighed, holding me tight. "Me, too."

Chapter Eighteen

COLE

I couldn't believe I just did *that*. With *them*. Rhys had a way of getting under my skin and making me do things outside my comfort zone. I'd never even shared a woman with my best friends.

I felt so out of control, anxiety tearing through my chest. Order calmed me and gave me a sense of peace. And at that moment, I felt anything but at ease.

When the gondola reached the bottom, Rhys helped Grace down to the landing and led her to the confession stand. I chased after them, still unable to catch my breath from mentally freaking the fuck out.

"I'm starving." Rhys rubbed his flat stomach over his shirt. "I worked up an appetite eating your pussy." He glanced at Grace and winked. "What do you want, princess?"

"Ummm…" She rocked back and forth on her heels, staring at the menu. "Funnel cake sounds good. What is it?"

Rhys pointed at the fried pastry covered with powdered sugar.

She licked her lips. "Yeah, I want one of those."

Rhys angled his body to look at me. "Marshall?"

"Hot dog," I told him.

What the fuck was going on with us? This was so out of

character for Rhys and me. We didn't act like friends. We didn't even hang out together at the academy.

I kissed Grace.

I touched Grace.

While Rhys watched.

Fuck.

If Rhys told anyone, I would be in deep shit. My father had warned me dozens of times about crossing the line. He constantly reminded me of what our family had at stake.

And it wasn't just us.

Fitzy would punish Drake since he was my cousin. He would also take it out on the Salvatores, who had not yet been admitted into The Founders Society. As the leaders of The Devil's Knights, they were responsible for my behavior. I swore to uphold the oath in front of Fitzy and the Knights.

I couldn't do that again.

Not with Rhys.

Not with Grace.

Rhys ordered three fountain sodas, two hot dogs, and a funnel cake. As they cooked the cake, he leaned against the counter.

"Cheer up, Marshall." He winked. "I'm not going to tell anyone."

I wanted to murder him.

Teeth clenched, I glared at the bastard. "You're just as guilty as me."

"There's nothing to tell." Grace flicked her long, blonde hair over her right shoulder. "I don't remember anything exciting happening. Your secret is safe with us, Cole."

She made it so hard.

How could I not want her?

Grace strolled over to me, a sexy smile tugging at her lips. She could light up a room with that smile. And as she stopped in front of me, my heart beat faster. After what we did together, we could never return to being just friends.

She put her hand on my bare chest since my shirt was

tucked in my back pocket, stained with our cum. Thankfully, I wasn't the only shirtless man on the boardwalk, so I didn't look like an asshole.

She wet her lips with her tongue. "Come to my room tonight."

"Grace," I whispered, hating what I had to say next. "What we did…" I shook my head and sighed. "We shouldn't have done that."

Her smile quickly transformed into a frown. "If you don't show up tonight, let me go. Don't try to stop me from finishing the list."

"The list was a stupid idea. I shouldn't have suggested it."

She shrugged, sliding her hand off my chest. "It's too late. I'm completing it with or without you. But I would rather it be you that takes my virginity."

I wanted that, too.

More than anything.

Rhys whistled, interrupting our conversation. "Marshall, get over here and help me with the food."

I looked at Grace once more, then rushed to the counter to grab her soda and funnel cake. She picked at the cake, giving me a sultry look as she stuffed a piece into her mouth. Grace wasn't the sweet, innocent girl who came to my house at the start of the summer.

Rhys tainted her.

I shoved the hot dog in my mouth as we walked the board-walk and headed to the parking lot. I was angry with myself for being human and letting that idiot play Truth or Dare.

Years of competing with Rhys created a lot of bad blood between us. He liked to play games, and we both wanted to win. It was a recipe for disaster when you put us together. Neither of us would concede to the other. And I wouldn't look like a pussy in front of Grace.

Because you're an idiot.

As we stepped off the boardwalk, I spotted two men I recognized on our way to the parking lot. They lounged against the wall, both tall and smoking cigarettes. They stood beneath a lamppost, the golden glow shining a light on them.

"Fuck," I whispered, throwing my arms out in front of them. "Don't move."

They would see us if we were to walk a few more inches into the light. The Russian men who worked for Grace's uncle could have easily gotten to us on the boardwalk. Andrey Romanov was a high-ranking member of the Volkov Bratva. Grace's grandfather was also part of the Russian Mafia before his death.

Her father was the only Romanov not to join the Mafia. Instead, he became a KGB operative, which was how he met Grace's mother. He supposedly changed for Grace and her mom, giving up his family's legacy. But after he fled imprisonment on Skull Island, he became even more sinister than his family.

He was a terrorist and number one on every Most Wanted list worldwide.

"Cole, you're scaring me," Grace whispered.

Rhys leaned over and whispered, "What is going on, Marshall?"

I inched backward so we could hide from their view under the boardwalk. "Do you see those men standing near the parking lot?"

Rhys nodded. "Who are they?"

"Volkov Bratva."

Grace gasped, clinging to my arm, her tremors shaking through me. "Russian Mafia?"

"Yes," I said at the same time as Rhys.

I pulled Grace into my arms to console her. "Look, I know you're scared. But you need to listen to me. This isn't my first time dealing with your uncle's men." I tucked the hair behind her ears and swiped at the tear streaming down her cheek. "I need you to do exactly as I say, okay?"

She nodded.

Rhys patted her back. "We'll protect you, princess. Don't get upset. It's going to be okay."

She shivered, wrapping her arms around her middle. "How will we get past them if they're blocking off our entrance to the parking lot?"

"We'll walk to the other side of the pier beneath the boardwalk," I said in a hushed tone, careful not to make too much noise. "And from there, I'll have Sonny pick us up."

Drake was out of town at a tech convention. And if I called my dad, he would lose his shit.

"Sonny Cormac?" Grace asked.

"Yeah. He's a Knight and a Founder. He lives down the street from me."

I told Grace about The Knights, but she hadn't officially met everyone. Sonny was the oldest son of a shipping tycoon and helped the Knights transport illegal products on their cargo ships. If anyone knew how to make someone disappear, it was Sonny Cormac.

As we walked beneath the boardwalk, I sent a 9-1-1 text to Sonny and received a response within seconds. He would meet us on the other side and let us know if we had any other threats awaiting us.

"Do you see why making that list was important to me?" Grace asked on our way to meet Sonny. "This has been my life for the past ten years. I never get to do anything without putting myself or someone else in danger."

I curled my arm around her. "This isn't your fault, Grace. Don't blame yourself."

"I can't take this shit anymore." She staggered away from me, nearly tripping on the sand. "I'm so sick of running."

It was so dark down here we only had the light from above to guide us. So when Grace's chunky sandal hit something hard, she fell forward. I reached out for her, but Rhys beat me to the punch.

"I got you, princess." He lifted Grace's feet off the ground, carrying her like a baby. He brushed his thumb across her wet cheek. "No one is going to hurt you. I will kill anyone who tries to touch you."

Until tonight, I thought Rhys was fucking with Grace and only using her to get back at her grandfather. But I saw a different side to him—a loving, caring person who wanted to protect her.

I considered what Grace said earlier. She wanted me to let her go or help her finish the bucket list. And I wasn't letting Rhys take her virginity.

Fuck him.

Chapter Nineteen

GRACE

They found me. After years of worrying about my father locating me, this was the closest he had come. His brother's men lurked near the parking lot, leaving us no choice but to dart under the boardwalk and trek through the darkness in the sand.

Despite my father's training, nothing had prepared me for a real-life situation. The thought of those men kidnapping me or even hurting Cole and Rhys terrified me.

"Almost there." Rhys's strong arms tightened around me. "Sonny's waiting for us in the SUV. Do you see it?"

A black SUV with dark-tinted windows was parked at the curb.

Sonny rolled down the window. "Hurry, I spotted more Bratva on my way here."

I got into the backseat, and Rhys climbed in beside me. Cole got into the passenger seat and took a handgun from Sonny, checking the clip before he tucked it into his back pocket.

"Vanderbilt," Sonny said as he drove down the street. "Wasn't expecting to see you here. I thought you left for California."

"Nope." Rhys patted Sonny's headrest. "I'm staying with Marshall for a while."

Sonny looked into the rearview mirror at me, shoving his fingers through his short, blond hair. "Nice to finally meet you, Grace." He reached his hand into the backseat for me to shake. "Sorry, it's under such shitty circumstances."

"That's my life," I deadpanned and shook his hand. "Nice to meet you, Sonny."

Sonny was classically handsome and clean-cut, like the blond version of Rhys but with less muscle. Even from where I sat, I could still see the definition in his biceps as he clutched the steering wheel. All of The Knights had a polished look that screamed money. Even Cole's usual cargo shorts and tight T-shirts looked expensive, the fabric a much higher thread count than anything I wore before arriving at Fort Marshall.

Sonny drove at an average speed past the harbor, and once we were in the residential part of Beacon Bay, he floored the gas. He took turns checking the mirrors. I turned my head to see what had gotten his attention. Two men in a black car peeled down the street.

"Motherfuckers," Sonny cursed. "Get ready, Cole. If they get too close, take out their tires."

I clung to Rhys's side and put my head on his chest. "I don't want to go back to him."

My father.

The terrorist.

"Keep your head down until I tell you it's safe." Rhys pushed down on my head, and I lay on his lap. He slipped his fingers through my hair to calm me. "It will be over soon, princess. Close your eyes and think of your favorite song. Can you do that for me?"

"Uh-huh."

Cole fired a bullet out the window at their tire.

"Sing it for me," Rhys said in a calming tone.

I couldn't hold a tune, nor could my adoptive father, so I hummed a song he sang for me when I moved in with him.

"Let It Be" by The Beetles helped soothe me at night, especially after another nightmare of the past. Flashbacks of my former life.

Cole turned in his seat and fired his gun out the window. I hummed even louder. The Colonel had taught me how to shoot, but the sound never bothered me.

Not until now.

It felt like the SUV was about to tip over when Sonny overshot the turn, the tires screeching. And with Cole dangling out the window, I tried not to look. I tried not to think about those men hurting him. I couldn't live with myself if anything happened to him because of me.

A bullet sank into the bumper.

I screamed.

"You're okay, Grace," Cole said with his head partially out the window. "Keep singing for us. We'll be home soon."

Rhys covered my ears. "Listen to Marshall, princess. Don't stop singing until I tell you."

I started at the song's beginning, humming the familiar tune. My dad loved that song, and it just so happened to calm me down whenever I had a panic attack.

Our first few years together were rough. I was traumatized, but he was patient and cared for me. The Colonel even enlisted help from his doctor friend to stop my nightmares.

Another bullet hit the bumper.

Cole fired more shots.

Sonny drove like a maniac.

Rhys stroked my hair.

I didn't stop singing.

Everything began to blur together, and I retreated to my happy place inside my mind. I was so angry sometimes about not having friends or boyfriends. But until now, I hadn't felt like I was in danger. The Colonel kept the target off my back. Whenever he thought my father was on to us, we moved again.

He gave up everything.

For me.

After Sonny took another rough turn, Cole sat in the passenger seat and rolled up the window. "We lost them."

Rhys removed his hands from my ears and rubbed my back. "You can sit up, princess. We're at the safe house."

I peeked up at him and wiped my face. "I want to call my dad."

"The Colonel is off the grid," Cole told me. "Even my dad can't reach him."

I sniffed back more tears. "He needs to come and get me. I'm not safe here."

Sonny parked in front of what looked like an abandoned apartment building. It was several stories tall and had no light on inside.

Does anyone live here?

"I made a promise to you the day we met." Cole shifted in his seat. "I will risk my life for yours. So you don't have to be afraid, Grace."

"But I am," I choked out. "We could have died on our way here. I don't want all of you risking your lives for me. That's my dad's job."

"Would you look at that?" Sonny said in a chipper tone, a smile plastered on his face as he pretended to inspect his arms. "Not even a scratch." He pressed his finger to my nose. "Boop! You look pretty scratch-free. Not bad if I do say so myself."

I laughed for what felt like the first time in too long.

"We know what we're doing, Grace." Sonny opened his door and flashed a golden boy smile that lit up his face. "You're in good hands."

Rhys pushed open the door. "C'mon, princess. Let's get you inside before you turn into a pumpkin."

<hr>

Cole held me in his arms until my body finally stopped shaking uncontrollably. If Cole hadn't taken the lead, I would have panicked. I felt shameful for not adapting to the situation. That was the whole point of the survival camp my dad sent me to each summer since high school. He would have been so disappointed.

I felt like a failure.

Sonny left to join other Knights in ridding Beacon Bay of the Russians. He said other men were driving around the town searching for me.

The Salvatores owned the entire apartment building, which The Devil's Knights used as a safe house. So we didn't have to worry for the rest of the night. Cole assured me The Knights were on watch outside and surrounding various parts of Devil's Creek and Beacon Bay.

The apartment was sparse, with only a couch in the living room, a dining table, and a bed behind a set of double doors. Compared to the luxury of Cole's home, this place was a dump. But maybe that was the point. No one would ever expect The Knights to live in a slum.

I sat on the couch in the living room between Cole and Rhys. They hadn't said much, allowing me time to consider the past hour's events. And the crazy shit I had done with them on the Ferris wheel.

I wasn't myself.

Since Rhys's arrival, I was bold and wild, a woman who wanted to explore her sexuality and live for once.

He made me feel alive.

So did Cole.

I wanted to experience everything life had to offer with both of them.

"I don't regret what we did." I placed my hands on their knees. "I just want you to know that."

Rhys smiled. "I'd never regret anything I did with you."

Cole breathed harder, his chest rising and falling as his

blue eyes met mine. "I feel like we're taking advantage of you."

Of course, he had to suck the life from this moment.

"You're not taking advantage of me. I wanted both of you on the Ferris wheel. I wouldn't have chosen your dare if I didn't want that to happen."

"Grace, you're inexperienced. Rhys and I knew better, but we did it anyway."

Rhys snickered beside me. "Speak for yourself, Marshall."

I slipped my fingers between Cole's and moved our joined hands to my thigh. "After tonight, I want to finish the list more than anything. I could be halfway around the world with my dad in a few weeks. I'll never get a chance to experience life this way. Don't you see that you and Rhys aren't taking anything from me? You're giving me a life I have wanted for years. And even if it's only for a few weeks, at least it's something."

"But…"

"No, buts, Cole. I want whatever this is between the three of us."

He glanced at Rhys and sighed. "You want both of us?"

I was attracted to them for different reasons. With Cole, it was those caring, loving moments between us. I could see how much he wanted to protect me because he didn't just show me with words. He was a man of action.

Rhys was fun and brought out another side of me—a wild, adventurous girl who felt free and alive. I became a different person with him, and I liked it.

I nodded. "Is that so bad? I doubt I'm the first woman to have feelings for two men."

"We're not supposed to touch you," Cole said after an awkward pause. "Rhys knows it. I know it."

"But that didn't stop you on the Ferris wheel," I pointed out.

"Stop overthinking everything." Rhys reached over to tap

Cole's shoulder. "Just go with the flow, Marshall. It won't kill you."

He narrowed his eyes at Rhys. "You're okay with this? Sharing a woman with me? We don't even like each other."

His broad shoulders rose a few inches. "We both want her. I can play nice if you can. And it's not like anyone will find out. So get out of your head and relax."

After that, Cole didn't protest and led me to the bedroom, and the three of us got into the bed. Sandwiched between Cole and Rhys, we lay on a king-size mattress in the dark. We couldn't risk turning on lights in an abandoned building. They didn't want to draw too much attention to this place.

It was so quiet I could only hear the sound of our breathing. I grabbed their hands, needing to feel them. After what we went through tonight, I sought comfort in their warmth. Cole's hands were rougher than Rhys's, the pads of his fingers calloused.

"Feeling better, princess?"

I nodded. "But I'm still worried about those men finding me."

"I don't care if we have to leave the country." Cole rolled onto his side. "I'm not letting anyone near you."

Comforted by his words, I smiled. "Thank you, Cole."

"Wherever you go," Rhys said, his lips inches from mine. "I'll follow."

After our scare with the Russians, Rhys was even nicer than usual. Not like he was mean. But he usually had something nasty to say to Cole, and he seemed to enjoy getting under his skin. The three of us had come together as a unit tonight.

It was nice.

"When can we go back to Fort Marshall?"

"Tomorrow," Cole replied, his hand holding mine on the mattress. "Sonny will come back for us in the morning. That should be enough time to get rid of the Russians."

"How do you know that?" I gulped down the bile rising from my stomach. "There could be more men waiting for us."

"They had the advantage tonight," Cole told me. "We didn't know they were waiting for us and couldn't plan." He squeezed my hand. "It's been a long night. You should get some sleep."

"I'm too awake to fall asleep."

"Me too." Rhys turned me to face him and put my leg over the top of his, running his fingers up and down my thigh. "But I have a few ideas to help us fall asleep faster."

Cole groaned beside me. "Do you ever think with anything but your dick, Vanderbilt?"

"Occasionally." Rhys snickered. "But when Grace is around? No, not really." He sucked my bottom lip into his mouth. "Her pussy is all I can think about."

"Which is why you make a terrible bodyguard," Cole muttered. "We just got chased through Beacon Bay, and you're thinking about getting your dick wet. You're un-fuck-ing-believable."

"I need the distraction, Cole." I moved his hand onto my leg, our fingers still joined. "Help me take my mind off everything."

Chapter Twenty

COLE

Grace wasn't wearing any panties. Her bathing suit bottoms were still stuffed into Rhys's pocket from earlier because the bastard refused to give them back.

She was so desperate for me to touch her. To kiss her. And with her legs spread, she begged me.

"Fuck me. Please," she whined, inching my hand up her thigh. "You already broke the rules tonight. Stop fighting it, Cole. I know you want me."

More than anything.

Since I hesitated for a second, Rhys took that as an opportunity to dip his hand beneath her skirt.

Grace wrapped her fingers around his wrist and pushed his hand higher. "Stop teasing me."

He sucked her earlobe into his mouth. "You can have whatever you want, princess."

I hated how he called her that like it was her name. But Grace didn't mind it and rolled her head to the side, moaning into the pillow.

"As long as you're a good girl and ask nicely." Rhys pushed up her skirt and thrust his finger inside her. "Tell me what you want."

"I want Cole to fuck me." She gripped my wrist and tugged. "Touch me."

Just for tonight.

I could fuck up tonight, and then tomorrow, I could return to how things used to be. At least, that was what I told myself.

"You've had a long night." I leaned forward, so our lips nearly touched. "Are you sure this is what you want?"

"It's all I've thought about this summer." She pressed her lips to mine. "Don't make me beg."

"I'd like to see you beg." Rhys sucked on her earlobe. "You purr like a kitten, princess."

Rhys shoved down her top and sucked her nipple into his mouth. And as my once archenemy made my girl feel good, I kissed her.

Grace unzipped my shorts. So impatient and greedy for more, she took my cock out and gave it a few strokes.

She peeled her lips from mine. "It has to be you, Cole."

I knew what she meant.

The list.

Her virginity.

We were alone in the dark apartment without anyone around to catch us. And after tonight, I wanted her to experience everything life offered.

Rhys made her sit up, so he could strip off her tank top, taking his sweet ass time untying her bikini top. The fabric dropped onto her leg, and he chucked it across the room.

"Are you sure you want to do this, Grace?"

If I didn't do it, Rhys would. And I wanted her first time to be with someone who cared about her. Someone who would risk everything to save her. She deserved a life she would never have, so this was the least I could give her.

Rhys bent down to lick her nipple. "Don't pussy out, Marshall. She's dripping on my hand, begging you to fuck her. I'd love to take your place, but she wants you."

"I want you, too," she lilted.

He nodded. "But you want Marshall to take your virginity."

She didn't correct him.

How did we get here?

Yesterday, I hated Rhys and was ready to kill him. And less than twenty-four hours later, they talked me into public masturbation and a threesome. Not something I wanted to check off my bucket list. But the list was important to Grace, and she wanted Rhys here.

So fuck it.

Rhys tugged on her nipple with his teeth, and her eyes slammed shut. She licked her lips, pulling at the ends of Rhys's hair as he stuck out his tongue and teased her.

I removed her skirt while Rhys played with her nipples, warming her up for me. We took turns kissing, licking, and sucking on her skin. Rhys kissed the left side of her body while I covered the right. Eventually, we both had our hands between her legs. Rhys tried to knock my hand away, but fuck him. I plunged my finger into her, right beside his.

She was *mine.*

"Oh, my God," Grace whimpered, rocking her hips to meet our hands. "Both of you feel so good."

"We need to break you in," Rhys grunted. "Your pussy is so tight."

"It's going to hurt, isn't it?"

Rhys planted a kiss on her lips. "At first."

"I'll go slow," I told her.

She was so tight, wet, and ready for me that I was dying to be inside her. As we fucked her with our fingers, she whispered our names.

Grace only had a week to check off another bucket list item before her dad picked her up. So I mentally checked off the item that mattered the most to Grace.

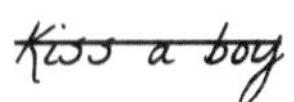

<s>Get asked out on a date</s>
<s>Lose my virginity</s>
Fall in love

She didn't have enough time for the last one. But what I felt for her could have been love. At least her first time would be with someone who would have given anything for her.

I grabbed a condom from my wallet and tore open the foil packet, rolling it down my length.

"Please, Cole." Grace reached between her legs, running her hands up my chest. "Fuck me."

I never thought I would break the rules. But staring at this beautiful woman beneath me, I couldn't stop myself even if I tried. All my self-control went out the window the second she took off her bikini bottoms on the Ferris wheel.

There was no turning back.

Chapter Twenty-One

GRACE

It was so dark in the bedroom I could only feel them. Hear them breathing in my ear as their hands navigated every inch of my skin. I felt like I was on top of the world with Cole and Rhys.

Like I could do anything.

As Cole settled between my legs, I sucked in a deep breath. The tip of his dick rubbed up and down my wet slit. He was trying to prepare me for how much it would hurt.

Between the two of them, I had checked off almost every item on my bucket list. I could return to my old life knowing I lived for a few months.

~~Kiss a boy~~
~~Get asked out on a date~~
~~Lose my virginity~~
Fall in love

I wouldn't get to fall in love, not with the time ticking down. But this was close enough.

Rhys held my left hand on the mattress while Cole

grabbed the other, inching into me slowly. My eyes snapped shut at the sudden pinch as he broke through my inner walls.

His thumb brushed my cheek. "You okay, Grace?"

I opened my eyes, breathing through my nose, and nodded.

"I don't want to hurt you." He kissed my lips, moving his hips in a rhythmic motion. "You're going to be sore."

While it was hard to see in the dark, I could feel him watching me.

"You're so perfect." He kissed me again. "Beautiful."

Rhys continued running his long fingers up and down my leg, keeping his mouth shut. For once, he didn't call Cole a pussy or say anything stupid to piss him off. It felt like I had lost my virginity to both of them.

Cole was my first crush.

Rhys was my first kiss.

They meant a lot to me.

So it was only fair they both got to be here, making me feel good on one of the most important days of my life.

Cole kissed me, cradling my head, but he wasn't as sweet as before. Our tongues still did that familiar dance, but there was even more passion this time. It felt like he was in pain… or as if he was saying goodbye.

I wasn't sure when we would be in the same town again. This summer was a once-in-a-lifetime opportunity, and I wasn't wasting a second.

Even with Cole being gentle, it hurt each time he moved in and out. But eventually, I adapted to his size, and it started to feel good. I enjoyed the ripple of pleasure that spread down my arms.

Rhys curled my fingers around his shaft and helped me jerk his big dick while Cole fucked me. They worked so well together you would have thought they were friends instead of rivals.

Cole picked up the pace and hooked my leg around his

back as my body completely relaxed. He slid deeper and deeper, groaning in my ear. He stuck out his tongue and traced the length of my earlobe before sucking on my neck.

Drunk on the pain and intense pleasure, I unraveled beneath Cole, losing myself to not one but two men. My orgasm took control of my body, creating an inferno inside me.

Rhys was close.

So was Cole.

I could feel Rhys on the verge of coming, and with each pulse of Cole's cock inside me, I knew it wouldn't be long.

Rhys' cum coated my fingers as Cole came inside me, his thighs trembling for a solid minute afterward.

Rhys rubbed my lips with his thumb. "You're such a good girl."

"No, she's a little brat." Cole massaged my breast, rolling his thumb over the sore bud as he pulled out of me. "You always get what you want, don't you?"

I nodded, a smile on my lips. "I'm going to have to be bratty more often because that was amazing."

I could have died at that moment and gone out with a bang. Losing my virginity to Cole was better than everything I had checked off my bucket list. Even better than making out in the pool with Rhys and getting my first kiss.

"How do you feel?"

I kissed Cole's lips. "Sore. But it felt good."

He dipped his hand between my thighs and massaged my clit. "Did I hurt you?"

"No," I whispered before sucking his bottom lip into my mouth.

Once our lips separated, Cole hopped off the bed and entered the bathroom. He returned a few seconds later with a warm washcloth and dabbed it between my thighs, cleaning me up. No one took care of me like Cole. When he said he would die for me, kill for me, he meant every word.

Cole got a little possessive and curled my body into his. "It's time for bed." He tucked my head beneath his chin, holding me against his chest, and whispered, "I hope you remember this night forever, Grace. I know I will."

I will never forget it.

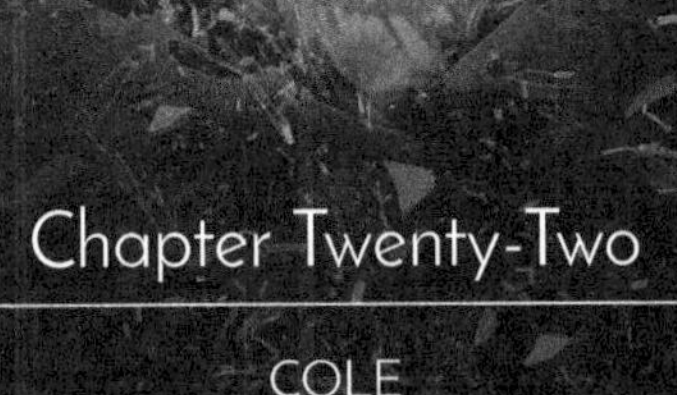

Chapter Twenty-Two

COLE

I woke up to my cell phone ringing and rolled onto my side to grab it from the nightstand. Drake never called this late unless it was an emergency. Either that or he made another breakthrough with one of his inventions.

"Cole," Drake bit out before I could say hello. "It's Alex. Her mom kidnapped her from the Salvatore Estate."

I shot straight up from the mattress as if it were made of fire ants and flicked on the lamp beside the bed.

Alex hadn't contacted her parents since her grandfather adopted her. She wasn't always a Wellington. The Queen of the Devil's Knights was born Alexandrea Fox and didn't come to Devil's Creek until six years ago.

Drake sighed. "Her fucking mom. Can you believe this shit?"

I stepped into my boxer briefs. "How did she find her?"

"The Salvatore brothers think Savanna Fox made a copy of the skeleton key before Carl Wellington exiled her from Devil's Creek."

All five founding families could easily access everything from The Devil's Knights' temple to the last house on Founders Way with one key. Of course, we would never invade each other's privacy without reason, but Savanna

117

wasn't a founder anymore and wanted revenge for losing everything.

"Vanderbilt, get up!" I shouted.

Grace turned over, her naked body wrapped in a sheet, and rubbed her eyes. "What's going on?"

I told Rhys and Grace about Alex's kidnapping.

"No." She gasped. "Someone kidnapped my cousin's girlfriend?"

Rhys was out of bed and grabbed her clothes from the floor. "Get dressed, Grace." He helped her tie the bikini top back into place before lowering the tank top over her head.

I put Drake on speaker and pulled on a shirt. "Do you have any leads on Alex?"

"We're tracking the chip in her engagement ring," Drake said, moving away from a group of men talking in the background. "She's on her way to the Il Circo auction."

"Alex is engaged?" I asked. "To which brother?"

"All of them," Drake said in a hushed tone. "I'll explain later."

The Salvatore diamond had a tracking chip and was worn by their mother before her death fifteen years ago.

"Sonny is on his way," Drake told me. "He should be there any minute."

"Is Alex's mom working with the Russians?" I asked Drake.

"No," he grunted into the receiver. "The Sicilian Mafia."

"The Sicilians?" My eyebrows rose in surprise. "The Salvatore brothers' uncle is involved in Alex's kidnapping?"

Lorenzo Basile was a dangerous Sicilian Mafia boss and an ally of The Devil's Knights, or so we thought. We'd been working with them for years on shipments of illegal merchandise.

Drake groaned in frustration. "This is another distraction. The real target isn't Alex. I'm telling you, Cole. No one will listen to me, not even the Salvatore brothers. They only see what they want to see."

I had been thinking about what Drake said earlier in the summer. He believed The Knights were chasing other leads so The Lucaya Group could steal his tech.

"Sonny is outside," Drake said. "I'll see you soon."

Thankfully, the safe house had clothes in my size. My shirt was hardened by Rhys and my cum. My shorts were also stained with dirt and sweat. So I dressed in sweats and a black, long-sleeve Under Armour shirt.

Grace wore the same outfit from earlier, and so did Rhys.

"Give back her bikini bottoms."

Rhys rolled his eyes and removed them from his pocket. Then, getting on his knees in front of her, Rhys tied the bathing suit into place. He kissed her pussy over the fabric before shoving the black skirt over her thighs.

He angled his body to look at me. "Happy, Marshall?"

Asshole.

We still weren't friends, but I hated him less. He had been good to Grace, so maybe all my worrying about him trying to hurt her was for nothing.

"Why would someone kidnap my cousin's girlfriend?" Grace asked, her top lip quivering.

Grace knew Bastian, but they'd only seen each other once over the years. She had yet to meet Alex and understood little about our world.

"There's an online auction," I explained. "Men are bidding on Alex. And if we don't find her in time, she'll be sold to the highest bidder. These men are dangerous. They're using her to hurt the Salvatore brothers."

"Will they come after me, too?" Grace's voice shook as we exited the bedroom.

"No," I said in a calm tone. "But we have to take precautions. We can't be sure who is working with who. The Sicilians don't like the Russians, but that doesn't mean they haven't joined forces against a common enemy."

"The Knights," she whispered.

I nodded.

Grace didn't know everything about her past life. But she knew Viktor Romanov was a terrorist. She came from a powerful family with money, connections, and no morals. They would do anything to get her back.

We rushed out of the apartment and downstairs to meet Sonny at the curb. He waited in the SUV, tapping his fingers on the leather steering wheel.

I helped Grace into the back seat, and Rhys got in on the other side, clutching her thigh with possession.

"Are the Russians gone?" I asked Sonny as we left the parking lot of the apartment complex.

"We scared them off earlier," he said with his eyes on the road. "They probably won't come back again today. But we have other enemies to concern ourselves with." He shook his head and sighed. "The Sicilians? I can't believe I've been helping those pieces of shit move illegal goods with Mac Corp containers."

Sonny sped through Beacon Bay and into Devil's Creek, flooring the gas up the steep incline into the subdivision called The Hills. He nodded at the guard who operated the gate that separated the other residents from Founders Way.

The gate opened for us, and Sonny continued in silence. He greeted the next set of guards at the Salvatore Estate, who carried machine guns and dressed in battle gear.

"Cole," Grace said as we parked next to the garage with a dozen other cars belonging to Knights. "Should I be afraid?"

I paused briefly, considering whether I should answer diplomatically or truthfully. The truth wouldn't do her any favors.

"Not as long as I'm alive."

Chapter Twenty-Three

GRACE

I thought Cole's family was wealthy until we arrived at the Salvatore Estate. The Salvatore brothers lived on a sprawling compound with an incredible bay view. The main house looked like a medieval castle. They had several guest houses on the property, including an infinity pool, which appeared to be spilling into the bay.

This place was unreal.

A large, covered veranda stretched across the back of the mansion. The sheer size of the house, combined with the stunning view, was impressive. It looked like a resort, not someone's home.

Cole led me to the helipad, where at least twenty men gathered on the blacktop. They wore suits and stern expressions that made them look even more intimidating. Guards lined the perimeter with machine guns in their hands.

I instantly recognized Drake Battle, Cole's cousin. He was a hacker and the brains behind the technology at Battle Industries. A real-life Batman and just as handsome.

Drake stood at the center of the circle, an iPad in his hand, with four other men gathered around him. They leaned over his shoulders to watch a video playing on the screen.

"They stole their own container," Luca Salvatore said.

Luca and Marcello could have been twins with the same black hair and angular jaws. Luca wore his hair spiked in the front, while Marcello's was longer and messy like he'd been tugging at the ends.

Both tall and well over six feet, Marcello had the build of an athlete, while Luca was lean but muscular. Expensive black suits fit them so well the fabric molded to their bodies.

Two more men stood next to them, one with hair as black as a raven's feathers and the palest skin I had ever seen. His lips were so red it appeared as if he had drunk blood. The man beside him had dark caramel hair and gray eyes.

My cousin.

Bastian Salvatore.

The man on his right was Damian. They were Salvatores but not by blood.

"The fifteenth anniversary of Mom's death is coming up," Luca said, the group's apparent leader with how he stood with the full attention of every man. "Lorenzo Basile has waited a long time to get revenge."

Cole had mentioned that name on our way over here. I couldn't believe they had gotten mixed up with a Sicilian Mafia boss, but I wasn't that surprised, either. I figured rich people did some shady shit to make their money.

"He was waiting for Alex to take her place with The Devil's Knights."

"Aiden, too. Does Wellington know yet?"

When Cole first told me about their queen, I almost laughed. Why did a bunch of grown men need a queen to rule them? But he explained it was a condition of the union between the Wellingtons and the Salvatores—a way for Carl Wellington to ensure his granddaughter's safety.

"With both of his pawns out of play," Luca said, "maybe he'll get off his ass and offer us the help of The Founders Society."

He walked over to Carl Wellington. The other men stayed behind and passed around the iPad.

"Any updates?" Cole asked.

Drake handed the iPad to Cole. "We just got a lead."

Rhys was on my right side, his palm on my ass as he leaned over to glance at the screen. When I looked up at him, he smirked. I liked when Rhys touched me. Anytime he was near, I couldn't get enough of him.

Everyone stared at the iPad and watched as the man on the screen stood inside an empty shipping container and held up a note.

> We captured your Queen.
> Took your Knight.
> Make your move.

I looked at Cole, confused. "What does that mean?"

"We've been getting played all along."

Shoes slapped the blacktop, drawing my attention back to the oldest of the Salvatore brothers. He approached us with an evil sneer aimed at me. "What the fuck is she doing here?"

"Luca, we didn't have a choice," Cole said. "She's not safe at my house."

His hate-filled eyes landed on me again before returning to Cole. "The Knights were too busy to see another threat coming because of her. We wouldn't have Russian scum on our doorstep if Fitzy didn't leave her for us to deal with. So get her the fuck away from me before I trade her to get Alex back."

What does that mean?

Trade with who?

The Sicilian Mafia?

My father?

I felt like I was going to be sick. All of this was my fault.

Luca was right.

Those men wouldn't have come here if my father hadn't been looking for me. Sonny and the other Knights wouldn't have been distracted. And maybe Alex wouldn't have gotten kidnapped.

Without another word, Luca stormed off, kicking up dirt on the blacktop.

"Don't listen to him," Bastian said with an apologetic smile. "He's just upset. Luca tends to overreact when he's angry."

I moved closer to him. "I remember you coming to dinner at Grandfather's house. I was around ten years old. You gave me a key and told me not to tell anyone."

He'd passed it to me under the table at dinner, but I was too afraid to use it. Even before I moved out, I never found out what the key unlocked.

"Do you still have it?"

I bobbed my head.

Sadly, it was the only thing anyone in my immediate family had ever given me. My grandfather didn't do birthdays or holidays. I remembered little about my life with my parents. The Colonel kept things simple and only gave me practical gifts we could take to our next duty station.

Bastian hooked one arm around me and bent down to match my height. "Unfortunately, we haven't gotten to spend much time together. But we'll change that after all of this is over, okay? You have my word."

I smiled. "Yeah, I'd like that."

"Good." He gave me a pained smile, and I assumed he was trying to contain his grief over losing the woman he shared with his brothers. "But I need you to do something for me, Grace."

"Sure, anything."

"Hang onto that key a little while longer. And when the time is right, I'll show you what it opens." I stared at him for a moment too long, and he cocked an eyebrow at me. "Deal?"

My face hurt from smiling so hard. "Deal." He gave my shoulders a reassuring squeeze. "Now, I need you to do one more thing for me. Go back to Fort Marshall with Cole."

"Actually," Rhys said with a crooked grin aimed at my cousin. "I can keep Grace company. Cole should go to the island."

Drake nodded to confirm. "I agree. We need Cole's aerospace knowledge. Let Rhys stay with Grace."

Cole frowned. "Go with Rhys. I'll be home soon."

I wanted to hug or kiss him goodbye, but I knew better than to make a scene, so I nodded and left with Rhys.

Chapter Twenty-Four

GRACE

After Luca's outburst, I returned to Fort Marshall with Rhys, still tired from waking up in the middle of the night. I didn't understand the danger The Knights faced until tonight. And if Alex could be taken from the Salvatore Estate, I wasn't safe here, either.

Cole and Rhys would do everything in their power to protect me. I knew I could trust both of them with my life. But I was still afraid of my biological father finding me.

We hadn't seen each other since I was eight. And after thirteen years, he became a distant memory—just a man from my past.

Yet, I could still recall the scar on his right thumb, the musky scent of his cologne, and his deep voice. He had a thick Russian accent that he concealed whenever we were in public. He said it was best if no one knew he was from Russia. Back then, I didn't know why. I had no idea he was a spy turned into a criminal.

To me, he was Papa.

My dad.

Rhys tucked me into bed and got in bed with me. He rolled onto his side and soothingly ran his long fingers down my arm. "I won't let anyone hurt you, princess. Close your eyes."

I grabbed his hand, needing to feel his warmth. "I wouldn't mind if you held me until I fell asleep."

"Yeah?" Rhys curled up behind me. "Like this?"

"Exactly like this." I leaned over and turned off the light. "Night, Rhys."

He kissed my cheek. "Night, princess. Sweet dreams."

<hr>

I couldn't sit still the next day, pacing across the great room. Rhys tried to distract me with a heavy brunch that filled my belly like a lead weight. He even spent some of the time giving me kisses that made me crave him even more. But with Cole on a private island trying to rescue Alex, I couldn't think straight.

Rhys sat on the couch and watched me like I was about to disappear. After about ten minutes of pacing, he grabbed my wrist. "Sit, princess. All of this worrying isn't good for you."

"What if Cole gets hurt?" I choked out. "Or worse, what if he dies trying to save her?"

"That's the risk he'll take," Rhys said calmly. "All Knights swear an oath to protect our queen." He patted the cushion beside him. "Now, sit before you wear down the floor."

"I need something to do to take my mind off everything."

He pulled me onto his lap, resting his hand on my thigh. "Wanna get in the hot tub with me?"

"Yeah, that sounds good."

Rhys lifted me in his arms, throwing me over his shoulder. I giggled, and he smacked my ass, finding ways to touch me on the way to the natatorium.

Rhys set my feet down in front of the hot tub. He pulled his shirt over his head, and I stripped off my sundress, standing before him in a black bra and panties.

I watched as he shoved down his pants. His body was like

a work of art, contoured and perfectly tanned. He removed his shoes and clothing, including his boxer briefs.

He winked. "Your turn."

I kept on my bra and panties because Willow, Mark, or the twins could have caught us out here. Maybe even some of the staff who lived on the premises.

"Don't be shy." Rhys gave me a cocky smirk. "Let me see that gorgeous body."

I glanced around the room, reminded of the cameras in each corner. "We're being filmed."

"Who cares?"

Once in the water, he hooked his arm around me and brought me to his lap. The warm, bubbly water felt amazing on my skin. And with Rhys touching me, my skin was on fire.

He ran his fingers through my hair and yanked on the ends as his lips crashed into mine, his tongue sweeping into my mouth. He tasted like mint toothpaste and smelled of his spicy cologne. Clutching the back of my head, he deepened the kiss, digging his fingers into my hips. Then, he got more aggressive, pressing his cock into my stomach.

I rocked my hips and rubbed against his shaft, desperate to create more friction. He took that as an invitation to put his hand in my panties.

He pushed two fingers into me and groaned. "You're always so wet for me."

His fingers slid in and out of me, and several moans fell from my lips, his name coming out in strangled breaths. I curled my hand around his shaft and gave him a few strokes, needing to make him feel good.

"Dammit, princess."

It wasn't long before I was coming, and so was Rhys.

Rhys kissed my lips, breathing hard. "Wanna take this upstairs?"

I was about to respond when his cell phone dinged. He reached into his pocket, and I read the message on the screen.

COLE

Alex is safe. I'll be home within the hour.

How's Grace?

RHYS

Thoroughly satisfied :)

"Rhys." I slapped his arm. "Stop provoking Cole."
He rolled his broad shoulders, a grin plastered on his lips. "I can't help it, princess. He makes it too easy."

Chapter Twenty-Five

COLE

After the longest twenty-four hours of my life, I didn't want to shower or sleep.

I wanted to see Grace.

If The Knights hadn't needed my background in aerospace engineering to rescue Alex, I would have stayed behind with Grace and sent Rhys to the island.

Grace waited for me in the living room, wearing a pale pink sundress highlighting her golden tan. She smiled as our eyes met and launched into my arms, hanging onto me like a koala.

"You're okay," she breathed against my neck. "I was so worried about you."

I hugged her back, loving to feel of her body against mine after one of the most challenging nights of my life. She was becoming an addiction for me.

Cupping the back of her head, I breathed in the delicious scent of her perfume and pressed my lips to her cheek. "I'm okay, Grace."

That's a lie.

I would never be okay knowing I could only watch her, keep her safe from her enemies, and never know what it felt like to lose myself with her again. The other night was a one-time thing. I couldn't allow myself to continue breaking the rules. Not without hurting both of us.

"I'm the last person you should worry about."

She released her grip around my neck and looked at me. "You're my friend, Cole."

Friends.

All we could ever be.

Rhys moved behind Grace and pulled her off me, cradling her in his arms like a baby before setting her feet on the floor.

Was he jealous?

"How did it go?" He placed his hand on her shoulder with possession. "Everyone alright?"

Not like he cared.

Rhys was only a Knight because he didn't have a choice. It was a requirement for all of us to become Knights before we could ascend later in life to The Founders Society.

"Alex is home safe with the Salvatore brothers. No one got hurt."

We arrived in time for the auction, only to discover Lorenzo Basile planned to marry Alex. He had dressed her in a white wedding gown and forced her to walk down the aisle while the Salvatore brothers watched. The Knights weren't allowed to bring weapons, and as planned, we used Alpha Command to outwit our opponents. The army of mercenaries worked for Salvatore Global and helped us with the element of surprise.

I offered my hand to Grace. "It's dinnertime. Eat with me."

She smiled and slipped her fingers between mine. I glanced at Rhys, who donned an irritated scowl.

Grace wasn't a game to me.

But she was to him.

Midway through dinner, Rhys received a call from his father and left the dining room in a hurry. His voice was strained as he spoke, and whatever they talked about sounded urgent.

So I soaked up the opportunity to get Grace alone and invited her to watch a movie with me in the theater. We hadn't done this since Rhys arrived, and I missed spending time with her.

She ate a handful of popcorn, staring at the projection screen with wide eyes.

I loved observing her.

Grace fascinated me.

The other night, I let Rhys talk me into breaking my oath. Years of fighting him for top marks and promotions at the academy turned me into a competitive asshole. But when it came to Grace, I had to bow out. Stepping over the line with her would only lead to my family being in the same position as the Vanderbilts.

They had nothing to lose.

I had everything to gain.

Grace screamed when the masked man jumped out from the closet on the screen, practically hopping into my lap. Her arms trembled from the fear rocking through her body.

I rubbed my hand down her arm to soothe her, and she snapped her head at me and giggled.

"Sorry, I didn't see that coming."

I didn't see you coming, either.

If I had known Grace would become special to me, I would have begged another Knight to take my place. I had no idea she would make me second-guess my oaths. That just being around her each day would become unbearable. I wanted her so badly and hated myself for having these feelings.

I wanted more of her time.

More stolen moments.

More of *her*.

Grace sat up, clutching my bicep. Sparks of electricity crackled between us, a palpable energy I felt each time. She leaned in closer, lips puckered like she wanted a kiss. Her hand cupped my face as she breathed harder.

My chest rose and fell rapidly when she parted those pink lips now inches from mine. "Grace," I said with a warning in my tone. "Please. We can't keep doing this."

"You took my virginity. Why stop now?"

After risking my life on the island, I deserved another taste —one kiss to satisfy the craving. Once was not enough. But crossing the line again with Grace would make it harder for us to say goodbye.

Grace didn't heed my warning and pressed her lips to mine, waiting for me to open up. Instead, I gripped her skinny biceps and pushed her off me.

"This can't happen again," I said firmly. "Your dad will be here soon to take you to his next duty station. If we keep this up, it will only end in heartbreak for both of us."

Grace rose from the chair, using her hair to shield her face. "You don't like me. You only wanted to fuck me, so Rhys didn't get the chance."

"That's not true." I reached out for her, and she recoiled. "I like you a lot. Maybe more than I should."

"Then, what's the problem?" Grace slid her hands onto her hips, her body angled, so I could only see the side of her face. A single tear streaked her left cheek. "My grandfather would never know. I won't tell him."

"Please understand that I'm not trying to hurt you." I stepped toward her. "We can't always get what we want."

She sucked back the tears and bolted down the aisle, leaving me no choice but to go after her. After putting myself in danger with The Knights, I wanted to relax and have a quiet night. But there were hardly ever dull moments in my life.

"There you are." Rhys entered the theater, holding open

the door with his hip. "I've been looking everywhere for you, princess."

"Now is not a good time," I said, trailing after Grace.

Rhys brushed the tears from her cheek and gave me an evil snarl. "What did you do to her, Marshall?"

I waved my hand. "You can go. I'm not done talking to Grace. And this doesn't concern you."

"No," Grace whispered, her back to me. "I have nothing left to say."

Rhys wrapped his arm around her, smirking at me as they left the theater.

He won.

Once again, I pushed her into the arms of my enemy.

Chapter Twenty-Six

GRACE

The following night, Cole knocked on my door. He stood shirtless in the entryway of my bedroom, with a pair of board shorts hung low on his narrow hips. He had the same ink on his muscled chest that Rhys had on his back. A skull wearing a gladiator's helmet, swords crossed. All of the members of The Devil's Knights had the same tattoo.

We hadn't spoken since I tried to kiss him, and he pushed me away. I couldn't bear to look at him after he made me feel stupid. At least with Rhys, I knew where I stood. I didn't have to wonder if he liked me.

"I invited people over." Cole shoved his fingers through his blond hair, keeping his distance. "I thought you'd want to check this off your list."

My list.

Because of Cole and Rhys, my bucket list was almost completed.

"We're partying in the natatorium if you want to hang out."

The enclosed pool house was on the first floor in the West Wing. Cole's place was so massive I hadn't heard any music, not even the doorbell or any indication people were arriving.

After he left, I grabbed the notebook from my nightstand and crossed off another bucket list item.

~~Attend a party~~

I could sense *him* from a distance. Cole always watched me, like he thought I would vanish into thin air. He stared at me from across the pool, flanked by two of his friends.

It was dark, the space lit by lanterns to hide the debauchery at the party. Everyone in town wanted an invitation to Fort Marshall. And from the look of it, most of Devil's Creek was in attendance.

I ordered a drink at the bar and surveyed the room. People were hooking up in the pool. A group of guys took turns passing around a rolled hundred-dollar bill, snorting lines of cocaine on the table. Two girls had their tops off, flashing their boobs to everyone. I felt so out of place among this crowd of lunatics.

But who was I to judge?

I got off with two men on a Ferris wheel and let one take my virginity while the other watched. I wasn't exactly a saint anymore. Years of hiding changed me.

"Hey, princess." Rhys hooked his arm around me, his fingers slipping beneath my bikini strap. "I've been looking for you. Where have you been hiding?"

I flashed a sexy smile. "Someplace you couldn't find me."

"And where's the fun in that?"

Rhys dipped his head down, and I couldn't take my eyes off his lips. They were soft and warm, and I wanted to kiss him. "We only have a few more days. I'm trying to make this a summer you won't forget."

"Hmmm…" I hooked my arms around his neck, and he

placed his hands on my hips, tapping his long fingers. "So far, you're exceeding my expectations."

Rhys was at least a foot taller than me and had about sixty pounds more solid muscle. Cut like an athlete, he was lean and toned, with a body so perfect I wanted to let my hands roam over every inch of him.

His hands moved from my hips to my ass. "You're so fucking sexy, Grace. There's nothing I wouldn't do to have one night with you."

"One night?" I gave him a sweet smile. "That's all you would want?"

"No man could only have one night with you. But I'll take whatever you're willing to give me."

I wanted to say *Cole could* but held my tongue. His reaction last night still pissed me off whenever I thought about him.

"Then, let's play a game." I flashed a smile. "If you can find me, you get to keep me for the rest of the night."

He winked. "Challenge accepted."

I got lost in the crowd and exited the room. A group of people stumbled down the hallway in my direction. I gripped the railing and ascended the staircase to the second floor.

My room was beside Rhys's at the far end of the hallway. His door was open, so I poked my head inside. The guest room had the same king-size bed and balcony overlooking the bay as mine. I liked to sit outside at night, breathing in the salty air.

I loved it here.

This town was perfect.

Like a fairytale world.

Since Rhys was downstairs, I inched into the room and flipped through the books on the nightstand. I knew better than to spy, but I couldn't help myself. Rhys was still somewhat of a mystery.

When I Googled his family, it returned thousands of search results. Most of the articles talked about their manufacturing company. One news outlet speculated they were bank-rupt, but it was only a rumor.

I opened the dresser drawers containing socks, boxer briefs, shorts, and T-shirts. The closet was filled with dress shirts, pants, suits, and jackets.

Nothing exciting.

I sat in front of the desk and flipped open his laptop. I wanted to know everything about Rhys because I was starting to have real feelings for him. Of course, the MacBook was password protected. I needed to know more than what he'd told me over the past few weeks to crack the code, so I didn't even bother.

I heard footsteps in the hallway moving closer to the room. *Shit.*

Panicked, I hopped out of the chair and dropped onto the bed, my heart pounding against my ribcage.

Rhys entered the room, humming a tune under his breath, a bottle of liquor tucked under his arm. He stopped when he noticed me, a sly grin illuminating his face. "There you are, princess. You didn't make it very hard to find you."

I spread my legs, placing my hands on my inner thighs. "Come claim your prize, Rhys."

His eyes darted across the room to the open laptop. *Shit, I'm so busted.*

Rhys set the bottle on the nightstand and crossed the room to type something into the computer. His fingers moved across the keys. I wondered if he knew I was spying on him. But he didn't say anything. Instead, he dimmed the screen and spun around to face me.

Rhys ran his thumb across his bottom lip, staring at me like a snack. "Fuck, you're hot." He moved between my thighs, bending down to touch my skin. "Wanna have some fun, princess?"

"Yes," I whispered, excited by the promise, and slid my hands up his chest. "Kiss me."

Without hesitation, his lips crashed into mine. He tasted

like expensive whiskey and smelled like spicy cologne. His lips were soft and warm, and as his tongue slid into my mouth, I moaned from the sheer pleasure blooming inside me.

He tugged at the strings of my bikini bottoms and slipped his hand between my legs. "You're so wet." Rhys slid his finger inside me, and I cried out as he added another. "Are you going to come all over my cock and scream my name like a good girl?"

"Yes," I whimpered.

He leaned forward to taste me, and intense waves of pleasure rolled down my arms. And with his mouth on my throbbing pussy, the heat from his breath sent chills down my legs as his tongue rolled over my clit.

He lifted his head, dark hair slightly obscuring his eyes. "Feel good, princess?"

"So good."

Rhys licked me the way he kissed me, slow at first before picking up the pace. Then, after tasting me, he climbed up my body and parted my lips with his tongue, kissing me like he wanted to be the last man to claim me.

Taking his time, he kissed my neck, his fingers pumping into me. Nothing compared to the feeling of hot and cold washing over me, the sensation building until it reached a crescendo. Rhys captured my moans with his mouth, making me dizzy with lust and hungry for more. When the last of my tremors ceased, my entire body felt numb.

"You taste good." He licked my juices from his fingers. "Watching you with Marshall nearly killed me. I need to be inside you."

I bit my bottom lip as he pushed his bathing suit over his hips, and his long, hard cock sprang free. He caged me against the mattress and covered my mouth with his. Sucking his bottom lip into my mouth, I rocked my hips, and Rhys groaned, threading his fingers through my hair as he deepened the kiss like he wanted to brand me.

Eventually, he stopped touching me and grabbed his wallet

from the nightstand. Rhys opened a condom and rolled it down his length, lining the tip at my entrance. He hooked my leg around his back and guided himself inside me. Only an inch or two, but it felt like more.

He stilled on top of me. "You have to relax."

"I am," I choked out, trying to hide the pain from my face.

"No, you're not." He rubbed my nipple with the pad of his thumb, his gentle touch helping to ease the tension in my body. "Open up for me, princess." Another inch. "You're so tight." His eyes closed for a moment before they opened again. "Fuck."

His eyes found mine as he stretched me out, careful not to move too fast. An intense wave of pain shot through my body. He kept his thrusts slow and steady, my body melting into his. After a while, I relaxed, no longer worried about the pain, because with it came intense pleasure. I unraveled beneath him, losing myself to a man I barely knew.

A carnal hunger flared in his pretty green irises, and his legs trembled. "I want you to get on top."

All of my sexual experiences could be summed up into a few nights. So I didn't know what Rhys expected from me. Thankfully, he took charge and rolled onto his back without breaking our bond.

His hands settled on my hips, and he moved us again, pushing into me. "Like this."

Straddling his thighs, I gripped the top of the headboard and followed his lead.

"That's it, princess." His hands moved to my ass, squeezing hard. "Ride me. Come all over my dick."

"Is this what you like?" I asked, picking up speed, no longer afraid he would hurt me.

"Fuck, yes," he grunted, matching my thrusts.

I lifted my head, greeted by my face in the mirror behind the bed. With a wild expression in my eyes, I looked possessed. Free. So out of my element, I didn't look like myself.

But that bubble burst the second the door opened. Cole

stood in the entryway, shaking with anger, arms crossed over his chest.

I didn't stop.

Maybe I should have.

But what was even more pleasurable than watching myself was knowing Cole was, too.

And I liked it.

Chapter Twenty-Seven

COLE

I would never forget the day Grace moved to Fort Marshall. She strolled into my home with her grandfather, dressed in a baby blue sundress. Grace looked like a porcelain doll with those pink cheeks, big blue eyes that practically jumped off her face, and long, blonde hair that spilled down her shoulders.

She was perfect.

I wanted to reach out and touch her, maybe even mess up her hair to put my mark on her. So quiet and shy, she only smiled as our families introduced us. At this moment, I wanted so badly to return to *that* day.

She was on top of Rhys, staring at me in the mirror while she came on his dick. I tried to be the nice guy, her protector. Her knight in shining armor. I took an oath and swore to uphold the laws of The Devil's Knights and The Founders Society.

That was my job.

It was Rhys's, too.

We agreed to share her, but I wasn't good at it. I wanted Grace to myself. And as I watched them, my heart thudding in my chest, I saw red. My vision blurred, and I thought I might black out.

I stormed into the room, trying to block out the sound of Rhys coming inside Grace. Anger surged through me like a storm.

Her cheeks flushed, and her long, blond hair brushed the tops of her breasts. Grace was the prettiest girl I had ever laid eyes on. I had met a lot of beautiful women, but no one compared to her.

"You better have worn a condom, Vanderbilt."

Grace covered her naked body with a sheet. "Cole, why are you mad? You said you were okay with this. And after last night, you made it clear you don't want me anymore."

"I never said those words."

Rhys tied off the condom, threw it into the trash can, and shot up from the bed. "She's wet, tight, and ready for you, Marshall. I got her all warmed up." He patted me on the back and smirked. "I know how much you like my sloppy seconds. Have fun."

It was all a game.

Of course, it was.

He even had me fooled for a little while. Rhys was so good at hiding his true nature. And as long as he wasn't hurting Grace, I stopped thinking about the words he said to me on the day he moved into my house.

A gentleman never kisses and tells.

He stood before me naked, his dick at half-mast and smirking as if he'd won. "Wait until I tell Fitzy about how you violated his precious granddaughter. All the dirty things she let us do to her." He shrugged. "You might as well fuck her again, for old time's sake."

With that, I slammed my fist into his jaw, knocking him off balance. He stumbled backward, but I hit him again before he could right himself. One punch after the other, swinging so hard my knuckles burned.

Rhys took a swing, and I ducked, his fist landing on my bicep. He tried to hit me with a right hook, which I evaded. "You're jealous. Get over yourself, Marshall."

"No, I'm not." My fist crashed into his cheek. "You fucked her out of spite."

He let out maniacal laughter that set me over the edge. Rhys Vanderbilt was the villain in Grace's story, not the hero. At least he showed his true colors, letting her see the real Rhys. The asshole I had grown up with at York Military Academy.

So I pounded my fists into his face, blood spilling from his mouth, staining his bare chest.

"Cole," Grace shouted, her voice a whimper. "Stop it! You're going to kill him."

I hope so.

Ignoring her screams, I punched Rhys until he couldn't take anymore and hit the carpet like a sack of potatoes. Clutching his bloody face, he lay on his side and groaned. His pretty face would be black and blue by morning.

Grace sobbed. "What did you do?"

Good question.

I violated my promise to treat other Knights as if they were my brothers. To put aside all differences and uphold the Charter of The Devil's Knights.

Fuck.

If Rhys reported this incident, I would face an inquiry from the higher-ups. But then Rhys would have to explain what he did to Fitzy, so it was a win-win.

We would both pay the price. At least it was worth it.

"Pack your bags." I stood over Rhys, wiping his blood down the side of my shorts. "I want you out of her life."

And mine.

I couldn't think straight.

Her naked body made it harder for me to focus. I did a shit job at protecting her because the one person she needed protection from was lying on the floor, naked and bloody.

I failed her.

"You better be gone by the time I wake up," I told Rhys.

Instead of one of his usual comebacks or insults, he nodded in defeat, wiping the blood from his lip.

I lifted Grace off the bed, cradled in the bedsheet that dragged across the floor as I left the room and headed into hers. "I warned you about Rhys. I tried to protect you because I know what he's like."

Tears stained her beautiful face, sliding down her cheeks. I didn't want to hurt her any more than Rhys already did. So I lowered her onto the mattress and sat beside her.

"You didn't deserve this, Grace. I'm sorry. This wouldn't have happened if I hadn't crossed the line with you. It's all my fault."

"No, it's not. It's mine." Grace clutched her chest and cried harder. "Why would Rhys do this to me? I thought he liked me. Instead, he acted like I mean nothing to him."

"Your grandfather has just as many allies as enemies." I put my hand over the top of hers on the bed and felt the tremors rocking through her body. "Let this be a lesson never to trust anyone."

<hr>

After Grace cried herself to sleep, I locked her bedroom door and cleared out the house. I waited for Rhys by the front door. The butler helped him with his bags and carried them to the car waiting by the curb.

Like nothing happened, Rhys whistled some stupid tune under his breath, approaching me with a victorious grin. "Why do you look so glum, Marshall? This day couldn't get any better, wouldn't you say?"

I wanted to kill him.

"If you breathe a word to anyone, I'll hunt you down and bury you."

He clutched the laptop bag over his shoulder, and despite his bruised face and bloody lip, he looked the same. Still smiling and joking, acting as if nothing had changed. The bastard hadn't learned anything. No amount of beat-downs would change Rhys Vanderbilt.

"You think I lost, Marshall?" His laughter filled the silence in the house. "Think again, old friend. This is only the beginning."

The wheels in his mind never stopped turning. By nature, Rhys was always plotting his next move, thinking about his strategy.

I got in his face and bumped my chest into his. "Whatever you're planning, leave Grace out of it."

"Don't you get it?" Rhys leaned forward, so our foreheads nearly touched. "She *is* the plan. I knew she was staying with you for the summer. My father arranged for me to be here. It was his idea."

I shook my head. "No, my dad offered to let you stay with us."

"How about I let you in on a little secret?" Rhys rubbed at his cracked lip, which was bleeding again. "My dad is terrible with money. But he's good at manipulating people. And I learned from the best."

I didn't understand what he could gain from having sex with Grace other than using her to get revenge. The Founders hadn't exiled his family yet. They were still one of us for now.

"I suspect my dad contacted Fitzy with the video I sent him." Rhys smirked. "One way or another, Vanderbilts get what they want. And we used *your* girl to get it."

I still wasn't following his train of thought. And then it hit me…

Grace.

Sex.

Video.

Fuck.

"You filmed her?" I muttered, still in disbelief, though I shouldn't have been that shocked, considering Rhys was a dirty motherfucker.

He winked. "Have yourself a good day, Marshall. I'll be seeing you soon."

And then, he walked out the front door, whistling that annoying tune under his breath. It wasn't until after he left that I realized I knew the song.

Amazing Grace.

Chapter Twenty-Eight

COLE

I hopped into my Ferrari seconds after Rhys drove off the property and went straight to Drake's house. He was family and the only person I could trust with this information. Luca made it crystal clear he didn't give a shit about Grace. And his brothers, apart from Bastian, would side with him.

I parked in the circular driveway and hopped out of the car, forgetting to kill the engine. My mind was scattered after the encounter with Rhys.

Several security guards lined the entrance to the house. They acknowledged me with a nod. I didn't have time for pleasantries, not when Rhys was plotting against Grace.

I had to save her.

The promise I made the day we met meant something to me. No matter what, I would always try to do right by her. I would do anything in my power to protect her. And if that meant finding a gray area to my rules, so be it.

Moments before sunset, I walked toward the Battle Fortress, the sky a purplish-orange hue.

Lovelace recognized me and opened the doors. "Welcome back, Mr. Marshall. You seem distressed."

"Because I *am* distressed," I told the AI as I entered the house. "Where's Drake?"

"Master Battle is in the Fortress of Solitude," she lilted. "He is not to be disturbed."

Drake rarely slept, so I knew he would still be awake.

"Disrupt him, please." I stood by the elevator, and it didn't light up when I hit the button. "Tell him I'm here and to turn the fucking elevator on!"

I was angrier than I realized and now taking it out on a computer.

"Master Battle gave specific instructions," she told me. "He needs complete concentration."

"Then tell him this is an emergency."

"Shall I wake Mr. Maxwell? Perhaps he can assist."

"No, Tate can't help me." I was ready to lose my mind. "Get Drake. Now!"

"One moment," she said, and the house fell silent.

Drake's assistant and her older brother lived here. But even Drake didn't expect them to work around the clock.

"Master Battle will see you now," Lovelace said.

The elevator light turned green, and when I hit the button this time, the car opened to allow me inside.

Dammit, Drake.

Pain in my ass.

I cursed him all the way down to the secret lab he called many things. The Battle Cave. The Fortress of Solitude. My cousin was a nerd at heart and loved his comics.

When the doors opened, I exited the elevator and almost ran into a disheveled Drake.

"Jesus," I muttered, studying his appearance. "You look like shit. When was the last time you shaved or showered?"

He scrubbed a hand across the dark stubble on his jaw, thinking over my question. "I don't know. I lost count after a few days."

He was serious.

I followed him into the room several floors beneath the house, built on the same level as the catacombs but not connected to them. My cousin wanted this place to have no exit points other than the ground floor.

Or so he said.

He would not spend this much time in a room with only one exit. So wherever the secret door was hidden, I didn't know its location. One of many mysteries my cousin kept to himself.

"What's the emergency?" Drake asked as he poured scotch into a highball glass.

I took the bottle from his hand. "The sun isn't even up yet, Drake. What the fuck is going on with you? Have you become an alcoholic since the last time I saw you?"

"No." He sighed, tugging at the ends of his hair that needed a cut and wash. Strands hung in front of his brown eyes, at least five inches longer than usual. "I've been under a lot of stress, Cole. I don't expect you to understand."

"Talk to me." I grabbed his wrist before he tried to walk away. "You can tell me anything, Drake."

"There's a reason I couldn't get the Il Circo website shut down," he confessed, his words slurred from drinking so much. He smelled like he fell asleep inside a copper whiskey still and went through the distillation process. "It's my fault that Alex got kidnapped and taken to the island."

I guided him over to the couch and sat beside him. "What are you talking about?"

He looked as if he were seconds from collapsing, leaning to the side, using the cushion for support. Stripped down to black boxers and dress socks, he wore a Superman T-shirt beneath an open white oxford. A red tie hung loosely around his neck, so I figured he was wearing a suit at some point.

I'd never seen him like this.

"Drake." I snapped my fingers as his eyes closed. "Don't fall asleep on me. Not after saying shit like that. What did you do?"

His eyelids fluttered. "I tried to get fancy. I thought I could out hack a hacker who goes by the name of Maverick. He runs the site for the owners of Il Circo."

"Wait, you knew all along?"

He bobbed his head. "You don't understand, Cole. Maverick is a ghost, a legend. I came across him on the Dark Web in high school. He's the reason I became a hacker."

"Yeah, but you're not black hat."

"I wasn't at the start," he confirmed. "I mostly stole porn, movies, and dumb shit to see if I could. But those days are over. The things I've done for The Devil's Knights crossed lines I never wanted to cross. I have broken so many laws I'd probably be in jail if not for The Founders." Drake scooted closer to me, looking more awake than before. "I didn't know I was going up against Maverick. Not at first." His Adam's apple bobbed as he swallowed hard. "Not until I saw his signature."

"What happened?"

"I tried to shut down the site, just like I told Luca and The Knights. But I wasn't fast enough. I didn't think like him. He was ten steps ahead." Drake groaned, once again pulling on his hair at the memory. "He skull fucked my entire system. When I said my board of directors leaked the demo of Lovelace, I lied. It was Maverick. He was only on my network for ten seconds before I locked him out, but it was enough time for him to get information."

"Fuck."

"Yeah," he whispered. "Fuck."

We sat silently for a moment, and I let it all sink into my brain. Drake blamed himself for everything that had happened to Alex. But was it his fault? He was only trying to protect her. If he made a few mistakes, it was because he was human.

"You were out hacked." I put my hand on his shoulder and gave it a reassuring squeeze. "It's not your fault Alex was kidnapped. You did everything you could to stop it."

"Cole, you're not listening." Drake shifted his weight on

the cushion and let out a deep breath. "Maverick got information from my server. Only The Knights know Alex is living with the Salvatore brothers. So how did her estranged mom, of all people, know where to find her? They haven't spoken in six years."

He had a point. While our enemies were intelligent, they weren't *that* smart.

"Think about it, Cole. How did the Russians know Alex was living with them? And how did they know her exact location? The Salvatore Estate has over twenty bedrooms and a team of guards who monitor by land, air, and sea twenty-four-seven."

I shot up from the couch. "Maybe I could use a drink after all."

"Pour me one." I narrowed my eyes at him, and he said, "Please. I promise I'll stop tomorrow."

I could tell the guilt over this had been killing him. Maybe now that he confessed to me, Drake could return to normal. Well, *normal* was a relative term with my cousin. He lived an unusual life, often without sleep or food for days. He needed a girlfriend, a therapist, or someone to keep his ass in check.

"Why are you shutting everyone out?" I added scotch to two glasses and strode to the couch, passing one to him. "You could talk to Tate or Olivia. They live in your house. Hell, you could have called me."

"This stuff upsets Liv. And Tate… Well, you know Tate."

I sipped from the glass, feeling the burn slide down my throat. "You can't keep secrets without them eating you alive."

"I told you," he said, relief washing over his face. "I already feel lighter."

"Maybe you'll get some sleep."

He bobbed his head. "But there's one more thing, Cole. It involves Grace."

My heart skipped a few beats at the mention of her. "What?"

He pounded the scotch in one gulp and set the glass on the

table, nearly falling into it. "Maverick got more than Alex's location."

Don't say it.

Please, don't say it.

"He knows Katarina Adams Romanov is Grace Hale."

I gasped, a shiver of fear rushing through me. "No."

"Yes." His expression darkened. "That's why Viktor is getting closer to finding his daughter. Maverick must work for The Lucaya Group. Or, at the very least, he made a trade for the information. People like Maverick do this for profit."

Viktor Romanov put out feelers on Grace on the Dark Web. He had been looking for her for so long that anyone who came across the request could have contacted him.

"I've been thinking a lot about why Fitzy has kept Grace around for so long," Drake said, his deep voice wavering. "He hates her. Treats her like shit. There's no love lost between them. I think Viktor has something on Fitzy."

I drank a few more sips and added the half-full snifter to the collection of empty glasses on the coffee table. "What does he have on Fitzy?"

He shrugged. "I don't know, but it's something big. Viktor was KGB, a trained intelligence officer. He came to the United States to get information on The Founders. Maybe he got more than he bargained for, and that's why Fitzy locked him up on Skull Island."

All Knights train on Skull Island before becoming members of the organization. I did horrible things there that still haunt my nightmares. We kept prisoners on the island who were too dangerous to allow a fair trial through the judicial system.

Plus, we couldn't kill them until we got what we wanted. Men like Viktor were not that easy to break. He was on the island for several years, made friends with a guard, and escaped.

The island was in the middle of the Atlantic Ocean. But he must have had help from others because we never found him—only the handcuffs he'd left behind. Like a ghost, he vanished. We thought he had returned to Russia until he appeared on our radar looking for Grace.

"We're missing something, Cole. Bastian should be the heir to the Adams fortune, not Grace. It has something to do with Viktor. Maybe even her mom."

I patted his thigh. "We'll keep digging. Eventually, we'll find something useful."

He laid his head back on the leather cushion and yawned. "You said there's an emergency. What is so important it couldn't wait?"

"Rhys had sex with Grace and filmed it."

Drake sat up, eyes wide with interest. "That's fucked up." He studied my face briefly and said, "What are you not telling me?"

"Remington Vanderbilt sent the video to Fitzy. I need to get Grace out of Devil's Creek before something happens to her."

Drake lifted an iPad from the table and started typing feverishly. "He could use this to leverage Fitzy into a payoff."

I nodded. "Exactly. They need the money. Can you help me get Grace out of here?"

Drake drunkenly pushed himself up from the couch, iPad tucked under his arm as he staggered to the desks on the opposite side of the room. At least a dozen monitors hung from the ceiling and on the walls. Around fifteen desktop and laptop computers were scattered throughout the messy space.

My cousin wasn't usually so unorganized. But he thrust himself into chaos whenever he went on a bender like this one. Staring at the chip bags, open soda cans, and snack wrappers gave me the sudden itch to clean.

"I can create a new identity for Grace." Drake sat in front of one of many monitors and started typing so fast the keys pounded. "A new passport and license. Medical and dental records. Credit history. The complete package."

"Yeah, great. Just do it. I don't have much time."

Eyes flicking between the monitors, he said, "But how are you going to explain to your parents and Fitzy that she just disappeared from Fort Marshall? It would start an inquiry with The Founders Society that could jeopardize your future. And who will protect her? She's more vulnerable now than before."

I propped myself against the wall by my hip and watched Drake work his magic. He was so brilliant I sometimes envied him until I realized his life was a complete mess. He couldn't have the woman he loved. People were trying to kill him for his technology. And because of his secrets, he carried the world's weight on his shoulders.

"I'll ask Hunter or Brax to help me."

He glanced over his shoulder at me. "And make your friends complicit in your crimes? We're family, so I don't mind being an accomplice. But you can't burden them with this. If you're unwilling to uproot your life and go with her, there's no point in sending Grace away."

He was right.

This was too heavy of a burden to dump on my friends. If I wanted to protect Grace, I had to do it myself. I had to give up everything for her.

Chapter Twenty-Nine

Rhys left Fort Marshall after we had sex. Cole hadn't been around since he caught us in the act. I wasn't even sure if he was home.

I couldn't wait for my dad to pick me up, so I could get as far away from my mistakes as possible. What I thought would be the perfect summer quickly became my worst nightmare. Rhys used me to get back at my grandfather.

I believed his lies.

Fell into his trap.

Cole was right all along.

If only I had listened.

Every time I thought about that night, I vomited. I couldn't even stand to look at myself in the mirror.

I cracked open my bedroom door and poked my head into the hallway. My nose tipped up at the scent of beef, so I wandered downstairs, letting my growling stomach lead the way.

I found Mark Marshall in the main dining room. He sat by himself at the head of the table, drinking a glass of scotch as he read the newspaper in his other hand. The opposite of my dad, he reminded me of a businessman, not a military academy's commandant.

"Did I miss dinner?"

Mark looked up from the newspaper. "No, you're right on schedule."

I sat in the chair beside him. "Is it just the two of us?"

He folded the paper in half and set it on the table. "For now. Willow is out with a friend. So are the twins. And Cole is... I'm not sure where."

The waitstaff set our plates on the table.

"Did Rhys go back to California?"

He dropped the cloth napkin on his lap and shook his head. "No, he's staying with a friend."

I sliced into my steak and chewed, delighted by the tastiness of the meat. "I'm sorry," I said between bites. "I didn't mean to cause trouble."

"It's not your fault." He put down the knife and stabbed at the meat with his fork. "Rhys has always been a troubled boy. His family is... Well, I guess I shouldn't make excuses for him. But Rhys doesn't come from a loving home. He's never been shown how to treat people properly. Still, that doesn't excuse what he did to you. You have my sincerest apology."

I didn't understand why Mark felt so bad. The Marshalls had been nothing but nice to me.

"When is my dad coming to get me?"

Mark scooped the fluffy potatoes onto his fork, speaking between bites. "I'm sorry, Grace. But I have bad news. The Colonel's mission has been extended by six months. So you'll stay here until he returns."

No.

Dad said he would be here at the end of the summer. I needed him. My stomach filled with dread, the food churning in my stomach. I put down the fork and wiped my mouth with the napkin, hoping I could hold down my food.

Cole stumbled into the dining room with a bottle of Macallan raised to his mouth. "I need to talk to you. Alone."

Mark glared at Cole as he pounded the expensive liquor

from the bottle. "We're in the middle of dinner. Sit and eat with us. We can talk afterward."

"No." Cole's jaw clenched, his grip tightening on the bottle. "We need to talk. Now."

"Excuse us," he said, then led a drunken Cole out of the dining room.

Mark left in the middle of dinner and never returned. So I spent the rest of the night in my bedroom reading. Whenever in doubt, I always turned to one of my comfort reads to take my mind off things.

I read half the book before I heard a disturbance in the hallway. It sounded like something slammed into the wall, followed by a thud.

What the hell?

I glanced at the clock, surprised it was well after ten o'clock. Time had escaped me. When I started reading, it was a little after seven.

I kept telling myself one more chapter. But the book kept getting better and better. I both loved and hated when that happened. Sleep was great, but so was getting lost in a good book.

Another loud noise made my heart race. The hairs on my arms stood at attention. I stuffed the bookmark into the fold of the book and set it on the nightstand.

Someone turned the doorknob. Cole had warned me never to open the door for anyone but him. He locked me inside each night for my protection.

Shoes tapped on the floor, moving away from my room. As they retreated, the tension in my body slowly faded. A few minutes passed without a sound. So I slid onto the mattress, grabbed the book, and laid my head on the pillow. I flipped to the last page I read and tried to relax.

My eyelids fluttered. I blinked a few times to stay awake,

slowly drifting. And when I heard another noise in the hallway, I didn't have time to react before the door flew open.

Cole stood in the entryway, dressed in jeans and a fitted black shirt that clung to his muscles. Even drunk, with one eye slightly closed, he still looked like a god, oozing sex appeal.

"What are you doing in here?" I demanded. "I'm sleeping."

He approached the bed. "You can't stay in Devil's Creek. You need to leave before he hurts you."

"I know you're mad about Rhys, but I have nowhere to go."

Cole pressed his palms to the mattress. "This is all Rhys's fault. I tried to warn you, Grace. You should have listened to me. What comes next could have been avoided. Rhys has sealed your fate."

I crossed my arms under my breasts, attempting to hide my nipples that poked through the silky pajama top. "What are you talking about?"

He shook his head, and the scent of hard liquor rolled off him. "You have to leave tonight."

"Why?" I croaked. "At least give me a reason."

Cole knelt on the bed between my thighs and lowered his voice. "We're leaving tonight."

"What's going on?" I struggled to catch my breath. "Why are you doing this?"

A dark expression cast over his handsome face like a storm cloud. "Because I said I would protect you."

"From who?"

"Rhys." His knee slid off the bed, and he inched backward toward the door. "Your grandfather. The Founders."

"What does Rhys have to do with my grandfather?"

He shook his head, scrubbing a hand at his jaw. "If you trust me, do as I say. Pack a bag and meet me in the game room at two o'clock. I'll explain everything."

Without another word, he exited the room.

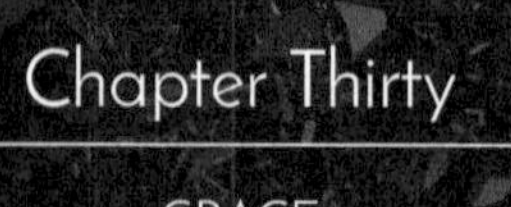

Chapter Thirty

GRACE

I packed whatever I could into a backpack and slung it over my shoulder. Creeping into the hallway, I kept my footsteps light, careful not to make a sound. This place had more rooms than I could count and enough staff to run a hotel. I couldn't risk letting anyone see me.

It was almost two o'clock. The upper floors were dark, with only the dimly lit wall sconces creating a golden glow on the hardwood floor. Using the light as my guide, I tiptoed in a pair of sneakers down the long corridor.

Clutching the thick, wooden railing, I descended the stairs with the grace of a dancer, light on my feet. Downstairs, it was much darker. I bumped into a table with my hip. A glass vase tipped over, but thankfully, it hit my stomach, and I saved it in time.

"Is someone there?" A female voice called out. "Mark, is that you?"

Shit.

I stumbled into the living room and waved to Willow. "It's just me."

"Grace," she whispered. "What are you doing up so late? You should be in bed."

I didn't know how to respond, so I said nothing.

Willow padded over to me, tugging at the belt of the silky robe. Her long, blonde hair flowed down her shoulders, slightly curled at the ends. Cole was the mirror image of his mother, who was still stunning.

Her eyes lowered to my bag. "Grace, you can't leave." She curled her fingers around my wrist, concern dripping from her tone. "If you were to disappear from our home, your grandfather would hold us responsible."

"Then why did Cole tell me to pack a bag?"

Her eyes widened with surprise, but she quickly recovered from the news and said, "Sweetheart, he's not thinking clearly, especially regarding you." She led me over to the couch. "Cole means well, but he's misguided."

I dropped my bag onto the floor and sat beside Willow, propping myself against a throw pillow. "What's so important that he wanted me to leave in the middle of the night?"

She smoothed a hand down the front of the robe. "Your grandfather is coming back to Devil's Creek."

My heart pounded so hard I wondered if Willow could hear the rapid beating. It felt like it was ready to punch a hole through my chest.

"Why?"

Willow sighed. "I'm sorry, Grace. Your grandfather has plans for you."

My mom died when I was eight, and after thirteen years, I barely remembered her. But having Willow around this summer reminded me of what it was like to have a mother.

I heard footsteps in the hallway, glanced at the room's entrance, and saw Cole's shadow. It was too dark to see his face or reveal his features.

Willow moved toward him. "Honey, I know you're upset about what Rhys did to Grace. But you can't plan things like this without speaking to your father."

I looked at him, wondering what I should do.

"It's okay, Grace," he said in a hushed tone. "My mom is

right. I shouldn't have asked you to go. I was drinking and not thinking clearly. This wouldn't have worked, anyway."

Willow turned to look at me. "Your grandfather would have found the two of you and punished our family for it. And I can't imagine what he would have done to you."

I lifted my bag from the floor and joined them. "I want to be free of him and go home with my dad."

Willow hugged me with one arm. "I know, sweetie. The Colonel will be home before you know it."

I glanced at Cole. "What is Rhys planning with my grandfather?"

He rolled his broad shoulders. "I don't know yet. But I wanted to get you out of the crosshairs before you find out."

There was something he wasn't telling me.

"What could Rhys possibly hold over my grandfather?"

Cole dug his teeth into his bottom lip and looked at his mother.

Willow pulled me closer. "Grace, I hate to be the one to tell you this… but Rhys filmed the two of you together."

Her confession sucked the air from my lungs.

"No one has seen the video," Willow added. "But Rhys mentioned it to Cole before he left. The Vanderbilts are trying to use you to extort your grandfather."

I balled my hands into fists at my sides, teeth gritted as the rage bubbled up inside me.

"The boys are not to touch you," my grandfather said when he dropped me off at Fort Marshall. "They are under strict orders to keep their filthy hands to themselves. And I expect you to act like a lady."

I broke his rules.

Fuck.

He was going to kill me or, worse, torture me. Could he use Rhys to do that? I didn't know the *real* Rhys Vanderbilt. After we had sex, he became a completely different person.

He used me.

Manipulated me.

Within seconds of Cole walking in on us, Rhys transformed into an asshole, making it clear I was nothing more than sex to him.

"Has anyone spoken to my grandfather?"

Willow nodded. "Mark received a call from him earlier. We're hosting a party in his honor tomorrow."

So, in other words, I had to wait for the other shoe to drop. With my grandfather, no sin ever went unpunished.

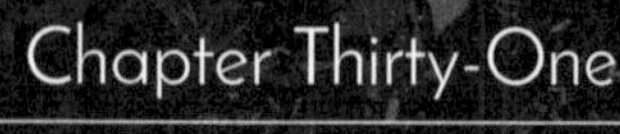

Chapter Thirty-One

GRACE

My grandfather forced the Marshalls to host a party in his honor, but no one knew why. All night, I couldn't sleep thinking about seeing Fitzy again. And as I sat in front of the vanity, my stomach churned. I couldn't keep down anything I ate all day.

Rhys would be here.

So would The Founders.

And The Devil's Knights.

Willow turned on the curling iron, humming a tune under her breath. A song I didn't recognize. From what I could remember of my mother, she was a lot like Willow—sophisticated and refined, from a wealthy family that expected her to marry well.

Like the Marshalls, my parents married for love. At least, I thought they did. If you asked my grandfather, he would say my father was our family's undoing. He was glad to be rid of him.

The circumstances surrounding the day my mother died remained a mystery to me. I could recall bits and pieces, fragments that didn't make much sense.

My grandfather didn't even let me attend her funeral. He told me she was cremated, but I knew that was a lie. The

Adams' plots took up half of the cemetery. One whole section was dedicated to my relatives. So I knew my mother was buried there.

Didn't matter, anyway.

Dead was dead.

She was gone.

After Willow curled my hair and dabbed makeup on my skin, I changed into a pretty red dress. It was floor-length, strapless, and fit me perfectly.

"Gorgeous." She wiggled her fingers, and I grabbed her hand. "Come, our guests are waiting."

"I thought I was free from my grandfather," I muttered, deflated.

"I wish I could say that someday you will be. But look at us." She waved her hand to where the second floor overlooked the foyer as men and women in expensive clothes entered the house. "We must follow The Founders' rules, same as you."

"Couldn't some of you rebel against The Founders Society?"

She shook her head. "It's not that simple. Our families have maintained wealth and power because of our connections. To break free from The Founders would be worse than exile. We could lose everything."

I was glad I had been spared this for the past ten years. Thanks to my adoptive father, I had a new name—a new identity. On paper, I was no longer an Adams.

I was pissed at first about my grandfather changing my name. But after I left town with the Colonel, I felt a sense of relief. My last name and family didn't follow me from city to city. I could move across the country with my new dad and live a normal life.

Until now.

As we entered the ballroom, I spotted Cole standing by the bar with his best friends from York Military Academy, Hunter Banks and Braxton Cade. They drank amber liquid from glasses, talking to a group of guys.

"Go say hello," Willow suggested, tapping me on the back. "I have to find Mark. We'll join you soon."

At least two hundred people filled the space. In a house this size, it didn't seem that claustrophobic. But I wasn't used to being around so many people.

I wasn't used to people.

Period.

"Hey, princess." Rhys curled his long fingers around my arm and pulled me into his chest. "Where are you going?"

I looked at his bruised skin that darkened around his eyes and right cheek. His split lip looked like it would gush at any second. Cole messed him up, and I was glad because I wanted to set him on fire.

Rhys tightened his grip when I ignored him and tried to walk away. "Hey, I'm talking to you."

Shooting him a nasty look, I swatted at his hand. "Take a hint, Rhys. I don't want to talk to you. Not after everything you've done to me."

He breathed bourbon in my face. "You're going to be mine. Stop fighting the inevitable."

I snorted at his comment. "Never gonna happen."

Rhys stared over my shoulder and laughed. I spun around to see what held his attention and found Cole with Hunter and Brax.

"You don't own her, Marshall," Rhys snapped. "So get lost."

"Neither do you," Cole countered. "Stop acting like you do."

I waved to Hunter and Brax, both of which returned my gesture. They drank from the highball glasses in their hands and eyed up Rhys.

Hunter was taller than Cole and had more muscle, his arms thick beneath his suit, like a professional athlete. Brax was around the same height. He was cute and had curly, dark brown hair that flopped onto his forehead and got into his eyes. His naturally tanned skin was several shades darker than Cole's summer glow.

Rhys dipped his head down, so his lips almost touched my cheek. "You're mine, Grace. Wait until the old man makes it official." He laughed in Cole's face. "Always the last to know what The Founders are planning. You heard me. Grace is *mine*. And there's nothing you can do about it."

Without another word, he disappeared into the crowd.

Chapter Thirty-Two

COLE

R hys fucking Vanderbilt. That asshole always knew the right thing to say to rile me up. And if his words held any truth, I would lose my mind.

Grace wasn't his.

She was *mine*.

From the moment she walked into my house, I felt the need to save her. She'd lived a horrible life before she became Grace Hale, and I promised to be there for her.

Anything she needed.

Her Knight.

Her protector.

Rhys didn't give a shit about Grace. He only cared about saving his ass.

Hunter put his hand on my shoulder. "Don't listen to Rhys. He's only trying to fuck with you."

Hunter was my best friend. We'd known each other for so long that I couldn't remember when we weren't friends.

"I know," I muttered. "But I can't stop thinking about it."

I downed the contents of my glass and nodded at the bartender for another. My eyes moved to Grace, who looked gorgeous in a strapless red dress.

She flicked her hair over her shoulder and giggled as Brax told her a joke. He'd been my friend almost as long as Hunter.

Most men in the room were The Devil's Knights or The Founders Society members. I caught plenty of guests' gazes darting in our direction. They wanted a good look at the only granddaughter of Fitzgerald Adams IV. This was Grace's first time in the spotlight.

"Fitzy invited The Founders and The Devil's Knights," I pointed out. "He only does that when he has big news. I think Rhys might be right."

Hunter shook his head. "No way. Fitzy hates the Vanderbilts. He wouldn't let a scumbag like Rhys marry Grace."

Pressing my lips together, I glanced at Grace. "She might be his heir, but Fitzy hates her. This could be another one of his punishments."

Drake sauntered over to me, drink raised to his mouth. "Fitzy is up to something. I overheard him talking to Carl Wellington about the flight that killed Bastian and Damian's parents."

"Probably arguing over shares of Atlantic Airlines."

"Maybe." He took another sip of scotch. "But it sounded more intense than shares in a company." Drake leaned into my arm and lowered his voice. "After this is over, we need to talk. Viktor made contact earlier."

My eyes widened. "Okay, yeah."

'This is good for Grace," he added. "I'll explain later."

I spotted Fitzy moving through the crowd, which parted for him. Everyone wanted to steal a second of his time. He was a powerful man and the richest in the world. The Adams family owned banks, railroads, tech companies, and dozens of holding companies. They were once governors, senators, and even presidents.

He ignored those who attempted to gain his attention, eyes fixed on Grace.

His target.

As Fitzy looked at her, hatred scrolled across his face.

Despite his age, the old man looked at least twenty years younger. His skin was nearly free of wrinkles, and his hair was without an ounce of gray. I often wondered if he was a cyborg.

Fitzy didn't seem like a real person. He didn't act like one, either.

"Gentleman," he said to the group, tugging at his cufflinks. "Staying out of trouble, I hope."

"Of course, sir," Hunter replied.

I nodded in response.

Drake raised his glass.

Fitzy's head snapped to Grace, and then he extended his hand. "It's time. Come with me."

Worry furrowed her brows as she looked to me for advice. I couldn't help with her grandfather, even though I wanted to take her away from this place.

"What's going on?" Grace asked him.

With a wicked glint in his eyes, Fitzy yanked on her arm. "You know better than to speak out of turn."

Chapter Thirty-Three

GRACE

My grandfather tightened his grip around my wrist, dragging me toward the stage at the front of the room.

"What's going on?" I asked.

"I already warned you once, Grace." He fired an angry look at me. "Don't make me tell you again, or there will be consequences."

"I'm not being difficult," I said in my defense. "I want to know how to act. I can't play my part if you don't coach me."

He never let me near anyone as a child, not without going over the proper way to sit, speak, and act. Grandfather even brought a woman to the house once a week to teach me how to be a lady. Of course, I tossed all those lessons out the window the second I moved in with the Colonel.

"Act grateful," Fitzy said as we walked toward the front of the room. "Like this is a dream come true, and you're thrilled to be here." He yanked on my arm the rest of the way. "And when you're asked a question, the answer is yes. Nothing else." He stopped at the stairs, his eyes burning a hole through me. "Do you understand me?"

"The answer is yes," I repeated. "I got it."

I followed him onto the stage. The Marshalls stood in the

front row beside the Salvatores and the rest of the town's founding families. Cole joined his parents and the twins, who wore bored looks and suits.

"Thank you all for coming," my grandfather said into the microphone. "Tonight, I brought you here to introduce my granddaughter, Grace, and share some exciting news for The Founders."

He raised his hand to beckon someone, but I couldn't see who until Rhys, his younger brother, and his parents joined us on the stage, smiles tipping up the corners of their mouths.

Grandfather patted my shoulder, smiling as if he didn't hate me. I slapped on the fakest smile in history and looked at the crowd. My stomach twisted into knots whenever I was around my grandfather, and I could hardly breathe.

Rhys moved beside me. We were so close I could feel his body heat radiating off him.

I wanted to run.

Scream.

I couldn't even look at Cole, knowing I would find a sad expression on his face. My grandfather gave a speech about The Founders and our duty to this country.

Midway through the speech, Rhys whispered, "You can relax, princess. I won't bite." His hand moved to my ass. "Not now, anyway."

I pressed my lips tighter.

To make a sound would only piss off my grandfather. Besides, I didn't want anyone in the audience to see me squirm.

On the outside, Rhys was a pretty boy and looked the part. But a monster lurked beneath his designer suit. He could give me that shit-eating smirk all he wanted because I saw right through his perfect exterior.

"Rhys has something he would like to ask Grace," my grandfather said at the end of his spiel.

Rhys lowered to one knee, holding out a black box with a massive diamond ring inside. It looked like the kind of jewelry passed down for centuries—not something you could pick up at the mall on your way home from work.

A diamond fit for a queen.

Rhys took my hand, and I jerked at the sudden connection. His skin was soft and warm like he'd never worked a day in his spoiled life.

I glanced at my grandfather. He tipped his head at Rhys and gave me a stern look.

Rhys clutched my fingers, rough and possessive. "Grace, will you marry me?"

And when you're asked a question, the answer is yes. Nothing else.

I let my grandfather's words roll around in my head. He would probably kill me if I said no. Maybe even lock me in his basement without light, food, or water.

It wouldn't have been the first time. And I wasn't going back there.

So I had to say yes.

I took one look in Cole's direction. His chest rose and fell rapidly as if he couldn't control his breathing. My heart ached at the sadness in his eyes, written all over his face.

I felt the same pain.

I turned away from Cole, unable to look at him when I said the word that burned my tongue. "Yes."

Rhys slipped the ring on my finger, a victorious grin in place. He rose from the floor and collected me in his strong embrace. I didn't pull away because I needed him to hold me up.

"You're mine now, Grace." Rhys's lips brushed my cheek. "Forget about Cole Marshall. You'll never see him again after the wedding."

Chapter Thirty-Four

COLE

Grace was engaged. To Rhys fucking Vanderbilt, of all people.

After the applause died down from the announcement, I stormed out of the ballroom. Hunter called out to me, trailing behind. I didn't wait for him to catch up and ignored everyone I passed.

The room was too small.

Too crowded.

I needed air.

Exiting the ballroom, I headed straight to the game room. Fuck Fitzy and The Founders Society.

Maybe it was karma.

Grace and I had one night together. One perfect night I would remember forever. I tried to do right by her and let her go. I could have had Grace but pushed her away, all because of the stupid rules.

Rhys broke them and won.

I should have told her how much I thought about her. Some days, she was all I could think about. Even when we were apart, she was on my mind.

And I fucked it up.

Fitzy had threatened my family. He said he would make

the lives of anyone who touched Grace a living hell. We knew he would make good on that promise.

I was a good Knight.

A good son.

And I still lost.

"Cole, wait up," Hunter called out as I entered the game room.

I ducked into the room, and he joined me seconds later, locking the door behind us.

"I know how you feel."

"No, you don't." I walked over to the bar and grabbed a glass. "You don't have to let someone else marry the woman you love."

Hunter handed me a bottle of scotch. "No, but I know what it's like to have someone else control my life. My dad plans every single detail. I don't have a choice either."

I poured the amber liquid into two glasses and passed one to Hunter. We sipped our drinks and plopped onto the leather couch.

I devoured most of the scotch in one gulp. It burned on the way down, but I needed to feel something.

Anything.

"I can't let Grace marry Rhys," I muttered between sips.

"Fitzy will destroy your family. Don't get in his way. It's not worth it."

I finished my drink and hopped up from the couch, feeling too fidgety to sit still. "I let Grace think I'm not into her when she's the only thing I think about."

"You know how this will end," Hunter reminded me.

I knew the cost of breaking The Founders' rules. I witnessed several banishments in my twenty-two years on this earth.

They lost everything.

Their status.

Their money.

Their power.

My cell phone buzzed in my pocket, a call from my dad, probably to yell at me for leaving so abruptly. Fitzy wasn't done making a spectacle of his granddaughter's engagement before I rushed out of the ballroom.

Fuck him.

My phone rang again, and Hunter got up from the couch, one eyebrow raised. "Who keeps calling you?"

"My dad."

"We should head back." He put his empty glass on the bar and tipped his head at the door. "Our parents won't be happy."

Hunter's dad was an abusive asshole. His only reprieve from his father's cruelty was the nine months he'd spent each year at York Military Academy. Now that we graduated, he was stuck living at home and forced to follow orders.

"Yeah, okay," I agreed because I didn't want him to get into trouble and knew he would stay with me, despite the consequences. "I guess I have to face Grace. She's probably looking for me."

Hunter nodded. "You can't hide forever. And it's not too late to tell her how you feel," he said on our way down the hallway. "She's not a married woman yet."

I expelled a deep breath to steady my nerves the closer we got to the ballroom. "Maybe it's better if she doesn't know."

Chapter Thirty-Five

GRACE

I latched onto Rhys's arm and forced a smile for the cameras. Dozens of people wanted to snap pictures of the happy couple. It killed me to pretend when I felt like I was dying on the inside.

The second I accepted Rhys's proposal, Cole stormed out of the ballroom and didn't look back.

My heart raced as Rhys paraded me across the room on his arm, like his perfect little pawn. I didn't understand why my grandfather wanted me to marry Rhys, of all people.

What choice do I have?

He made the rules.

We had to follow them.

"Smile," Rhys whispered, "everyone is watching you."

I thought I was smiling, but maybe it was harder to fake enthusiasm than I thought. Every inch of my body heated from the anger coursing through my veins. If given a chance, I would claw out Rhys's eyeballs with a spoon and feed them to him.

Rhys was beautiful on the outside, but his heart was as black as coal.

Black heart.

Black mind.

He was evil.

Fitzy often threatened to arrange my marriage to the highest bidder. Instead, he sold me to a man whose family was going broke.

After we made our rounds around the room several times, my feet were killing me from the stilettos. I gripped Rhys's muscular bicep to steady myself. He took that as a sign of affection and smiled. But it wasn't a normal smile, not the one he used to charm his way into my panties. This one was sinister and terrified me.

I spotted Cole entering the ballroom with Hunter at his side. He scrubbed a hand through his blond hair and scanned the room. Our eyes met briefly before Rhys steered me in the opposite direction.

I glanced over my shoulder at Cole. My expression said, *Save me*. But I knew he wouldn't come running when there was nothing he could do. Even Cole couldn't interfere with this wedding and walk away unscathed.

The Salvatore brothers approached us with a beautiful blonde woman between them. Alexandrea Wellington was flawless. She practically glowed in a champagne-colored dress that hugged her waist.

Luca, the oldest of the group, held her hand like he was afraid someone would steal her again. Marcello clutched her right hand. Bastian was my cousin on my mother's side. He had a warm smile and dark caramel-brown hair that flopped onto his forehead. His gray eyes met mine, and he winked.

He was Fitzy's only living grandson and should have been his heir. I wasn't sure what Bastian had done to get on the shit list, but it didn't take much with our grandfather.

For most of my life, I wanted a family. Having a relationship with my cousin was another thing Fitzy deprived me of. It was like our grandfather was afraid we would swap war stories about him.

Bastian stood beside Damian, who was gorgeous and had the palest, unblemished skin I'd ever seen. His lips were so red it was as if he drank blood. He had the kind of face you put on magazine covers—a Roman nose, a jaw that could cut diamonds, and ridiculously high cheekbones, every inch of his face perfectly symmetrical.

The wicked look in Damian's green eyes terrified me. Whatever was rolling through his mind must have been dark and scary. And the way he stared at Alex was even more sinister.

I wasn't sure why my cousin and his adoptive brothers wanted to share one woman, but I could see the appeal. Alex had the face of a runway model and the body of a porn star.

"Vanderbilt," Luca said with a cocky smirk, his hand extended. "Congrats on the engagement." They shook hands, but it looked forced and uncomfortable. "Your parents must have something on Fitzy to slime your way into the Adams family."

Rhys swiped a hand across his jaw and smirked. "Jealous The Founders chose my family over yours?" Wicked laughter spilled from his mouth. "Last I checked, The Founders refuse to admit the Salvatores into the society. You're not one of *us.*"

"Not yet," Luca snapped, and his gaze turned to Alex lovingly. "But Alex will be my wife soon."

Women were treated like possessions in our world. From an early age, most of us were groomed to become the wives of powerful men.

People like us didn't have a choice. Our marriages were arranged for us.

We didn't marry for love.

We married for power.

Rhys slid his arm behind my back and pulled me closer. My skin felt as if tiny spiders were crawling over me.

I hated his touch.

Luca and Rhys exchanged a few more nasty quips. They had an undeniable hate-hate relationship. No one seemed to like Rhys or his family.

So why did he get to marry me?

I was dying to know why my grandfather had agreed to this nightmare. Either he wasn't done torturing me and wanted me to suffer even more, or there was something he hoped to gain from the Vanderbilts.

Maybe their silence?

Their cooperation?

It could have been anything. Money never motivated him.

Cole strolled over to the group with Hunter and Brax at his sides. I felt every bit of his anger as he locked eyes with Rhys. His lip curled into a snarl, the rage bubbling beneath the surface.

"Did you run off to cry, Marshall?" Rhys tipped his head back and laughed, his eyes moving from Cole to his friends. "Did your boyfriends make it all better?"

Cole's jaw clenched as if trying to keep from losing his cool. He wouldn't let Rhys get under his skin. At least he wouldn't show how much he affected him.

"Not like it's any of your concern, but I had business to handle for my family," Cole said, even though it sounded like a lie.

Rhys grabbed my wrist and raised my hand to let Cole see the diamond. The ring on my finger weighed down my left hand. I felt every ounce of responsibility and everything that came with it.

Cole inspected my finger, and a wild expression danced across his face. If looks could kill, Rhys would have been dead.

His eyes drifted to me for a second, then back to Rhys. "Whatever game you're playing, Vanderbilt, I will find out. And when I do, this engagement is over."

"Nothing is going to get in my way of marrying Grace." He squeezed my shoulder and pushed me in front of him. "This is a done deal."

I hoped Cole was right about this being a game—because that meant he could win.

"Nothing is final," Cole said through clenched teeth. "You're not married yet."

"When is the wedding?" Hunter asked, his voice deep and smooth.

"At the end of the month," Rhys commented.

Cole breathed through his nose and stared through Rhys. "You won't last until then."

He laughed. "You should know better than to bet on me, Marshall. I always win."

The conversation ended with Fitzy summoning us to meet some of his wealthy friends. And since I was expected to play the dutiful granddaughter, I clung to Rhys's side and followed his lead.

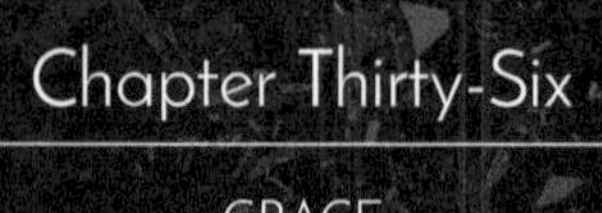

Chapter Thirty-Six

GRACE

Rhys swept me into his arms and paraded me around the ballroom. His glittering smile aimed at our guests said, "Look at my prize. Isn't she beautiful? Isn't she the luckiest girl in the world to be marrying me?"

He won, but he didn't play fair. The bastard tricked me into thinking he wanted me. That he liked me for more than what my family could give him.

I felt so stupid for walking right into his trap. Cole tried to warn me about Rhys when he'd first arrived at Fort Marshall. But I was too blinded by his good looks and wicked charm to see he was a snake.

He lied to me.

Manipulated me.

Used me.

Once we made our rounds, Rhys guided me to where his family waited. Remington, Helena, and Grayson Vanderbilt looked like Founders. Rhys had inherited his father's good looks—even the same evil glint in his green eyes.

Helena wore a black gown that reminded me of couture you'd only find on a runway. Her long brown hair was curled at the ends, hanging in a perfect knot over her shoulder.

His brother, Grayson, was two years younger and the

mirror image of their father. Except Grayson didn't have the same villainous expression. He had kinder green eyes and smiled when he spotted me with Rhys.

"Congratulations, brother." Grayson patted Rhys on the back. "Well done." His gaze flicked to me, and he extended his hand. "Welcome to the family, sis."

Sis?

Gross.

I wanted to cry.

With some hesitation, I shook his hand and forced a smile. Then I pulled my hand away like his skin was on fire, rubbing my palm down the front of my dress when Grayson wasn't looking.

I had to find a way out of this marriage. There was no way I would walk down the aisle, put on his ring, and become a Vanderbilt.

Grace Vanderbilt.

I hated how it sounded.

Rhys dipped his head down to speak against the shell of my ear. "Be nice, princess. My brother might not see the wheels turning in your pretty little head, but I know you better than you think." His hand moved to my lower back, inches from my ass. "I'm a master manipulator, but I learned from the best. So before I introduce you to my parents, you better get your shit together."

Last week, I would have moaned just having him this close. My panties would have been soaked. But now, my skin crawled as if bugs were on me.

"I don't care what you or your sleazy family thinks of me," I shot back, keeping my voice low. "You might think you won. But this isn't over, Rhys."

"Oh, princess, you underestimate me." He twisted a lock of my hair around his finger, yanking me toward him. "The Rhys Vanderbilt you met over the past month was an imposter. Everything I said and did was a lie. All for show." His lips curved into a mischievous grin, lighting up his emerald eyes. "I feel *nothing* for you. Not a single thing. You were always a means to an end. And after we're married, you will never know what it's like to have the freedom Marshall gave you this summer." He tugged harder on my hair. "Get used to your gilded cage."

My mouth opened, lips parted in shock, the words I wanted to say dying on my tongue. With a few hateful remarks from Rhys, I felt my soul being sucked from my body. Everything I felt for him this past month still lingered.

The longing.

The desire.

The need.

I even thought I was falling in love with him for a short time. I was so foolish. Grandfather would have called me a silly girl.

My gilded cage.

Was he planning to hurt me? Without my father here to protect me, I was at the mercy of ruthless men. The Colonel should have been home by now. His missions never went on for this long.

Was it intentional?

He worked for The Founders. That was the reason he agreed to become my legal guardian. Which meant he would stay gone for as long as my grandfather wanted.

Would I see him again?

Rhys looped his arm through mine and led me over to his parents. He tipped his head at his father. "Grace, I'd like you to meet my dad, Remington." Then his doting gaze landed on his mother, who was smiling at her son like he was a god. "And this is my mom, Helena."

I was raised with manners, so I offered my hand to his father. "Nice to meet you, sir."

His fingers slipped between mine, and he shook my hand like he was trying to break my knuckles. "Welcome to the family, *daughter*."

He didn't lovingly say that word. No, it sounded sinister and hateful, like how Rhys had been speaking to me all day.

His mother didn't offer her hand nor hug me as our eyes met. Helena Vanderbilt seemed like a woman who could hold her own without a man. But standing beside Remington, she was even more powerful and disarming. She eyed me up as if I were nothing.

Less than her.

I should have treated them with the same disdain they showed me, but I was better than that.

Better than *them*.

"Rhys, darling." Helena's bright red lips turned up into a smile. "Fetch your mother another glass of champagne." She glanced at me for a moment. "I'd like to have a word with your bride. *Alone*."

Rhys brushed his thumb over my cheek. "I'll be right back. Remember what I said earlier."

He disappeared into the crowd, leaving me alone with his parents.

Remington grabbed Grayson by the shoulder. "We'll give you two a moment." He steered his youngest son toward the bar without another word.

Helena sipped from the champagne flute, inspecting my face. "My Rhys is a good boy," she said after a moment of silence. "He does whatever his mother tells him." She slid her hand beneath my jaw to get a better look at me, her cold, blue eyes hardened into slits. "You're a beautiful girl. The perfect trophy wife for my Rhys." Her hand dropped to her side. "But I hear you're a troublemaker. You do whatever is necessary to get what you want."

"That's not true," I said to defend myself. "Your son used me."

"He was only doing what he was told," she lilted. "Rhys played his part perfectly. This is exactly the result we expected. And if you do anything to mess with my plans, you will pay for it."

Rhys said his dad was the manipulator, but maybe the real mastermind of this family was his mother. She was cunning and cruel, the love child of Cruella de Vil and Voldemort.

I could see why Rhys was so fucked up. His parents were terrible people and didn't have good intentions.

Rhys reappeared seconds later with a fresh glass of champagne for his mother and a plate of canapés. "I thought you might be hungry. You always work up an appetite when you're scheming."

They were so messed up.

She took the drink and appetizers with a glowing smile. "So thoughtful, my dear boy. Always thinking of your mother's needs."

Vomit.

My mother died before I could form a real relationship with her. But I couldn't recall her ever acting so strange. You would have thought Helena had a thing for her oldest son.

Maybe she had a Jocasta complex, which would have made Rhys Oedipus. I'd read that in high school and got sickened by the thought of a son marrying his mother. Helena could have her son because I didn't want his lying, traitorous ass.

After the party ended, my grandfather pulled me into the great room by my arm. His fingers created a thick rope of red marks on my skin. When he treated me this way, I felt like the scared girl he dragged from the wreckage of my old life.

"If you think about messing with my plans," Grandfather said with a cold stare aimed at me, "I'll kill your boyfriend and his family."

"I don't have a boyfriend," I choked out, startled by his word choice.

"I heard the story from Rhys," he said as he inched toward

me like a hunter about to seize prey. "He told me every dirty detail about you and Cole Marshall. Everything you did this summer. You're disgusting." He shook his head. "Filthy animals, all of you. Corrupted by the Devil."

Bile rose from my stomach, and I had to cover my mouth so I didn't puke on the floor at his feet. Whenever he was around, my insides turned to slush.

"You are your mother's daughter," he said in a nasty tone, his top lip curled up in disgust. "She was a whore, too. I had to clean up her messes regularly. Abigail was simple-minded and liked to party. She threw herself at that conman you call a father." His nose scrunched. "And then she came to me with the horrible news that she was pregnant with you. I told her to get an abortion, but did she listen?" He shook his head. "No, of course not. She kept you and married that thief."

Tears welled in my bottom lids, and I desperately struggled to hold them back. Grandfather hated weakness. He didn't tolerate crying or any behavior that he deemed inappropriate.

Like having feelings.

So I sucked down the anxiety spreading up my throat and bit back the tears. Standing straighter, I held my chin higher. He would only get meaner if I caused a scene. And God forbid I talked back.

"The past is repeating itself," he continued, his voice deep and angrier. "You gave your virginity to Cole Marshall on an old mattress in a safe house with Rhys beside you." He nearly spat on me as he spoke. "I gave the Marshall boys strict orders not to touch you. And what did he do? Defiled my good-for-nothing granddaughter. You're a disgrace to my name. How dare you embarrass me like this?"

"It's not Cole's fault. Don't take this out on him."

Grandfather's palm crashed into my cheek, knocking me backward. I tripped, staggering into a table. Thankfully, I turned my body just enough to fall onto the couch. The soft fabric brushed against my cheek, and my lips stung from how hard he hit me.

"Get up, you stupid slut," Grandfather seethed. "You have three seconds. On the count of one—"

I was off the couch before he could say two, tears streaming down my cheeks.

He wrapped his cold fingers around my throat, his face inches from mine as he sucked the air from my lungs. "I have kept you alive for the past thirteen years for one reason."

What was that?

Even Cole had suspected my grandfather had some master plan for my life. He assumed that was why none of The Knights were allowed to touch me. Had he planned to marry me to Rhys all along? It made no sense why Rhys was rewarded for doing the same thing as Cole.

Would Cole have gotten to marry me if he had sent a sex tape to my grandfather?

"Don't think for one second I'm giving you a free pass," he said, breathing scotch in my face. "Marrying Rhys is your punishment for being a whore. Remington has assured me you will suffer at their hands. You will pay for all of your dirty deeds. This marriage is nothing more than a business arrangement. I have no reason to keep you alive the second you serve your true purpose. After that, your husband can do whatever he wants with you."

What is my purpose?

I considered asking him for the truth, but I knew he wouldn't tell me his plans. Besides, my face hurt from getting the wind smacked out of me. Another slap would probably knock me senseless. So I clamped my mouth shut and let him speak.

He released his grip on my neck, and I choked, struggling to catch my breath. I coughed a few times and bent over to take in a few mouthfuls of air. Something wet dripped from my lip and down my chin. When I dabbed at it, I gasped at the sight of blood.

"You will stay at Fort Marshall until the wedding," Grandfather said, running a hand across his jaw. "So will Rhys. And if I hear another bad word about you, I will lock you in my basement until your wedding day." He removed the handkerchief from his pocket and threw it at me. "Clean yourself up. You make me sick."

Chapter Thirty-Seven

GRACE

After my grandfather left Fort Marshall, I ran upstairs and cried until my tears stained the sheets. My door opened and closed, footsteps moving toward the bed.

"Go away," I shouted into the pillow.

"It's me," Cole whispered as he got in bed with me.

I lifted my head, and mascara ran down my cheeks as I cried. "I'm sorry, Cole. I made you do this. I talked you into breaking his rules. And now, he will hurt you and your family if I don't do what he wants."

He swiped at my tears, his touch soft and loving. "I chose to break them. *Me*. You didn't make me do anything I didn't already want to do, Grace."

"I wish we had run away the night you suggested it." I buried my face in the pillow and sobbed. "This is all my fault. I should have listened to you about Rhys."

Cole stroked my back with his fingers. "Grace, I don't know how to fix this, but I will try. I can't let you marry Rhys. You don't deserve a life of misery." He leaned closer, his lips inches from mine. "But you deserve so much more than I can give you."

"What are you going to do?" I muttered, sniffing back the tears.

"I don't know yet." He traced circles on my back and sighed. "The wedding isn't for a few weeks. That should give me enough time to figure something out."

"How will we do anything without Rhys reporting back to my grandfather?"

"I have some good news. Your father made contact," he said in a hushed tone, checking over his shoulder to ensure the door was closed.

"The Colonel?"

He shook his head. "No, Viktor. He used a hacker named Maverick to send a video of your grandfather to Drake."

"What was on it?"

"Your grandfather talking to a man. His head was turned away from the camera. But Drake is doing his best to get a match using his artificial intelligence software."

"Well, what did the man say?"

"He was blackmailing Fitzy, forcing him to sign papers that made you the beneficiary of his estate."

"But why?"

Cole released a deep breath. "We don't know yet. But I think Viktor is giving us breadcrumbs that lead back to Fitzy because he wants us to know why the old man has kept you around."

Laying across the bed on my stomach beside him, I put my hand over his. "I can't do this anymore." I curled my fingers around his wrist, shaking so hard that I needed to hold onto him for support. "If this summer has taught me anything, I want to live. I'm sick of hiding. Maybe I should come out to the world as Katarina, so my father will stop chasing me. Maybe he can save me from this marriage."

"No." Cole was in my face, his mouth so close we could have kissed. "You don't have to sacrifice yourself. Let me figure this out."

A tear slid down my cheek, and I let it fall. "I'm a pawn in a rich man's game and don't know how to play it. My entire life has been spent running from a ghost I barely remember."

"Drake thinks your father has something on Fitzy," he confessed. "You're the heir to the Adams fortune, not Bash. This tape proves it. We'll contact Viktor again and see if he can tell us more."

My heart hammered in my chest as I considered everything I knew about my father and grandfather. And until Alex Wellington got kidnapped, I had forgotten all about my cousin Bastian and the key.

"I have an old key," I told Cole. "Bastian gave it to me when I was a little girl. He handed it to me under the table at dinner when our grandfather wasn't looking and said to hold onto it for him."

"Did he say anything else?"

I closed my eyes and focused on the night Bastian came to my grandfather's house, allowing my mind to drift to that moment.

I'm close to ten years old and excited about meeting a relative for the first time. No one ever comes to the house for dinner. It's always the staff and me. And on rare occasions, I eat with my grandfather at the opposite end of the banquet table fit for a king.

He doesn't talk.

He never looks at me.

I exist, but I don't.

I'm like wallpaper.

Bastian strolls into the great room, dressed in a black suit, his caramel hair styled off his forehead. His gray eyes are so striking I notice them immediately. He carries himself like an adult, not a teenager.

My grandfather hasn't come downstairs yet. He's still in his office on a business call.

Bastian offers his hand to me. "I'm Bastian Salvatore. Your cousin. Our mothers were sisters."

Before they died…

I smile and shake his hand. "Nice to meet you, Bastian. I'm Katarina."

His expression mirrors mine. "That's a pretty name. You know, you look like your mother. The two of you could have been twins."

I hear my grandfather clear his throat, and I turn my head to see him standing in the entryway. He looks polished and expensive, the kind of man who demands to be noticed. The type of man you can't help but wonder if he's a god.

He looks at least twenty years younger than his age and with no gray hair. Never without a suit, my grandfather wears it like armor.

"You're alone?" Grandfather asks him. "Where is that dirty, filthy animal you call a brother?"

Bastian's nostrils flare, and I have no idea which brother he's talking about. Until tonight, I didn't know I had a cousin. I was told I only had my grandfather and his charity.

"Damian is at home," Bastian says with disdain as he crosses the room. "And he's not any of those things you claim. You don't know him."

Grandfather rolls his eyes. "He's not worth knowing."

"Fitzy," Bastian says to our grandfather as if he were one of the old man's business partners. "Let's cut the shit, shall we? I'm here because I want to start working at Atlantic Airlines. I'm old enough to learn the ropes."

He plays with his gold cufflink and sighs. "You're a child. An imbecile like your father. Like I would ever let you run that company. You would drive the stock price into the ground."

I have no idea what they're talking about. Grandfather uses words like stock, portfolio, and diversification all the time.

He doesn't even let me leave the house to attend school. My education comes from private tutors. I like reading and writing, anything that gets me extra time in the library. It's the only freedom I'm allowed.

As they turn to leave the room, I notice Bastian slip his hand inside my grandfather's jacket pocket. Grandfather doesn't see Bastian has taken an object from him.

It's shiny.

Silver.

A key?

A shiver rushes down my arms. My grandfather will blame me. He holds me responsible for anything that goes wrong in this house.

He loses money.

It's my fault.

He doesn't like the food.

It's my fault.

I follow them to the dining room and take my place at the table. Since we have a guest, I'm allowed to sit closer than usual.

Bastian takes the chair beside me. He has a warm smile and seems friendly, but I can see there's a lot more to him. My cousin has guts and doesn't put up with our grandfather's attitude. He gives it back to him, and I wish I had the same nerve.

Midway through dinner, my grandfather receives an urgent call and leaves the room. I stuff my face because I don't know when I'll get to eat like this again. There's enough food to feed a small city and only the three of us.

"Katarina, I need you to hold onto this for me," Bastian whispers, opening his palm to reveal the key he stole. "It's your birthright just as much as it is mine." He opens my hand and curls my fingers around the cold metal. "Guard it with your life."

"But it belongs to him," I whisper, nerves shaking through me. "What if he finds it? He'll kill me."

"I only lived here for a month after my parents died," Bastian says in a calm, low tone. "But I know what you're going through. We even shared the same bedroom."

There are at least twenty bedrooms in the house. How could he possibly know which one is mine?

Lowering his head, he says in a hushed tone, "There's a loose floorboard in the right corner of your closet. Keep the key there until you get out of this godforsaken place. When we meet again, I'll show you what to do with the key."

"But why me?"

I hear my grandfather's Berluti oxfords tap on the tiled floor in the hallway, coming closer to us. Bastian must hear him, too, because he speaks faster.

"One day, this key will buy your freedom. It's the only thing that will keep you alive." He kisses the top of my head. "I wish I could do more for you, Katarina. But this is the best I can do for now."

Tears streamed down my face as I snapped back to reality.

Cole held me in his strong arms, cradling me like a baby. "What just happened? Where did you go, Grace?"

"I had a flashback of the day Bastian gave me the key."

He partially released me from his grip and brushed the hair away from my face. "Does this happen often?"

I shook my head. "I used to have terrible night terrors and flashbacks from the past. So the Colonel took me to see a specialist, a Marine doctor he knows."

He nodded. "Dr. Beck is a friend of my dad's."

"After I saw him a few times, the nightmares lessened. And now, I sometimes have trouble remembering anything from my past. It's like Dr. Beck blocked my bad memories."

He held me at arm's length, his chest rising and falling faster than usual. "What did you see?"

"Bastian stole a key for me, and I never saw him again. But I never forgot him or the key. I just didn't know what to do with it."

"Fitzy must have suspected you stole the key."

I bobbed my head to agree. "He tore the house apart the morning after the dinner. I remember him waking me up before sunrise, ripping the sheets off my bed. Even had the staff flip over every piece of furniture. They searched the house for days. He would have found the key if Bastian hadn't told me where to hide it."

I shot up from the bed and entered the closet, searching for the key. It was tucked beneath a stack of folded T-shirts. Cole moved behind me, his warm breath on my neck. The second I retrieved the skeleton key from the velvet pouch, Cole took it from my hand.

He held it up to the fluorescent light. "It's an Elders key."

"Do you know what it opens?"

He nodded. "A door that leads to a vault. Only the five Elders of The Founders Society have access to it. Some of the secrets hidden inside date back to the late 1700s and have kept The Founders in power for centuries."

I grabbed the old key to inspect the metal with strange markings. "Why do only the Elders have a key?"

"The Founders Society formed not long after the signing of the Declaration of Independence. There are five keys, one for each of the original families."

"Weren't there seven Founding Fathers?"

He nodded. "But only five of them had their own children. Your grandfather is the head Elder because the Adams family is the only bloodline that has remained untainted after all these years. Most of us are not directly related to the Founding Fathers, at least not in the same way you and Bastian are."

"I'm not an Adams anymore," I told him. "My grandfather changed my name."

He shook his head. "You were born an Adams. This key is your birthright." Cole opened his palm. "Let me hold it for you. I have a safe in my room. You don't want the wrong person getting their hands on it."

I placed the key in his hand. "No one locks a vault with a skeleton key."

"The key opens a door. Only one of the Elders could tell you what's behind it. I've heard stories but not much more." He stuffed the key into his pocket and guided me to the bed. "The Founders are a little old school. Our real net worth comes from the things we've acquired over decades. We have a saying in Devil's Creek. Secrets are commodities. And the more you collect, the more power you have."

I cocked an eyebrow at him. "What do you think is in the vault?"

"Who knows what Fitzy is hiding?" Cole deadpanned.

"Probably dead bodies."

"I'll keep it safe for you," Cole promised, stroking his thumb over my cheek. "Bastian saved your life. You are expendable to Fitzy without this key, and he knows that."

"At the Salvatore Estate, Bastian said he would show me what the key opens when the time is right."

We sat turned toward each other, and my heart beat a little faster with him invading my space. My life felt like it started the day I met Cole. And it sucked to want something I could never have.

"Grace, I wish you would have mentioned the key sooner." Frustration dripped from his tone. "If I had known you have an Elders key…"

"Cole, what are you not telling me?"

"This changes everything."

My pulse quickened as I waited for him to elaborate, and when he didn't, I said, "How so?"

He blew out a breath of air, shaking his head. And when our eyes met, he smiled as if this wasn't the worst day of our lives. "You're the heir to the Adams fortune because Fitzy thinks your dad took the key. Not you. If he thought you had it, he would have tortured you."

I cocked an eyebrow at him. "How does this help us?"

"Grace, this key is your freedom." His hands cradled my face. "Do you trust me?"

I nodded. "With my life."

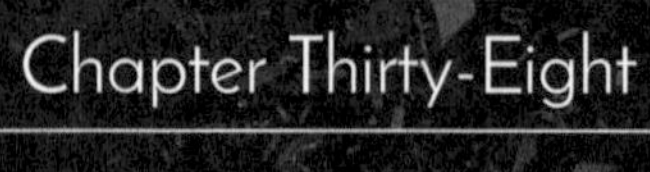

Chapter Thirty-Eight

COLE

We had an Elders key. Our winning ticket. The only thing that could free Grace from a horrible life with a man she hated.

With Grace safe, I headed into my bedroom to hide the key. I had secret hiding spots all over the house. Pull on a candlestick, and you might tumble down a dark staircase. Tap the right button on a fireplace, and you might open a door. If I ever needed to escape quickly, there were trap doors everywhere.

Hidden safes.

Random doors.

Winding staircases.

Families like mine could never be too careful. Not all our money was made legally, and we had to take precautions. When the Founders of Devil's Creek built the town, our families were bootleggers and gunrunners, anything to make a buck.

Inside my bedroom, I pushed the oak chest away from the wall and felt around for the groove in the wooden panels. Finally, my fingers caught on the latch. I hit the trigger point, and the door creaked open.

I pressed my thumb to the safe and entered the combination. It contained five handguns with ammunition, stacks of cash, jewelry, and random items I didn't want to leave out for someone to find.

I locked the Elders key inside, still in disbelief that I had the power to crush Fitzy. Grace was only alive because of this key. Without it, her grandfather had no reason to keep her around.

After seeing the tape sent to Drake by Viktor, I knew Grace's father had something to do with the key. But how did he know Grace had it? Bastian hadn't been in contact with him. Her cousin was the only other person who knew she had it.

Fitzy undoubtedly questioned Bastian, who would have lied through his teeth. Maybe that was why Fitzy let Bastian run Atlantic Airlines after he graduated from Harvard University.

Did he force Fitzy's hand?

According to his parents will, Bastian couldn't access the trust until his twenty-fifth birthday. But he became the CEO at twenty-one. At that point, Fitzy stepped away from the company and only attended board meetings when required.

Bastian could have taken the fortune for himself. But, instead, he gave it to Grace. But why? Out of the kindness of his heart?

I couldn't ask him over the phone. The Knights only shared information in person. We could never be too careful, even with all of Drake's safeguards to protect us.

After I slid the panel into the wall and moved the chest back into its proper place, I sat on the bed. I considered all of Grace's options. She could come clean with Fitzy and barter her freedom for the key. But then, that would leave her vulnerable to her bio dad and The Lucaya Group.

Fitzy and The Devil's Knights would wash their hands of her. On paper, she wasn't an Adams anymore. Her grandfather might let her go, but I doubted he would let her live. The old man left no stone unturned and wasn't above resorting to murder.

I needed to talk.

To tell someone.

With the key secured, I went straight to my father's office without speaking to anyone. Rhys was talking on the phone outside by the pool, smoking a cigar as if he had something to celebrate. I could see him sitting at the table on the patio through the French doors, thinking about putting a bullet in his traitorous skull.

I moved Rhys to a room on the first floor to keep him away from Grace.

Lying prick.

I was right not to trust him, despite him being a Knight. The piece of shit even had me fooled but not for long. And to think I was stupid enough to share her. Grace hated herself for letting him trick her, but I let him blindside me, too.

And I knew better.

I entered my dad's office, and his head snapped to me, shock scrolling across his face when I locked the door behind me.

"Cole, what are you doing?"

"We need to talk."

I sat on the couch across from him and explained everything I had learned from Drake and Grace tonight.

The key.

Bastian.

Fitzy.

Viktor.

All of it.

Dad scratched the corner of his jaw, deep in thought. He hadn't spoken a word for several minutes, taking it all in.

"At least now we understand some of Fitzy's behavior," he said after a few more minutes of contemplation. "But Grace having an Elders key doesn't change anything."

"Yes, it does," I shot back.

"This only puts more of a target on her head."

"Grace has leverage over him," I insisted. "Something none of us have on the old man."

He sat back in the oversized armchair, resting his dress shoe on his knee. "Even without the key, Fitzy is still worth over two hundred and fifty billion dollars. Grace won't inherit a cent until he dies. Besides, women can't become members of The Founders Society."

"It's not about the money. That key *is* power. And we both know Fitzy won't allow anyone to have that over him. He hasn't killed Grace because if he had, he would never know what she did with the key."

"I understand the predicament," my dad said with an attitude. "I don't need my son to explain it to me."

I inched toward him, anger surging through me. "Then do something about it! We finally have a way out from under the old man. No more following his stupid rules."

Dad placed the highball glass on the desk and rose from the chair. "This is about your feelings for Grace. What have I told you about mixing business and pleasure? The two can never go together without one jeopardizing the other."

"I don't have feelings for Grace," I lied. "I'm just doing my job."

Grace had asked me if she was just a job to me.

Of course not.

She was everything.

I'd never met a woman I wanted to keep around for more than a few weeks. Grace was special and not in a clichéd way. It wasn't because she wasn't like other girls. My attraction to her came from something more profound, a need to connect with her on a cellular level.

I asked her to write a bucket list so that I could learn everything about her. What were her dreams? Her desires? And I wanted to be the person to give them to her.

"Grace is important to you, Cole." Dad rose from the chair and put his hand on my shoulder. "I understand. I felt the same way about your mother when we first met. I would have done anything to protect her. Still would. But you have to let her go. Grace isn't like your mother. She doesn't have the same freedom to choose who she wants to love. Her grandfather will never allow it."

"That's why she needs to use the key," I said with anger dripping from my tone, my body shaking. "She'll never be free of the old man if she doesn't cash it in."

"Cole, I said no. You have no right to that key, and neither does Grace. Where are you keeping it?"

"It's well hidden."

He raised an eyebrow at me. "Don't play games with me, Cole. That key could land you into a world of trouble."

"I'm already in trouble for what I did with Grace. So what difference does it make?"

Before he could ask any more questions about the key, I left his office. He called for me to come back, but I kept going. If my father wouldn't help me, I had to find another way to save Grace.

***

After leaving my father's office, I went straight to Drake's house. I sent him a 9-1-1- text, and he replied immediately for me to come over.

Sitting beside Drake at his desk, I watched as his fingers moved quickly across the keyboard. He typed so fast I could hardly make out the words. The second I told him Grace had an Elders key, Drake hopped onto the Dark Web and started looking for Maverick.

Dozens of monitors sat on the desk. Some hung on the wall and even dropped from the ceiling of the Battle Cave. The place was clean and organized, unlike the last time I sat in the same spot.

Drake blamed himself for Alex getting kidnapped and Grace's father finding her. But at least he looked well-rested and didn't have open soda cans and candy wrappers littering the desktop. He wore a freshly pressed suit and smelled like body wash and cologne.

"Okay, we're in." Drake turned to look at me. "Maverick spoke to Viktor. He's agreed to talk with us."

"Viktor sent you that clip because he wants to see Grace." I shoved a hand through my hair to shove it off my forehead. "Maybe we don't need the key to take down Fitzy. We can use Viktor for whatever information he'll provide in exchange for letting him see his daughter."

"She'll never agree to it." Drake seemed uncertain, but I knew Grace would do anything to get away from her grandfather. "It's also too risky. What if Viktor hurts her?"

"He won't," I said with certainty. "Viktor wouldn't have gone to such lengths to find her if he was going to hurt her. We'll only let him see her for a few minutes and with The Knights protecting her."

"But he's a terrorist," Drake reminded me. "Viktor is trying to steal my tech and sent Bratva to Devil's Creek for Alex on multiple occasions. He might have been a good father once upon a time, but he's not a good person. And he will kill all of us to get Grace back."

"Let's see what he says. Then we'll go from there."

Chapter Thirty-Nine

GRACE

Rhys broke into my bedroom and stood in the entryway, wearing a smirk that screamed, *I won*. He strolled toward my bed, dressed in expensive black slacks, a hand-woven golf shirt, and boat shoes. His face was so pretty and perfect, except for the dark bruises and the cut on his lip.

Cole fucked him up.

And he deserved it.

"What do you want?" I sat up on the bed and folded my arms beneath my breasts.

His eyes dropped to my cleavage, and he licked his lips. "I haven't seen you since the party. Just checking on my fiancée."

I rolled my eyes. "Like you give a shit about me."

He sat on the bed and grabbed my wrist. "Where's your engagement ring?"

I glared at the massive diamond on my dresser, and he followed my line of sight with his eyes. The second the party ended, I stripped it off and showered for thirty minutes to get the feel of Rhys off my skin.

I wanted to cry.

Scream.

Run away.

Once again, my grandfather condemned me to a life of

misery. Like it wasn't bad enough that he ruined my childhood and forced me to live in fear. He looked so smug as I said yes to Rhys, soaking up every second of my pain.

"Put it on," he hissed. "The ring belonged to my great-great-grandmother. It's a family heirloom. I wouldn't put that ring on just any woman's finger."

"No?" I cocked my head at him. "What makes me so special?"

He slid off the bed, grabbed the ring from the dresser, and shoved it onto my finger so hard my knuckle hurt. "I'll get more than this ring is worth when the old man gives me the dowry."

I laughed. "Dowry? This isn't the Middle Ages."

"You didn't know, did you?" He waggled those dark, sexy eyebrows at me, and I hated how much I used to love it when he did that. "Fitzy owes three billion dollars to your husband in exchange for taking you off his hands."

I held back my shock, staring at the comforter so he couldn't see my reaction. "My grandfather is worth a lot more than three billion. That's pennies to him."

He rolled his broad shoulders like he didn't have a care in the world. A pretty boy like Rhys never did. He was used to everything being handed to him on a silver platter.

"So you got close to me for the money?"

He nodded. "This was never personal, princess. I have a pretty face and a big dick, which I used to manipulate you. You met my parents. They're sharks. For me, this has always been about survival."

"I was just a game to you? Didn't feel like it that night on the Ferris wheel."

I folded my legs beneath me, biting back the urge to punch him in the face.

"You only turned into an asshole after we had sex. Why did you even bother getting to know me? Why did you take me on dates? You could have lied and told my grandfather we had sex to get what you wanted. You didn't have to use me. Film me. Humiliate me, and make me feel like shit."

"I like you," he said with his fingers inches from mine on the mattress. "That's never been the problem. You're a sexy little thing with a tight pussy and lips that were made to suck my cock." He leaned closer, and the scent of his cologne filled my nostrils. "But you were always a means to an end for me. This won't be a traditional marriage. You'll fuck me, suck me, and do whatever I tell you if you want to stay alive. Because once your grandfather washes his hands of you, no one will save you. Especially not him."

Rhys took one last look at me before pushing himself up from the bed. Without another word, he left my room, keeping the door ajar.

Cole usually locked my door for protection. But since my monster of a fiancé forgot to close the door, I decided to see if Cole was home. We hadn't spoken since he left to meet with Drake the night before. He'd been busy with stuff for The Knights, leaving me alone with his mom for most of the day.

Dressed in black booty shorts and a skimpy tank top that barely hid my nipples, I padded downstairs. It was dark and late, so I didn't expect to run into anyone. And I wanted to catch Cole off guard if he was home.

We hadn't been together since he took my virginity. I wanted him, even if it was only one more time. I needed to experience everything I would be missing once I married Rhys. Cole had once told me I would find him in one of two places—the library or the game room.

So I opened the door to the game room, which was more like an adult arcade with a bar and couches, and locked it behind me.

Cole was alone on the leather couch with a drink in his hand. His blue eyes traveled up and down my thighs several times before landing on my face. "It's late, Grace. You should go back to bed."

He looked slightly drunk, and he must have been because

he didn't seem to realize my door should have been locked.

"I don't want to sleep." Inching toward him, I pushed out my breasts, which weren't big but were falling out of the tight top. "I wanted to see you."

He turned away from me. "I'm not in the mood to talk. I have a lot on my mind and need to think." He raised the glass in his hand. "And get drunk."

"I don't want to talk." I stopped before the coffee table and blocked his view of the television, which turned his attention back to me. "I want to show you something."

Cole put the half-empty glass on the table. "What's that?"

I gripped the hem of my tank top, pulled it over my head, and threw the shirt onto Cole's lap. He fisted the fabric, jaw clenched. I couldn't tell if he was angry or turned on, but the silence was killing me.

He grabbed himself over the top of his shorts and grunted. "Fuck, Grace. What are you doing?"

"I want you. It's always been you, Cole." I pushed down my shorts and kicked them off. "I only let Rhys touch me because I wanted to make you jealous. If I could go back in time and take it all back, I would."

Standing naked before Cole, I'd never felt so exposed and vulnerable. But I liked the way he carefully inspected every inch of my skin.

"You can watch." I wet my lips. "Then you're not breaking any rules."

"I don't think you understand what you're doing to me," Cole bit out as his eyes moved to my pussy, and he licked his lips.

"I know exactly what I'm doing." I rubbed the pads of my thumbs over my nipples. "We're both victims, Cole. But we don't have to be. Not anymore. I don't want to marry Rhys. I want you."

Quickly, his resolve faded. Breathing hard, he shoved down his shorts and fisted his hard cock. "Sit on the chair. Spread your legs nice and wide for me."

I did as he asked and flicked my hair over my shoulder to give him a better look at my breasts. "I'm so wet." I propped my legs up on the arms of the chair and then pushed one finger inside my pussy, then another.

"You're such a brat. Always torturing me to get what you want." A wild look lit up his face. "Coat your fingers with your cum for me."

He stroked his dick, gripping the base so roughly it looked like it would hurt. Maybe it did because he spit in his hand and rubbed it up and down his shaft to lubricate his skin.

"Spread your legs wider." He jerked harder as if trying to match my movements. "Squeeze your fingers. Pretend they're my cock. Give me your orgasm."

I followed his orders, pumping my fingers as I circled my clit with my thumb. "Oh God, Cole…" His name was a whimper on my lips. "I want to feel you inside me again."

His legs shook like the pressure inside him built until he couldn't stand it anymore. "It's time to come." He stared at me with those pretty blue eyes and licked his lips. "If you don't come right now, I'll spank your ass and pussy."

"Cole," I moaned, lips pressed into a thin line, my eyes slightly closed as the tremors rocked my body. "I'm coming."

"Good girl."

He came right after me in his hand and then stripped off his T-shirt, using it to clean himself up. Neither of us spoke for a solid minute, still breathing hard. I couldn't even think straight, drunk with pleasure, high on the sounds he made when he came for me.

Cole stood and pulled up his shorts, a seductive look in his eyes. "Did you make a mess for me?"

I spread my legs so he could see the cum dripping down my thigh.

He scrubbed at his face and grunted. "My dick is jealous."

I beckoned him with my finger. "Then come over here and fuck me."

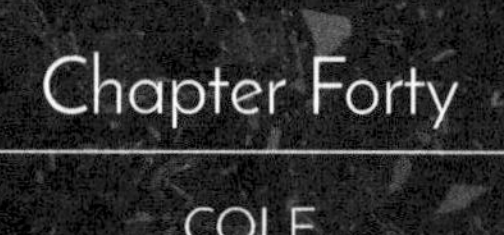

Chapter Forty

COLE

Fuck, she was killing me. I hated the old man and his rules. Hated the fact he was forcing Grace to marry Rhys for whatever sick reason. Still, a part of me was so used to following orders I couldn't allow myself to break them.

Order gave me control.

It comforted me.

With Grace naked and her cum glistening on her pussy, I couldn't take my eyes off her. She was gorgeous, a fucking knockout.

I was done.

Hooked.

I'd thought about Grace from the day we met, even though I knew feeling anything for a girl I could never have was pointless. But I needed to feel her one more time.

Just once.

Standing over her, I looked between her legs and watched the cum dripping out of her.

"You're making a mess, Grace." I fisted my shaft, staring at her flawless body. "Look at you. Fuck, you're so wet."

She reached out to touch my dick. "Break the rules for me."

That was all I needed. Seeing her naked and wet, begging for my dick, got me rock-hard again.

Grace's lips parted for me. "I want to know how you taste."

I grunted and grabbed her hand, helping her stroke my shaft. So sweet and pure, Grace was nothing like me. She'd been preserved like her grandfather's rare art. Untouched and perfect until Rhys and I defiled her.

Fuck Rhys Vanderbilt.

Fuck The Founders.

Fuck Fitzy.

My resolve faded with each second she moved her hand in unison with mine, making my dick so fucking hard. I was sick of playing my part and being a good Knight.

As she stroked me harder, I said, "Do you want me to kiss you?"

Grace bobbed her head, and blonde hair dropped into her blue eyes, forcing her to push the strands behind her ears. "More than anything."

I peeled her fingers from my shaft and bent down in front of her. She looked surprised I stopped her. But if I kept letting her touch me like this, I would come soon, and I wanted to do that inside her.

So I dropped to my knees in front of her and gripped her thighs, staring at her pretty face. "I'm not going to kiss your lips."

She gave me a perplexed look. "Where do you want to kiss me?"

Her inexperience was cute, and she smelled as sweet as she looked.

I rolled my tongue over her clit. "I want to kiss you here." Then I dragged my tongue between her wet slit. "And here."

I'd never licked another girl's pussy, but I wanted to drown myself in her scent. If I couldn't keep her, I could savor this memory.

Her mouth opened wide, her chest rising and falling with

each breath. She whimpered, legs shaking as I placed them over my shoulders. "Cole, please."

"Feel good, brat?" I kissed higher, and her soft skin pebbled with tiny bumps of arousal. "Don't be shy. Tell me how it feels."

"Amazing," she whispered, staring up at the ceiling as if she couldn't bare to look me in the eyes while I licked her. "Don't stop."

I feasted on her pussy, my tongue darting between her slick folds. Her hand fell to the back of my head, and as her body relaxed, she gripped the ends of my short hair and tugged hard.

"Cole," she moaned, and my name sounded like a sweet melody on the tip of her tongue.

I thought I would hate myself for breaking the rules. Structure mattered to me. Yet, after watching Grace get engaged to Rhys, that part of me was slowly dying.

Rhys broke every rule.

And he still fucking won.

The Vanderbilts were barely holding onto their legacies, and somehow they weaseled their way into Grace's family.

It didn't make any sense.

So fuck them.

Grace was mine.

I heard a loud crash that snapped my attention away from Grace. Lifting my head, I looked toward the door and tried to listen. She was breathing so hard I thought maybe I imagined the sound.

But then…

I heard another noise.

A scream.

Female.

Mom.

Grace sat up. "Did you hear that?"

I nodded and shot up from the floor, wiping my mouth

with my hand. Tucking my dick into my shorts, I headed toward the door.

"Wait," Grace called out. "I'm going with you."

I pushed out my hand to stop her. "No, stay here."

Our fight with The Lucaya Group was far from over. We might have gotten Alex back from the auction, but Drake and The Knights were still dodging constant threats. So I couldn't take any chances with her life.

Grace slipped into the tiny booty shorts, a tank top, and no bra. "I'm coming with you."

I cupped her face in my hands. "Grace, please."

Another loud bang.

A crash.

I didn't have time to tell her no again because I was running down the hallway with Grace at my side. Halting in front of the door to the natatorium, I could smell my mother's sweet perfume.

I opened the door, and the familiar scent quickly transformed into something vile.

Chlorine.

Metal.

What the fuck?

I could practically taste both scents on my tongue as I entered the room.

Blood.

Grace screamed.

So much blood was on the floor, splashed across the white tiles, and ran into the pool. My eyes followed the trail of blood straight to… my mom.

She was floating on the pool's surface, dressed in a one-piece black bathing suit with her arms at her sides. We had the same white-blonde hair, now fanned out around her once pretty face, drained of color. She looked so still but not peaceful. A look of complete horror froze on her face.

And there was blood.

Everywhere.

I dropped to my knees, not giving a single fuck about the pain radiating up my spine.

I felt nothing.

And everything.

Fucking numb.

Dead inside.

"Mom…"

Grace screamed.

I hopped into the pool, wading through the blood to get to her. Holding my mother's dead body in my arms, I turned my head to the side and spilled my guts into the water. This wasn't the first time I saw a dead body. It wasn't even the first time I smelled this much blood. Not even the first time I had seen this much blood.

But this was my mom.

Not one of my enemies.

Chapter Forty-One

GRACE

It broke my heart to watch Cole holding his mom's bloody body. He kept saying, "This is why there are rules." And then, "Mom, I'm sorry. I failed you. I won't make this mistake again. Just open your eyes. Please. Come back to me."

Cole broke the rules with me and felt responsible for her murder. Not like he could have prevented it.

Rhys must have heard my screams because he lifted me off the wet floor, cradling me in his arms. "It's okay, princess. I got you."

My asshole fiancé was the last person I wanted to console me, but I needed someone to hold onto with how hard I shook. I didn't care that it was Rhys.

"Drake will be here soon." He carried me to the surveillance room and grabbed two guns he had stuffed into his waistband. "Don't open the door for anyone else."

I nodded, and he locked me inside to search for the intruder.

Drake arrived at Fort Marshall minutes later. He entered the room, dressed in a black suit with a red tie hanging loosely around his neck, a black Spider-Man shirt beneath his partially open oxford. "Where's Cole?"

I wiped at the tears dripping down my cheeks. "In the natatorium. Rhys is looking for the person who killed Willow."

Drake raked a hand through his dark hair and sighed. "I'll find whoever did this to her."

Drake's eyes were red-rimmed and glassy from crying. Willow was his aunt. She was a mom to all of us—including me.

I'd already lost my parents and understood Cole's pain. My mother's death was the worst thing that ever happened to me. That awful night sparked a chain of events that led my life to spiral for years. Not until I arrived at Fort Marshall did I finally feel like I had a family again.

Now it was broken.

Drake sat behind a desk with several computer monitors. He entered his credentials, his fingers flying across the keypad. I couldn't read what he typed on the black screen with white writing. It didn't look like any program I had ever used.

Drake was a hacker and The Devil's Knights' secret weapon. He flipped between five screens, entering code to jump to specific points in the camera feed. My jaw dropped in surprise when he found the assailant entering the property from the backyard.

The mansion sat on the edge of a cliff, which had to be at least fifty feet from the beach. And yet, he made it look effortless as he climbed the hillside.

I pointed at the screen. "How is he doing that?"

"Special tech that lets you grip the rocks. I produce something similar at Battle Industries."

I stared at the dark-haired man with ink on his arms climbing onto the grass in Cole's backyard. "So, he just walked in from the veranda without the guards noticing him?"

Drake nodded. "He must have known the guards' shift changes."

"Grace, you should leave." Drake paused the video. "I don't want you to see what comes next."

"No, I need to see it."

He tipped his head at the door. "Trust me. You don't want to see this. It will haunt your dreams for the rest of your life."

Drake sounded as if he spoke from experience. And after considering what this would do to me mentally, I took his advice and stepped into the hallway. I still had flashbacks of my mother's murder, though I still couldn't piece together all the details of that night.

I heard Willow's scream on the surveillance video through the crack in the open door.

"No, you can't have her!" Willow yelled. "She's not here. So get out!"

"*Kisa* is here," the man said in a thick Russian accent.

My dad called me *kisa*.

Russian for kitten.

A few more minutes of conversation ensued, where he ran after Willow. It sounded like she put up a good fight, only to end up in the pool. I was glad Drake spared me the gory details of her death.

After he turned off the video, Drake sobbed. This was a private moment for their family, so I moved farther down the corridor to give him space.

Drake emerged from the room a minute later, scrubbing at his eyes. He refused to meet my gaze and grabbed my shoulder, guiding me down the hallway.

"Who is that man? He called me *kisa*."

"Your uncle."

"What?" I blinked rapidly, still trying to digest his confession. "My uncle killed Willow?"

"Andrey Romanov is one of the leaders of the Volkov Bratva. This summer, his men almost raped and kidnapped Alex Wellington at his request. I assume he came here looking for you and found Willow. She wasn't his intended target."

I bent forward, clutching my stomach to still the waves of nausea sweeping through me. Any minute, I was either going to faint or vomit.

"Go upstairs and lock yourself in your bedroom. Don't

open it for anyone but me or the Marshalls," Drake ordered before continuing down the hall toward the natatorium.

The house was unusually silent. Not a sound from Cole's brothers, not even the staff. This place was always so warm and lifelike. It was as if the house knew she was gone.

I was about head upstairs when I caught something moving out of the corner of my eye. Not a something but a *someone*.

He was still in the house.

The blood in my veins turned to ice, and fear washed over me.

"Come, *kisa*," the Russian man whispered with a thick accent. "Your father is waiting for you."

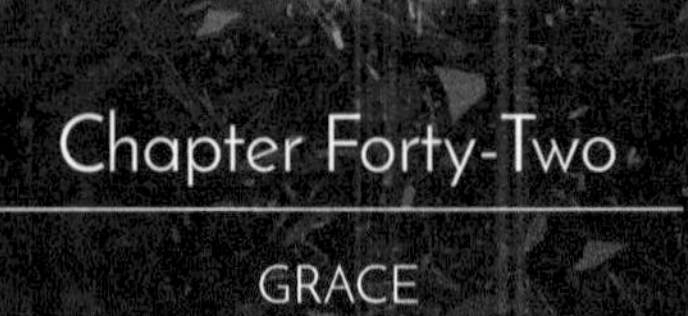

Chapter Forty-Two

GRACE

I hauled ass down the hallway, screaming for Cole, Rhys, and Drake, hoping one of them would hear me. With my uncle blocking the direction of the natatorium, I had to run toward the East Wing. If I could climb the stairs, I could cut across the second floor and get help.

My uncle stalked in my direction, his movements slow and controlled like he had all the time in the world. He was well over six feet tall and built strong like an ox. If he were to pin me down, it would be game over. He had at least eighty pounds more muscle and was close to a foot taller than me. I did the math and knew it was a losing battle.

I raced toward the stairs.

"Stupid, stupid girl," the man taunted from behind me.

A chill rushed over me like spiders crawling down my spine.

Fuck.

"Do not disappoint your father, *kisa.*"

Taking the stairs several at a time, I lost my footing and crashed into the metal railing. It stung like a bitch, the pain radiating up my arm. But I had to keep going. There wasn't a second to waste with Andrey Romanov on my tail.

He had a scar running down the right side of his face and

dark ink covering most of his body. I could tell he had done some really bad shit in his lifetime.

At the top of the landing, I gripped the railing to steady myself. Andrey was seconds behind me, but he didn't bother to reach out for me. Instead, he dipped his hand into his pocket and produced zip ties, snapping them in front of his face.

"*Bayushki Bayu*," he sang in a deep tone, a song that often haunted my dreams. "Have you forgotten your favorite song, Katarina?"

I hadn't heard the song in years. Not since my dad sent me to a psychiatrist specializing in dream therapy. Someone the Colonel knew from his time in the Marine Corps.

After months of waking up screaming, covered in sweat, and my heart pounding out of my chest, the Colonel got me help. I was only eleven years old and had terrible nightmares that felt real. Those memories were a distant remnant of my past.

But as the man sang the familiar song to me, pieces of those dreams flooded back. His Russian accent reminded me of someone from my past. Someone who caused me a lot of sleepless nights.

A blinding pain tore into the right side of my head. My vision blurred, and I had to blink a few times to clear my vision. I saw a man in a suit, not the one cornering me. His cufflinks brushed my cheek as he pushed the hair off my forehead.

I couldn't see his face, but I heard his voice. He sang *Bayushki Bayu*, a Russian lullaby. I knew all the words and understood every syllable as he spoke to me in his native tongue.

Sleep, my darling, sleep, my baby, close your eyes, and sleep.

"It is time for you to remember, Katarina," he said in broken English. "Your father has been looking for you for a very long time. He is not a patient man. Come with me before you hurt yourself."

As I snapped back to reality, I tried to block out his words. He was using the lullaby to fuck with my head.

I needed a weapon.

Something.

Anything.

Panicked, I smashed my fist through a mirror hanging above a table. My blood dripped onto the floor as I swiped the largest chunk from the pile. I'd never killed a man before. But if it came down to him or me, I would always choose me.

He laughed as I held the shard in front of me, using it to create distance between us. "*Kisa*, you disappoint me. You wouldn't kill your uncle."

I extended the sharpest point at him, teeth gritted. "I don't even know you."

He clicked his tongue. "I see they brainwashed you. Leave it to the Americans to turn you against us." He inched toward me, careful to keep his distance. "Give it time. You will remember Uncle Andrey. Viktor has been searching for you for a very long time. The Devil's Knights have been hiding you from us. They will suffer for stealing our precious *kisa*."

There was something oddly familiar about this man. His scent, maybe? A mixture of pine needles and citrus. It was such an odd combination. I caught a whiff of his natural musk as he moved toward me.

Uncle Andrey.

"Tell me, Uncle Andrey," I said to gain his attention and make him think I remembered him. "Who is Viktor Romanov?"

"Your father," he said without hesitation.

"But who is he? Is he a good man? A bad man? Why would The Devil's Knights hide me from him?"

I knew the truth but wanted to hear it from him.

Andrey took a deep breath, his long fingers gripping the railing as he advanced, forcing me to walk backward with the glass pointed at him. "Viktor is a powerful businessman. In Russia, he is like a tsar. A king among men."

"Is he dangerous?"

A smirk tipped up the corner of his mouth. "To you? Not at all."

"Tell me about my biological father. What is he like?"

Deep in thought, Andrey stroked his jaw with his long, tattooed fingers. "He disappointed our father when he went to work for KGB. Our father disowned Viktor. Eventually, my brother got an assignment that brought him to America. He worked in intelligence. It was his job to collect information. When your grandfather exposed Viktor, things got messy."

I lowered my arm to my side, maintaining my grip on the glass. He hadn't moved from the same spot since he started telling me stories about the past. I could tell he wouldn't hurt me unless provoked.

"What happened?"

His gaze dropped to the glass, and his eyes met mine again. "Viktor loved your mother and you. When your grandfather sent men to capture my brother, he tried to protect both of you. But one of the men shot your mother. She died instantly."

I heard footsteps coming closer, pounding the tile downstairs until Cole, Rhys, and Drake were on the landing behind Andrey. They aimed guns at his head.

Cole stood between Rhys and Drake. "Step away from her, Romanov."

Andrey angled his body to look at them before turning back to me. "Tell your friends you are not afraid of Uncle Andrey, *kisa*."

I locked eyes with him, my heart pounding so fast my pulse thumped in my ears. Andrey took another step toward me. Cole and The Knights walked toward us, leveling Andrey with a cold stare.

Cole's eyes flicked between Andrey and me as he pointed the gun. "Get the fuck away from her."

Andrey reached into his jacket and produced a gun aimed at Cole's forehead. With Drake right behind him, Cole didn't even flinch. He held his ground. Rhys was a few paces behind and off to his left, armed and ready to shoot.

In a flash, Andrey grabbed me before I could run. He held me firmly and pressed the gun to my temple. "Do not fucking move. I will shoot her."

"No, you won't," Cole challenged. "Your brother wouldn't allow you to live if you did."

"I will tell him you killed her," Andrey snapped.

"If you touch a hair on her head, you won't live long enough to tell Viktor shit."

Cole took another step toward us, breathing deeply through his nose. His eyes found mine, and a hint of sadness crossed over his face.

Andrey curled his muscular arm around me, pinning me into a position that made it impossible to move my arm.

"You have one second to get your fucking hands off her," Cole shouted, his image blurring as Andrey clamped down harder on my throat.

They couldn't shoot Andrey without risking my life. One wrong move, and he could lodge a bullet into my skull. His finger was on the trigger, and I broke out in a cold sweat from head to toe.

Rhys cleared his throat, drawing my attention to him. He dipped his head down as if trying to communicate with me. I didn't understand what he was telling me.

At least not at first.

His eyes drifted to my hand. And then I realized I was still holding the piece of glass.

I angled my body to the right and dislodged my arm from Andrey's grasp. Just enough to drag the glass across his throat. One swift slice into his skin, and his blood sprayed my face. His gun fired as he staggered backward.

Cole ran toward me and tackled me to the ground as another shot was fired. He covered me with his muscular body and cradled the back of my head. "I got you, Grace."

Andrey lay in a pool of blood, his eyes open and staring back at me.

He was dead.

Dead.

Dead.

Dead.

Cole helped me sit up and pulled me between his legs. I didn't realize I was shaking so severely until he wrapped his arms around me and hugged me to his chest.

I killed my uncle.

The man with the scar on his thumb drifted into my mind. I didn't want to go back there.

No.

No.

No.

But I couldn't stop the thoughts.

The blood on the floor. There was so much blood pooling around my dead uncle. And as I stared at the crimson glistening on the marble floor, my brain transported me to another place.

Men storm through the front door, rushing into the house with weapons. A red dot shines on my father's forehead. He grabs the gun at his waistband and raises it to defend himself.

The men shoot at him, but the bullet grazes his arm and goes straight into my mother's chest. She tumbles to the marble floor. Her blood seeps through the white blouse and onto my cheek. Blood pools around her body that is painfully still.

She looks so pretty.

Like one of my dolls.

"Mommy," I cry, touching the blood blooming on her chest. "Mommy, wake up!"

My mom doesn't move.

Her chest stops rising and falling, and her arms lay flat at her sides. I feel something wet on my face and dab my finger, screaming when I see blood on my hand.

One gunman tackles my dad to the ground, forcing him to submit, while another man lifts me off the floor.

"Papa, no. Help me!"

"Katarina," he bites out as his eyes meet mine, ignoring the man holding him down. "Papa will find you. I will never stop looking for you, kisa."

Chapter Forty-Three

COLE

Grace had a dead look in her eyes as if she went someplace else in her mind and wasn't here with us anymore. She sat between my legs with her head resting on my chest. But mentally, she was *not* okay.

I did this to her.

If I hadn't contacted Viktor, her uncle wouldn't have come to my house. Drake masked our location, but Maverick was a black hat hacker—one of the best in the world.

I told Viktor I wouldn't let him see Grace until he provided concrete evidence to help us with Fitzy—anything to prove why he'd made Grace his heir. Viktor had information on Fitzy and his dirty deeds, and until we had something to nail the old man to the wall, I wasn't letting Grace near Viktor Romanov.

And now…

She wasn't Grace.

That girl was gone.

Her eyelids fluttered as she looked up at Rhys. She stared like he was a stranger. Did she even recognize him?

Tears leaked from her eyes and dripped down her cheeks. Rhys bent down in front of her on one knee and swiped away her tears. She opened her mouth for the first time in over twenty minutes and whispered words in a foreign language.

Rhys looked at me and shook his head. "Why is she speaking Russian?"

"Because it's the language Katerina spoke."

He let out a deep growl, knowing what that means. Grace hadn't spoken Russian since she was a little girl. The fact she even remembered more than a few words surprised me.

Which meant she wasn't Grace. She was Katarina.

Drake hunched down beside me. "I called Dr. Beck. He's on his way."

I tucked her head under my chin and rocked her in my arms. "I can't lose her."

"You won't." He waved his hand in front of Grace's face. "She's in there somewhere."

Rhys dropped to his knees. "Grace, can you hear me?" He waved his hand again. "Hey, look at me, princess."

She focused on him and blinked a few more times. Finally, her mouth opened, and words tumbled out, but they weren't in English.

"Grace." I pressed my lips to her forehead. "Can you understand us?"

We thought she'd forgotten her father's native language. According to my dad, it had been years since she remembered anything from her past. She hadn't mentioned anything to me about her past life. Not even the nightmares I watched her have on the nights I popped into her bedroom.

Did she not remember?

Was it too painful?

"Grace." I cupped her cheeks with both hands, pleading for her to return to me. "Are you in there?"

She blinked, her eyes moving to my lips.

"What did Andrey do to her?" Rhys asked. "It's like he fucking brainwashed her."

"Who knows with the Russians? They're sneaky fuckers."

The pad of Drake's thumb grazed her cheek. "I have to

try this." He locked eyes with me. "So we know if she's that far gone." He stroked her skin. "Katarina?"

At the sound of her real name, her eyes met his. "*Da?*"

Yes.

She blinked a few times, then closed her eyes as if the lids were too heavy to keep open. Then, she rolled her head to the side and whispered, *"Bayushki Bayu,"* speaking entirely in Russian until she sang herself to sleep.

After she passed out in my arms, I kissed her forehead, clinging to her for dear life. I needed her more than anything.

More than oxygen.

More than life.

My mother's body was still warm when I held her. She hadn't been dead for more than a few minutes before we found her. I couldn't lose the two most important women in my life on the same day.

I rose from the floor with Grace's head cradled on my chest. "She can't go back to being Katarina."

I *needed* her.

"She won't," Drake said, though it sounded like a lie.

"What if we did this to her?" I choked out, keeping my voice low so Rhys couldn't hear us as we walked toward Grace's bedroom. "We shouldn't have contacted Viktor. We led them straight to us. Now my mom is dead, and Grace is…" I glanced at her sleeping in my arms, tears staining my cheeks as I lowered her to the mattress. "I love her, Drake. I won't give her up."

"There's an explanation for what happened tonight. When we talk to Viktor again—"

"I'm not talking to him," I shot back. "Or making any deals. Not after what he did to my mom and Grace. He doesn't deserve to see Grace again."

"Think this through," Drake said with concern furrowing his brows. "Viktor is cooperating. If we refuse to speak to him after making contact, we have no idea what he will do."

"We already saw what he's willing to do tonight. He sent his brother to my house."

"We don't know that for sure." Drake clutched my shoulder and guided me out of Grace's room. "I'm sorry about your mom. She was an amazing woman. If you need me to do—"

"Actually, there is something you can do." I led him to my bedroom and opened the safe. He gave me a quizzical look when I put the velvet pouch containing the Elders key in his hand. "Give this to Bastian. Tell him Grace needs his help."

I woke with a jolt. Adrenaline flooded my veins, my heart racing so fast I could hardly catch my breath. A man I hadn't seen in years stood over me with a syringe in his hand.

He was an older man with dark, graying hair, maybe somewhere in his fifties. Like my dad, he had dark tattoos on his forearms and biceps. We were in my bedroom at Fort Marshall.

I blinked a few times and sat up. "Dr. Beck?"

"Oh, good." He let out a relieved breath. "You remember me." He sat on the edge of the bed, a thoughtful expression on his face. "Are you Katarina or Grace?"

My nose wrinkled as I looked at him, and I had to consider his question. I was both girls at different times in my life.

"I'm Grace." I scooted closer to him. "Where's my dad?"

"He's on an assignment and doesn't have access to a phone," he said in a hushed tone. "Drake Battle called me after you…"

Murdered your uncle.

"I killed someone," I choked out, tears staining my cheeks. "My uncle. The man who killed Willow Marshall."

He bobbed his head to agree. "In my line of work, we call that a justified kill."

In his line of work?

Is he not a doctor?

Dr. Beck flattened his hand against my forehead as if checking my temperature. "What do you remember after you killed Andrey? You were speaking in Russian."

I hadn't spoken Russian in so long that I wondered if I could converse anymore. My dad taught it to me almost as soon as I could talk. It was his native tongue, and he often spoke to his friends in the same language. He said it was to keep people from overhearing them.

"I saw the day my mother was murdered before I blacked out." Putting my face in my hands, I sobbed as the horrible memory flashed before my eyes, playing in my head like a movie. "She was…"

"Stay with me, Grace." Dr. Beck put his hand on my forearm. "Can you recall any details of that day?"

In all the years of our therapy, this was the one memory I could never unlock. It was as if my mind hid it behind so many doors I could never reach it. Only those rare moments when I saw blood. Saw her body on the floor. But I couldn't piece it all together.

I nodded. "I saw my father." I closed my eyes and breathed deeply through my nose. "And there was blood."

"That's good, Grace." He pressed his lips into a thin line, his dark eyes on me. "Can you tell me anything else? Do you know how she died?"

"She was murdered," I said, sure of my response.

When I asked my grandfather who murdered her, he said my father shot her. But in my visions, my father didn't hurt her. I felt his love for my mother and me. That man, my papa, was my hero. And before we were separated, he promised never to stop looking for me.

He kept that promise.

Dr. Beck reached into his pocket and removed his cell

phone. "I think I know what triggered your flashbacks. Are you okay with me playing a song for you?"

I nodded.

"Tell me how this song makes you feel."

Dr. Beck hit a button on his cell phone. Seconds later, a familiar but haunting tune filled the silence between us. *Bayushki Bayu*, a man sang in a deep but soothing voice. Then, with only a few words, images flashed before my eyes.

I'm watching TV with my parents in the living room when a loud bang sounds at the front of the house, ripping a scream from my throat. My father shoots up from the couch and looks sternly at my mom.

"I will handle this, Abigail," he tells my mom.

I reach out to him. "Papa, don't go."

He extends his scarred hand, and I slip my fingers between his. "It's okay, kisa." He bends down to kiss my forehead, his cologne filling my nostrils. He smells like the woods. "Papa is going to see where the noise is coming from. Stay here with your mother."

Seconds after he leaves, my mom curls her arm around me. "It's okay, Katarina. No reason to be scared. The monsters are afraid of Papa." She laughs, and it sounds like a melody. "He will make them go away."

A man shouts in the hallway.

"Where is my daughter?" Shoes click on the tiled floor. "Abigail, where are you hiding?"

It's my grandfather.

He scares me.

I hate him.

Mom sweeps me into her arms and rushes into the hallway, headed toward the front door. Armed men have swarmed the house, the red dot from their weapons shining on my father's forehead.

Papa grabs the gun at his waistband and raises it to defend himself. His gaze moves between the gunmen to my mom and me.

"Abigail," Grandfather says as she sets me on the floor, keeping me at her side. "You knew the entire time, didn't you?" Disgust drips from his tone, and as he approaches her, his lip curls upward into a snarl. "You let a criminal into our family. Into your home." He shakes his head. "You're not as smart as you think, my dear. I uncovered all of your lies."

She stood straighter, chin raised. "I never lied to you, Father."

Grandfather clicks his tongue. "Save it, Abigail. You're a terrible liar. Almost as bad as your conman husband." He inches toward her. "You and your sister are such a disappointment. The two of you could have been anything. I gave you every opportunity, and you both married poorly against my counsel."

My mother throws out her arm in front of me.

Grandfather smirks. "You can't keep her from me. And you won't be seeing her where you're going."

"I'll never let you have her." Mom pushes me to the side, but I still see her face. "Katarina is my daughter."

The red dots on my father's head shift toward my mom. Her eyes go as wide as her mouth. Then, Grandfather turns on his heels, his dress shoes tapping on the floor.

"Get rid of them," he orders.

A shot fires and the bullet grazes his arm and sinks into my mother's chest. She falls backward and onto the marble floor. Blood seeps through her white blouse, a puddle pooling around her body that goes painfully still.

"Mommy!" Tears sting my eyes, her blood coating my skin as I cry for her. "Mommy, wake up!"

There's so much blood.

On my face and fingers.

All over my clothes.

"Abigail," my father yells, sinking to his knees on the floor beside her lifeless body. "No." He breathes air into her mouth, but she's not moving. "Abigail, please." He presses his palms on her chest and takes turns breathing into her mouth. "Come on, my darling. Open your eyes."

"Back away from her, Romanov," a man dressed in camouflage growls at my father, pointing a gun at his head.

Dad rises to his feet and faces off with the man. "You killed her." He effortlessly steals the gun from the man's hand and turns it on him. Then he glances over at me. "Katarina, go to your special place."

I know what that means, but I'm shaking so badly I can't move. My dad created a hiding spot just for me. He said it would keep me safe if the bad men came looking for us.

When I don't move, Papa attempts to lift me off the bloody floor with one hand while holding the gun in the other. "Katerina, I want you to close your eyes and sing our song. Can you do that for Papa?"

I close my eyes and sing my favorite Russian lullaby, Bayushki Bayu.

Sleep, my darling, sleep, my baby, close your eyes, and sleep.

Papa sings it to me every night. It's how he taught me to speak Russian.

I'm still singing when my dad fires his weapon at the men. He gets a few more shots in before a gunman on his right tackles him to the ground. I crash to the floor with them while another man forces him to submit.

A different man grips me beneath my armpits and lifts me.

"Papa, no!" I kick, scream, and even try to bite the man carrying me toward the door. "Help me!"

"Katarina," he says as his eyes meet mine, fighting against the weight of the men holding him down. "Papa will find you. I will never stop looking for you, kisa."

My eyes sting from all the tears as we step outside. And from a distance, I hear the voice of a man I hate.

"Take Viktor to Skull Island," Grandfather says to someone I can't see. "Get whatever information you can from him and then put a bullet in his head and dump his body in the ocean."

"What do we do with the girl?"

"She's my insurance policy," he says in a deep, scary tone. "Put her in the back of the SUV and bring her to my home in Sagaponack. And if you tell anyone she's alive, I will destroy you."

The scene faded into black around me, dissolving until nothing was left. I blinked a few times to regain my focus, and when I did, Dr. Beck was sitting beside me.

Who's bedroom are we in?

Where am I?

It takes me a second to realize I'm at Fort Marshall and am not an eight-year-old girl anymore.

"Tell me what you saw, Grace." Dr. Beck set his cell phone on the bed, a weary expression on his face. "How do you feel? What did you see?"

Thick tears slid down my cheeks, which I wiped away with

the back of my hand. I told him every detail of the memory, and he stared at me with his mouth hanging open.

"Do you know what my grandfather meant? He said I'm his insurance policy."

He shook his head. "No, but we can work on your memories. It's possible you heard more of the conversation and chose not to remember it."

"My head hurts," I told him, on the verge of breaking down in tears again, desperate for some alone time. Clutching the side of my head, I rose from the bed. "I feel sick. I need to use the bathroom."

The second I enter the bathroom, I sink to the floor and cry.

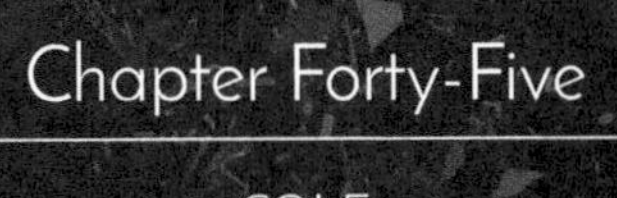

Chapter Forty-Five

COLE

I heard Grace crying from the hallway. My chest ached as I listened to her whimpers. Dr. Beck had been trying to wake her for hours with little success. The few times she had snapped out of her head, she thought her name was Katarina.

Grace didn't exist.

Dr. Beck popped his head into the hallway. "Did you hear what Grace said?"

I nodded. "Fitzy is keeping more from us than we realized."

"I can try to get the information out of her, but after what she's been through, I'm afraid to push too hard. Seeing your mom…" He put his hand on my shoulder. "By the way, I'm sorry for your loss."

"Thank you."

He dropped his hand to his side. "Seeing two dead bodies in one night and all that blood triggered her memories. Grace may begin to remember details on her own. But she's fragile right now."

"I have to go in there." I tipped my head at the door. "She needs me."

He bobbed his head. "Go ahead. I'll be downstairs with your father."

I stopped in front of the bathroom door. For a moment, I hesitated, my stomach twisting into knots at her voice.

She was talking to herself.

I turned the knob, surprised to find the door unlocked. Grace sat on the floor beside the tub, her knees pulled into her chest, tears streaming down her cheeks. She looked up at me, her entire body trembling.

She didn't speak.

Not a single word.

Just blinked.

I closed the door behind me and sat on the floor beside her, leaning my back against the tub. The silence hung between us, thick like smoke. She didn't stop me when I put my hand on her knee, right over the top of her hand. We just stared at each other, communicating without words.

Grace was so quiet and shy when we first met. Just the sound of her voice would excite me because she used it so infrequently. But as we got to know each other, she trusted me. She opened herself up and let me know what she needed.

"I killed a man." Her voice trembled as she spoke. "My uncle." With tears in her eyes, she glanced at me. "I did it without even blinking. Not a second thought about taking another human life. What does that say about me? Am I like my biological father?"

"No, Grace." I laced my fingers between hers. "You're not like him. He's a monster."

"Why don't I feel different?" She shook her blonde head, biting her bottom lip. "I thought killing someone would change me. It must be in the Romanov blood to be a cold-blooded killer."

"You're not a killer, Grace. Sometimes, we don't have a choice. Andrey pushed you to make that decision. You did the right thing. He would have turned you over to Viktor." I curled my arm around her, stroking my fingers through her blonde hair. "This is my fault, Grace. I contacted Viktor with Drake's help."

"What?" Grace gasped, eyes wide. "You talked to my father?"

I nodded. "Through a hacker named Maverick."

"Well, what did he say?"

"He wants to see you in exchange for information about Fitzy and why he made you his heir."

"Set it up," she said without a second thought. "I want out of this marriage. And I want to get away from my grandfather. I'm sick of him controlling my life and everyone in it."

"I don't think we can trust him. For all we know, he sent your uncle here. And now..." I nearly choked on the words, holding back tears. "My mom is dead. And I almost lost you, too."

She laid her head on my chest. "How are you doing, Cole? Your mom... I'm so sorry. Willow was amazing. She was like a mother to me."

A single tear slid down my cheek, which I wiped away before she could see it. Years of emulating my father had taught me how to stay strong. How to not show emotion or fear.

"I'm glad I still have you."

She was the silver lining. The only thing keeping me going.

Strands of blonde hair dropped before her eyes, forcing her to tuck them behind her ear. "Cole, I don't want to lose you."

I slid my fingers beneath her chin, and she turned her head to look at me. "From the moment you walked into my house, I knew I couldn't have you." My heart slammed into my chest with each breath I took. "I knew you were important to The Founders and that you would live the rest of your life in danger and need my help. I thought I could do my job. Be the perfect son. The perfect Knight. That's because I never expected to feel something for you."

I didn't realize a tear had slipped past my bottom lid until

Grace reached up and swiped her finger across my cheek. Every word was the truth.

I loved her more than life itself. And yet, we had no future.

I grabbed the back of her head and pushed my tongue past her lips, stealing the air from her lungs. She climbed on top of me, breathing hard as she rocked her hips to meet mine. I was so fucking hard with her grinding on my cock and those soft moans I captured with each kiss.

"My little brat," I whispered between kisses. "You drive me crazy."

She reached between us to unzip my shorts and whip out my dick. "No more rules. No more debating if we should do this." Sliding her shorts and panties to the side, she pushed the tip of my cock into her wetness. "Fuck me. Make me come. And promise you'll never stop fighting for me."

"I promise," I grunted as she rode my dick like a good girl, marking my shoulders with her fingers.

She could mark me all she wanted. I was hers just as much as she was mine.

Chapter Forty-Six

GRACE

I woke in the dark to a pair of strong, muscular arms wrapped around me, lifting me from the mattress. Rolling onto my side, my face smashed into a hard chest. He was solid muscle beneath his suit.

Scrubbing a hand at my eyes, I peeked up at him. "Cole?"

"No, it's me."

When I saw his face in the moonlight peeking into the room through the patio doors, I breathed a sigh of relief. Not some crazy person coming to kill me.

And not Cole

Bastian.

My cousin.

I looked up at him. "Where's Cole?"

After sex, I got into the bathtub with Cole and let him wash every inch of my body before fucking me again. Exhausted, we got out and laid in my bed. I fell asleep with his fingers interlaced with mine on the mattress.

"With his family." Bastian shifted my weight in his arms and kicked open the door wider for us to pass. Judging by the lack of light in the house, it was the middle of the night. "The Marshalls can't protect you anymore, Grace. You're not safe here."

I tried to sit up, shifting my pajama top into place, and he tightened his grip. "What? No. I have to stay with Cole. His mom just died. He needs me."

"Cole asked me to come here," he said emotionlessly. "I can protect you better than he can."

"But…" I gripped his shoulder as we approached the grand staircase. "Where are you taking me?"

"To one of The Knights' safe houses. No one knows it exists. You'll have protection around the clock."

"I'm not going anywhere." I tapped his arm. "Cole needs me. Put me down."

Bastian shook his head. "I'm here because of the message Cole sent me."

"What message?"

He ignored me and rushed downstairs and into the living room, which was dark and silent.

"But I need my stuff," I protested, tugging on his arm.

"Damian already packed your bags," Bastian said on our way out of the house. "They're in the car."

Bastian deposited me into the backseat of a black SUV and got in beside me. He patted the driver's headrest. "Let's go, D."

The tires screeched as we peeled away from the house, whipping around the circular driveway and down the long pathway illuminated by solar lights.

"Where is the safe house?" I asked as the gate opened, and we turned left onto Founders Way.

"Beacon Bay," Bastian answered. "About fifteen minutes from here. The one Sonny took you to not that long ago. If Willow wasn't safe at Fort Marshall, neither are you. This is for your protection, Grace."

Her death was all my fault.

How did Cole not hate me?

Instead of me comforting him, he sat on the cold bath-room floor with me. He kissed me and tried to make every-thing better. My heart ached at the thought of everything he had given up to be with me. And if my grandfather got his way, we would never have a life together.

I put on my seatbelt and settled in beside my cousin. "What message did Cole send you?"

He reached into his pocket and produced the velvet pouch that held the skeleton key.

Surprised, I raised an eyebrow at him. "Cole gave that to you?"

He nodded. "It's time you learn the power of this key."

Chapter Forty-Seven

COLE

My mother's death was my fault. If I hadn't contacted Viktor, his brother wouldn't have come to my house looking for Grace. He wouldn't have killed my mom.

I stared at my mother's casket, tears spilling down my cheeks. We ordered dozens of calla lilies—her favorite flower, which littered the space. It was a small funeral, with only family and close friends.

Grace would have wanted to be here. And my mother would have liked that, too. But The Knights couldn't risk Grace's safety. Viktor and his men could have been watching, waiting to kidnap her. So we had to do everything in our power to protect her.

She was at the safe house in Beacon Bay with Bastian and Damian on guard twenty-four hours a day. It was just as much their duty to protect her as mine. The Devil's Knights answered to The Founders Society. We had to defend our Grand Master's heir.

My heart felt like it cracked open from losing my mother. The pain was so intense my entire body was numb. I felt like I was dying. Like I couldn't fucking breathe. I wanted to climb into the coffin with her.

Without my mom around, the house wasn't the same. I

never got along with my father. Neither did my brothers. She was the glue that held our family together.

A small group of people gathered around the gravesite. It was a shame we couldn't give my mother the funeral she wanted.

The funeral she deserved.

My dad stood at my side, the same height as me, and touched my shoulder for support.

Like I needed him.

It was my mother I went to for comfort. He was often the source of my anger or frustration. My mom let me vent and made everything better.

After the funeral ended, people offered more condolences. I just wanted to get the fuck out of here and forget about the past week and drown my sorrows in more alcohol.

You could cut the tension with a knife on the ride home. The awkward silence was almost unbearable. Knox and Sloan sat across from me with tears in their bottom lids.

The boys hadn't spoken more than a few words since they heard about our mom. Sloan yelled at Dad and blamed him for her death. Knox ran to his bedroom and stayed there until this morning.

All of us were handling her sudden death in different ways. We didn't know how to communicate with each other without her. Mom made living with our father bearable. Don't get me wrong, he wasn't the worst dad. He also wasn't the best.

My dad cared more about being the commandant of York Military Academy than being our father. Sure, he loved our mom. But he didn't see her for most of the school year since he lived on campus.

I lived at the academy for ten years, only coming home for Christmas and summer breaks. My mom spent most of her time alone in our house while we were at school.

And now, she was gone.

Dad lounged by the window with his ankles crossed, the

black dress shoes so shiny I could see my reflection. I didn't own a pair of dirty shoes. All of mine sparkled, clean enough to use as a mirror.

"We'll pick up Grace tomorrow morning from the safe house," Dad said on our way home from the cemetery. "Fitzy expects us to arrive by two o'clock sharp."

"What?" I narrowed my eyes at him. "Arrive where?"

My father folded his hands on his lap, holding my gaze. "At his house to discuss eliminating Viktor."

"And how does he plan to do that?"

He blew out a deep breath. "By using Grace to draw him out of hiding."

"No," I shot back. "It's too dangerous. Look at what Viktor has already done. He killed Mom. We can't let him anywhere near Grace."

"Andrey Romanov killed your mother," he snapped. "He wouldn't have come to our home if Viktor hadn't sent him for Grace. We have lost everything because of her. I'm done playing this game with a terrorist, and so are Fitzy and The Founders. They have agreed it is in our best interests to give Grace to Viktor."

"But Viktor has information on Fitzy that can take him down," I pointed out. "We could get rid of the old man with his help."

Dad shook his head. "No, Cole. Fitzy isn't the problem here. It's Viktor and his attachment to his daughter. The Knights are in the middle of a war we have no business fighting. This is not our problem anymore. Look at what protecting Grace has cost all of us."

"Fuck Grace," Sloan interjected, speaking for the first time in days. "She's the reason Mom is dead."

"Why do you even care about her?" Knox hissed. "Stop trying to save her. She's the daughter of a fucking terrorist."

"You don't know Grace the way I do. She's not like her father."

Until she met Rhys, she was quiet and sweet. I doubted

she could harm anyone. What she did to Andrey was years of her training with the Colonel. He showed her to defend herself and would have been proud of how she handled Andrey.

"Could have fooled me," Sloan fired back. "She slit her uncle's throat."

"Killing runs in the Romanov DNA," Knox added. "If it were up to me, I'd get rid of her. Mom would still be here if it weren't for her."

Sloan shook his head at me, disgust scrolling across his face. "What the fuck is wrong with you? How can you stand up for her? She's just like her piece of shit dad."

"No, she's not," I said in her defense. "You don't know her. So shut your stupid fucking mouth."

"Why do you think Fitzy let Rhys have her?" Sloan snickered. "She's damaged goods, just like her loser fiancé."

"Enough," Dad cut in, hand raised to end the conversation. "I will not have the three of you fighting on the day we buried your mother."

Sloan folded his arms over his chest and rolled his eyes. Knox stared out the window, tapping his fingers on his knee, breathing through his nose like he was ready to explode.

I glanced at my dad before my gaze swept over my younger brothers. "Mom wouldn't have wanted this. So for her, how about we all try to get along?"

The twins didn't respond.

Dad nodded.

Chapter Forty-Eight

GRACE

After a week at the safe house, I was sick of watching TV and playing board games with Bastian and Damian, who usually ignored me and let Bastian take his turns. My cousin was funny and made Monopoly interesting, but I wanted to return to reality.

I wanted to see my dad.

Except that wasn't possible.

Until the Colonel returned from his mission, I had to live under the protection of The Devil's Knights.

Bastian poured me a cup of coffee and set it on the table. "The Marshalls are picking you up within the hour."

I drank from the mug and nodded.

Bastian chewed on his bottom lip, his eyes on Damian, who stood in the kitchen's entryway. "When we captured Alex's mom, she gave us the name of her accomplice."

My cousin gave me the scoop about Alex's kidnapping and the family drama I missed. I finally felt like I was part of something. Like I had a real family. It had been so long since I had more than my dad that I didn't know what I was missing until the past week.

I added sugar to my coffee and stirred in creamer. "Who helped Alex's mom?"

"She didn't know his real name, only that he called himself Mr. Fitz. I had a gut feeling it was Fitzy. So I showed her a picture of him."

My eyes widened at his confession, although I shouldn't have been surprised. "She identified him?"

Bastian bobbed his head. "He's working with the Sicilian Mafia and arranged for Alex to marry Lorenzo Basile."

"The Mafia boss?"

Another nod. "Carl Wellington has a black book that our grandfather wants."

I took another sip of coffee and licked my lips. "What's in the black book?"

"Secrets," he said with genuine concern in his gray eyes. "Fitzy made a deal with Lorenzo to marry Alex in exchange for the black book that he would have gotten if he had succeeded in marrying Alex off."

"Why would Lorenzo care about the book?"

"It wasn't about the book for Lorenzo. He blames my adoptive father for his niece's death."

Bastian was adopted by Arlo Salvatore when he was a kid, not long after his parents died in a tragic plane crash. He'd been a Salvatore for the past fifteen years and, like me, had to change his name. So did Damian. None of us could be the people we once were. Our lives changed dramatically after our parents' deaths.

I shifted my weight on the chair as Damian entered the kitchen. He dressed in all black, a suit that hugged his lean muscles like body armor. If possible, I tried not to stare. Despite his outer beauty, something was off with him.

Damian hadn't spoken much since we arrived, only at night when he thought I was sleeping. I'd seen and heard some shocking things when the apartment was silent. They had a very unusual relationship that went beyond the bond of brotherhood.

"What do you think Fitzy wants from the book?"

Bastian shrugged. "Could be anything. But my guess is

Wellington has something on him. Drake overheard him talking about the flight that killed my parents at your engagement party."

Bastian pulled out a chair from the table, gesturing for Damian to sit. He gave off some weird vibes, like he couldn't stand to be around people. But when Bastian told him to do something, he did it, no questions asked.

"We're going to confront Fitzy," Bastian said with his gaze on Damian. "But it will have to wait until after today's meeting. The old man will get suspicious if I discuss a different topic."

Our grandfather hated being ambushed, and if he had an agenda, Bastian's questions would only be met with hostility.

"What will you do if he confesses to kidnapping Alex?"

"Kill the old bastard," Damian said with a creepy grin.

Bastian's cell phone dinged. "Time to go." He rose from the chair and peeked out the blinds, staring at the parking lot. "Your ride is here."

Bastian lifted a gun from the table and escorted me downstairs with Damian in tow, carrying my bags. Outside, a black limo was parked in front of the building. The driver took my bags from Damian and opened the back door for me.

"I'll see you soon." Bastian hugged me. "Try to stay strong when you see the old bastard. Don't let him get under your skin. Remember, we have all the power. The key gives us that."

Last week, Bastian told me all about the key and why it was so important to have it in our possession. I asked him to keep it safe for me until the time was right. He said that time would be soon but didn't fill me in on his plan. So I had to wait until he revealed all the missing pieces.

I kissed his cheek. "Thank you for everything. Even though we were forced together under shitty circumstances, I had fun getting to know you this week."

He smiled. "Me too, Grace."

I got into the limo and sat on the bench across from Mark.

He acknowledged me with a nod, then his eyes dropped to the newspaper.

Cole scooted closer to me, dressed in a suit and smelling like body wash and cologne. "How are you holding up?"

"I should be asking you that." I rested my forehead against his and sighed. "I wish I could have been with you at the funeral."

He breathed through his nose, the warmth of his breath brushing my skin. "I'm just glad I have you back. That's all that matters right now."

Chapter Forty-Nine

GRACE

On our way to Sagaponack, silence hung in the air. Cole sat beside me in the limousine, his fingers flying across the keyboard of his cell phone as he played a game.

The three-hour drive from Devil's Creek to The Hamptons worsened my nerves, anxiety tearing through my chest. I needed to calm myself down before I saw my grandfather.

We drove down a long road, which overlooked the water, eventually stopping before a tall wrought-iron gate with *A* at the center.

Adams.

The driver hit a button on the call box in front of the gate. A deep male voice blared through the speaker. He exchanged words with the driver, and then the gate moved inward, allowing us passage onto the property.

We traveled down the driveway lit by lampposts, casting a golden glow on the flagstones. I recalled the first time I came here. How naive to think that my grandfather would love me and treat me like his heir. Instead, I endured years of his mental and emotional abuse.

Locked rooms.

Dark basement.

No food.

No toys.

Grandfather had trapped me within the walls of his mansion, enjoying my screams of terror.

My stomach ached as we rolled toward the house, a sick and twisted place that held all my worst nightmares. The house was too big for one person. Even when I lived here, it felt like a museum, not a home.

My grandfather had two daughters, both of which were dead. He never remarried after his wife passed away from a heart attack. From what I gathered, people believed she died from a broken heart—the pain of losing her children.

The driver parked in the circular driveway. Another limousine was in front of ours. Seven people climbed out: Carl Wellington, the Salvatores, and Alex Wellington. She was beautiful and stood between the four Salvatore brothers.

Each of them made a point of touching some part of her. Bastian brushed his fingertips against hers. Marcello swiped her curls over her left shoulder. Luca dug his fingers into her hip and pulled her closer like he was afraid someone would try to steal her again.

Damian stood behind her with a crazed look in his eyes. It said, *touch her and die*. He was even scarier than Luca if that was even possible.

My cousin didn't have as hard of a look as his brothers. Neither did Marcello. Sure, they both looked like they'd killed a few people without a second thought. But there was something in Bastian's eyes, a softness around the edges.

Two other men I recognized from the helipad at the Salvatore Estate stood beside each other. Carl Wellington and Arlo Salvatore. Mark walked over to them and shook their hands.

Cole tapped my back and guided me toward the group.

Bastian looked right at me and tipped his head. "It's going to be okay, Grace. I got your back in there."

I wiped my sweaty palm on my dress and smiled. "Thanks."

Bastian stepped out from the pack, now standing in front

of me. As tall as Cole, he towered over me. "Don't let Fitzy get into your head. That's his specialty."

I breathed through my nose and forced a smile. What else could I say? I had never been good at handling our grandfather. He was the type of person who commanded every situation and left you feeling powerless.

"Gentleman," Carl said in a deep tone that snapped my attention to him. "And ladies. It's time."

Arlo and Mark followed him into the house, where two men held open the double doors.

Bastian threaded his fingers between Alex's while Marcello held her other hand. As we walked into the marble foyer, no one spoke. The main hallway reminded me of an art gallery.

Alex commented on each piece as we passed, her eyes wide. She pointed at a few of the sculptures and gasped. "How did he get his hands on that?"

"If you want it," Bastian told her, "I'll take it."

She laughed. "No, Bash. That's okay. But I appreciate the thought."

"I would do anything for you, Cherry."

I couldn't help but wonder how she'd gotten that nickname. It was sweet. My cousin loved and adored her and worshiped the ground at her feet. He stayed with me at the safe house for the past week, but he took turns with other Knights, so he could go home and see Alex. I felt terrible because I could see how much he missed her.

Guards posted up at each end of the hallway. Some even stood beside sculptures and art encased in glass. Finally, we stopped at the elevator.

My old bedroom was on the top floor. The memory of being tossed into this elevator and locked in the basement still haunted me. I pushed down the bile rising from my stomach at the thought of ever returning to that tiny space. Four walls that practically suffocated me as a child.

There wasn't enough room for all of us. So Carl and Alex got into the elevator with the Salvatores.

After the car returned to the first floor, I got in with Mark and Cole. We were quiet, eyes on the doors as they opened on the second floor. At the end of the hall, we entered a large office that looked like something from an Old Western movie. A long wooden bar spanned the right side of the space. Dead animal heads were mounted on the walls and over the fireplace's mantle.

Alex sat between Bastian and Damian on one of the worn brown leather couches. Their hands were on her thighs as they shifted uncomfortably in their seats and drank from snifters.

A shudder ripped through me as I looked across the room. Grandfather was close to eighty years old. Yet he looked as if he were in his late fifties.

Dark hair that didn't have an ounce of gray. His skin was still taut, his cheekbones high, and he had a pronounced jawline. He was in great shape, with a solid frame beneath his black suit.

My grandfather looked closer to Arlo Salvatore's age, who was very good-looking. They drank scotch by the bar, speaking between sips, but Fitzy's eyes held mine.

Cole tapped my back, urging me to move farther into the room. My legs felt stuck in quicksand, its force pulling me down. Horrible memories of my grandfather resurfaced every time we were together.

He was there the night armed men invaded my parents' home. They took my father out of the house in handcuffs. My mom lay in a pool of blood. I cried and begged the men to bring my father back. I prayed my mom would wake up from her nap.

He killed my mom.

His own daughter.

Cole hooked his arm through mine and led me over to the couch. We sat across from Bastian, Alex, and Damian.

Damian had his eyes on his drink, which he barely touched. Something was off about him. Bastian kept glancing over at him as if checking on his mental well-being. They had a strange dynamic, a bond they didn't seem to share with the other Salvatores.

Marcello bent over the back of the couch and handed Alex a bottle of water. She took it from him, and he kissed her cheek. I couldn't understand how four men could share one woman until I saw how much they loved her.

Fitzy sat in the armchair at the center of us, tipping a glass of amber liquid to his mouth. "Viktor is on the move. And since he's trying to get in my way, I'm expediting the wedding to draw him out of hiding. He won't stay away from his daughter's wedding."

Now it all made sense. This wedding was never about Rhys. Grandfather only wanted to marry me to that lunatic to find my father. And he was right. This was the perfect way to do it.

"With that said," my grandfather continued, "I expect all of you to be on high alert at the event. Be prepared to take Viktor out by any means necessary. He's been a thorn in my side for too long."

I gulped down the nerves clawing at my insides. The thought of seeing my biological father again made me sick to my stomach.

Grandfather crossed his legs at his ankles and sat back in the oversized chair that made him look regal, like a king. With his finger pointed at me, he said, "And you better be on your best behavior, silly girl. You're so much like your mother. It didn't take much convincing for you to hop into bed with Rhys Vanderbilt. And you will not fuck with my plans. Do you understand me?"

I nodded.

Everyone was tense, especially Damian and Bastian, who seemed the most affected by my grandfather. It was easy to understand why he bothered them so much. They lived with him briefly after their parents' tragic deaths. Fitzy had tortured both of them for the month they lived in this house.

He locked them in his basement without food and water and treated them like animals.

Alex sat between them and stared across the room at Luca as if she were waiting for him to take charge. Because he always knew what to do, no matter the situation. He was the leader of The Devil's Knights.

"Have you given any thought to how vulnerable this makes Grace?" Bastian interjected. "We've been hiding her for years to keep her away from Viktor Romanov. If you plan to drag her in front of the media, it will put her back on the radar of The Lucaya Group."

An evil grin tugged at Fitzy's mouth. "I'm counting on it."

"But why now?" Luca cut in with the million-dollar question.

"Why not?" Fitzy rested his expensive, shiny dress shoe on his knee and scanned the room with a hunter's look in his eyes. "It's time for Viktor to show his face. And until now, he hasn't been properly motivated to do so."

"Are you going to kill him?" I asked, my voice sounding small. "He's my father. From what I remember, he wasn't always bad."

"You didn't know any better," Fitzy fired back. "But I can assure you the man you hold dear in your heart is a cold-blooded killer. He killed your mother right in front of you. He murdered Bastian and Damian's parents. And he will kill you if I don't dispose of him."

I gasped. "He killed their parents?"

I couldn't even bring myself to look at them.

How could I?

Bastian had been so nice to me. Damian, not so much, but I got the sense that he wasn't a big talker. At least now I understood why Damian glared at me the entire time we were forced to live at the safe house.

"Viktor is also a problem for The Knights," Luca chimed.

Mark turned to look at me. "We kept you from Viktor because he's a dangerous man. Even if he got you back, he wouldn't have put you above his interests. He's the leader of a terrorist organization, Grace. Colonel Hale and other men and women who served in the armed forces have fought for the same thing. To keep men like Viktor from hurting others."

His words sank deep into my skin like a bullet piercing my heart. Because he was right. I'd spent years living on military bases around the world. Even if he wasn't my biological father, Colonel John Hale was still my dad in every way that counted. He risked his life to save me.

"Okay," I whispered. "Do what you have to do. But I'd rather not see another parent killed in front of me."

"So it's settled," Grandfather said with a victorious smirk. "You'll marry Rhys Vanderbilt this weekend. And then we'll be done with The Lucaya Group once and for all."

This weekend?

Fuck.

Chapter Fifty

GRACE

Cole was up to something, pacing the halls all day and speaking on the phone with his cousin in hushed tones. He said he had a plan that would hopefully save me from this misery.

But I accepted my fate.

I had to marry Rhys.

We drove to the Salvatore Estate to discuss our strategy the morning before my wedding. Two armed guards stood outside the call box with machine guns strapped to their backs.

The guards waved us forward, and Cole floored the pedal down the long, paved driveway and halted in front of a covered garage. He parked beside Marcello's Maserati GranTurismo and got out of the Ferrari.

The old mansion was built on the edge of a cliff in the early 1900s and reminded me of a medieval castle. All the houses on Founders Way differed. Fort Marshall had the feel of a military base by design, hence the nickname. The Cormac Compound was a stone monstrosity that looked like something from *Coastal Living*.

Then there was Drake's house. The Battle Fortress replicated Tony Stark's Razor Point mansion from the Iron Man movies. Wellington Manor was to my right, the last house on the street, and it looked like a Southern plantation.

As we strolled up to the front doors, they swung inward as Bastian moved through them. Dressed in his usual ten thousand dollar suit, he looked like the CEO of Atlantic Airlines.

We looked nothing alike. The women on the Adams side were all blonde with light blue eyes. Bastian had his father's looks. Tall, well over six feet, with short chestnut brown hair and gray eyes you would never know he was an Adams.

"Grace," he said with a smile. "I hate how we keep seeing each other under shitty circumstances. But you need to hear this before the wedding."

He was jittery, tugging at his black tie and awkwardly shifting his stance. We followed him into the house, down the main hallway tiled in Carrara marble.

The Salvatores were second-generation Americans. Of all the Founders, they were the least legitimate. Arlo Salvatore took their family from criminals to businessmen. Though they still dabbled in many shady deals, especially those involving The Knights.

We entered a large sitting room off the main corridor. Arlo, Luca, Damian, and Marcello sat on couches and armchairs with glasses of amber liquid in their hands. Alex clung to Luca's side. She was beautiful, a blonde bombshell.

I waved to Alex and smiled. A gesture Alex returned with her free hand, rubbing her stomach with the other. She was pregnant with one of the Salvatore brothers' babies, but I didn't know which one was the father.

We sat on a couch across from Luca, who studied us with a drink raised to his mouth. He was always so cold.

"Our grandfather is luring you into a trap," Bastian said after a long silence. "He's been lying about everything. Last night, we received proof that your father is not The Lucaya Group's leader. And he has no ties to the Russian Mafia." My cousin scrubbed a hand over his face, his eyes meeting mine. "Your father didn't send his brother after you. He didn't order

Andrey to kill Willow. His brother planned to use you to get Viktor to do something illegal for him."

I turned to look at Cole. "Is this what you've been keeping from me?"

He nodded. "I wanted to wait until I had all of the information from Drake to tell you. And it's only fair you hear it from Bastian since this news affects him, too."

My eyes flicked back to Bastian. "Then why is Fitzy using my wedding to get to my father?"

"Because Viktor was an intelligence officer." He shifted the glass to his other hand. "He discovered something about our grandfather, so Fitzy eliminated him."

"So my dad is not a bad guy?"

Bastian rolled his shoulders. "Viktor's family is Russian Mafia. But no, your dad isn't part of their business. He had nothing to do with Alex's attempted rape or Willow Marshall's death."

I covered my mouth with my hand, eyes wide. "Rape?" Then I turned to look at Alex. "I'm so sorry."

"Nothing happened." Alex shrugged. "Damian killed him before he could touch me."

"Oh," I whispered. "Still, I'm so sorry that happened to you."

"Marcello got shot and almost died because of the Bratva," Luca said with anger dripping from his tone. "Because they were looking for you."

So did Cole's mom.

"This isn't your fault, Grace." Cole pulled me into his arms and rubbed my back. "You didn't do anything wrong. No one blames you for anything."

Luca's nasty attitude said otherwise.

I glanced at Bastian. "How do you know my dad isn't a terrorist?"

Bastian took a swig from his glass and set it on the table. "Viktor sent intel that proves Pierre Moreau is the group's leader. Your father was never involved with The Lucaya

Group. His only downfall was your mother. He wasn't willing to let you or her go, and Fitzy tried to detain him on Skull Island."

I sat back and curled up beside Cole, needing his warmth. He tightened his grip on me and traced the infinity symbol on my palm to calm my nerves. I once told him that it was something my adoptive father did to soothe me.

"I'm not telling you this to upset you," Bastian said after a brief pause. "But you need to know what you're walking into tomorrow." He waved his hand around the room. "We'll be with you at the wedding. So will other Knights. But your father will show up, and we can't predict what he will do once he sees our grandfather."

"Do you think he'll hurt me?"

He shook his head. "No, we don't see him as a threat. His information about The Lucaya Group checks out. We have no reason to believe he's lying to us or will be violent. He only wants to see you again. And in exchange, he will give us information about Fitzy."

My heart clambered in my chest, pounding so hard it felt like it was about to break through my skin. I had dreamed of my father for the past thirteen years. And now that I knew what happened on the day my mother died, I wanted to see him again. He wasn't a bad guy, only a father trying to get back to his daughter.

"Does any of this have to do with the Elders key?"

Bastian rolled his broad shoulders. "Fitzy believes your father stole the key from him. That's why he made you the beneficiary of his will. Viktor blackmailed him into doing so. And once the old man is out of the picture, I'll show you what the key opens." He gave me a tiny smile. "It will change your life, Grace. I hope you're prepared for what comes next."

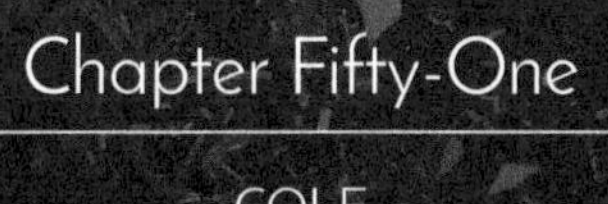

Chapter Fifty-One

COLE

Grace hadn't spoken since we left the Salvatore Estate, breathing harder than before. She kept sighing and staring down at her feet as we walked toward her bedroom at Fort Marshall.

"It's going to be okay, Grace. I won't let anyone hurt you."

"My grandfather will kill me if this plan goes wrong," she said, her body shaking from fear.

"It won't," I assured her.

Grace dropped my hand and entered the room, plopping down on the bed with a sigh. Her eyes drifted to the notepad she left on the nightstand.

The bucket list.

"What are you thinking?" I moved in front of her and slid my hand beneath her chin when she didn't respond. "You can talk to me, Grace."

She leaned over and grabbed the notepad. "This list is the reason I have to marry Rhys." Eyes downcast, she blew out a deep breath. "Rhys wouldn't have sent a sex tape to my grandfather if I hadn't given him the ammunition. This is all my fault. I wanted so badly to experience life that I didn't consider the consequences of having freedom."

She'd never been free a day in her life. As long as her

grandfather was alive, she would always have to follow the rules.

"Hey, don't blame yourself." I sat on the bed beside her, yanking the notepad from her hand to throw it onto the mattress. "None of this is your fault. The list was my idea."

She wiped at her eyes. "Yeah, but you didn't know what I would put on it. I'm the one who wanted to date both of you. I'm so stupid." Grace wrapped her arms around her middle and sobbed. "It was selfish of me to think I could have it all. That I could have two men without paying the price."

While I wasn't fond of sharing her with Rhys, I would have done anything for her.

Caressing her cheek, I stared into her pretty blue eyes. "Listen to me. You did nothing wrong. It's okay to want things. Your grandfather took every life experience from you so you would be miserable like him. If you want to blame someone, it's Fitzy."

"And Rhys," she bit out. "He manipulated me. Made me think I mattered to him." She looked at me with watery eyes and rubbed her nose. "No bad deed ever goes unpunished with my grandfather. He knows about us. What if he tries to hurt you, too?"

"I can handle him," I lied to keep her from beating herself up. "Don't worry about me."

Grace climbed onto my lap, and I held her against my chest, running my fingers down her back to calm her nerves. "Until this summer, I hadn't seen my grandfather for ten years. No calls on my birthday. No Christmas presents. Not a single word from him. And now, the Colonel is on an extended mission, and my life is slowly falling apart."

I cupped the back of her head, staring into her pretty blue eyes that captured mine. "I promised to protect you. And I will continue to do that until I take my last breath."

"Cole," she whispered, her lips inched from mine. "I need to be with you." She clawed at my shirt, pulling me closer. "I think you need this, too."

I pressed my lips to hers, wanting to lose myself with the girl who stole my heart. She was the only person with the power to hurt me.

I tugged at her clothes as she removed mine until each piece of fabric dropped to the floor. We explored each other's bodies, taking our time.

I rested my forehead against hers as my hand slipped between her legs. "Are you going to come for me, brat?"

She licked her lips and nodded. "I like when you call me that."

My finger slid inside her, and she cried out as I drew back and added another finger. "You gonna come all over my cock like a good girl?"

As her lips parted, her eyes snapped shut. "Yes."

Her small hand gripped the base of my cock, giving me a few strokes. We worked in harmony until I could feel intense pressure spread up from my lower back, causing my legs to tremble. I didn't want to come like this, so I peeled her fingers off my shaft and sat back to look at her.

Naked and beautiful, her blonde hair fanned out around her heart-shaped face. She was thin but had curves and breasts that filled my hands perfectly. I mentally captured every inch of her body and committed her to memory.

Grace rocked her hips, so the tip of my cock breached her folds. She was so wet and tight, and she whimpered as I pushed into her. I gripped her hips and thrust deeper as my lips crashed into hers, tasting a hint of mint toothpaste on her breath.

Clutching her hand on the mattress, I moved in rhythm with her, my heart clambering in my chest. "No matter what happens, this means something."

She wrapped her legs around my back, a moan slipping past her plump lips. "I don't want this to end. Cole, I've made so many mistakes. I'm sorry."

I swiped my thumb at the tear streaking her cheek. "Whenever you feel alone, think of this moment." I kissed her lips and made love to her. "Think about how I make you feel. Remember that if your heart is breaking, mine is, too." I placed her hand over my heart, so she could feel it beating faster. "This belongs to you."

We kissed until we both lost control, and I was coming inside her, riding out our orgasms. After I slid off her, Grace sat up, lifted the notepad off the bed, and pointed at the nightstand.

"Can you hand me the pen?"

I placed it in her palm, and she crossed off the last item on the bucket list before ripping the page out of the book.

"For what it's worth," she said as she stuffed the page into my hand, "I got everything I ever wanted. No matter what happens, you made all of my dreams come true. My grandfather can't take this list from me."

I stared at the page, mouth hanging open at the last item.

~~Kiss a boy~~

~~Get asked out on a date~~

~~Lose my virginity~~

~~Fall in love~~

"Rhys helped me with the first two. And at the time, I thought those things mattered. But sex is meaningless when it's not with someone you love."

She didn't have to say the words. This was her confession.

Grace loved me.

Chapter Fifty-Two

Sweet orchestra music filled the ballroom. At least two hundred guests sat in the white chairs on each side of the aisle.

"Smile," Grandfather snapped. He begrudgingly took my hand as the song changed to the bridal chorus. "Pretend like you want to be here. This is your wedding, you ungrateful bitch."

I slapped on a fake smile as we moved forward to the song.

Tears stung my eyes.

I wore a beautiful white dress I would have worn for Cole. And as I walked down the aisle, I clutched the bouquet, trying not to cry when I spotted him in the crowd. He looked like he wanted to stop the wedding. I even thought he might try.

But I knew he couldn't.

Not without hurting me.

And when we got to the altar, I was greeted with the wicked smirk of Cole's rival.

The man I loved to hate.

If I refused to marry him, my manipulative, controlling grandfather would hurt the man I loved. He had already taken everything from me, so I knew he would make good on his threats. So I put on my new husband's ring.

I said I do.

I expected my biological father to appear before the minister said, "You may now kiss the bride."

Rhys clutched my hip and pulled me to him, staring into my eyes with one of his villainous grins. "Don't make this worse than it needs to be, princess," he whispered. "Kiss me."

My gaze flicked to Cole for a moment. He nodded his approval, even though he looked like he wanted to snap Rhys's neck.

So I pressed my lips to Rhys's and opened up for him, letting this traitorous piece of shit put his tongue in my mouth. It had to look real for my grandfather. The old man had to believe he had won.

Now a married woman, I let Rhys parade me around the ballroom on his arm. I changed into a shorter dress for the reception and smiled at our guests. I chugged champagne and prayed my father would save me.

Even my grandfather seemed tense. He must have expected Viktor to show before we said our vows. The old man had to pay Rhys the dowry. Three billion dollars. All because my dad didn't get here in time.

Sucks to be him.

Two hours into the reception, I snuck away from Rhys and met Cole in the hallway. We rounded the corner, and Cole clutched my shoulder from behind and shoved me inside a dark room.

It was a bathroom.

His lips brushed my ear, his cock as hard as steel. "You look beautiful in this dress, Grace. Fuck, the things I want to do to you."

"Cole, what are you doing? The wedding isn't over."

"Taking what I want." He fisted my hair in his hands and pulled my mouth to his, prying my lips apart with his tongue.

Then, Cole grabbed my wrists and raised my arms above my head, pinning me against the wall with his muscular chest. "I hate that you're married to him. I wanted to put a bullet in his skull as I watched him kiss *my* woman in front of everyone. We'll get the marriage annulled as soon as this is all over."

He slipped his tongue into my mouth, kissing me like I consumed him. Each kiss was more intense and impatient as we clawed at each other's clothing, our hands and tongues doing the talking.

"I should never have let Rhys kiss you," he said as our lips separated. "It should have been me. I was so fucking stupid for thinking that following the rules would get me ahead."

He slid his hand up my stomach over the top of the dress to feel my nipples. I melted into his touch as he pinched the tiny bud between his fingers, leaving a trail of kisses on my neck.

"You're mine, Grace." Sucking my bottom lip into his mouth, he tugged hard on it, earning a few moans. "Mine. I'm never letting you go."

He wrapped my leg around his back and shoved my panties to the side. My tongue tangled with his, and I moaned as he pushed two fingers inside me. I was so wet that his fingers slid in and out.

Burying my face against his neck, I gripped his thick arms for support. "Cole," I whimpered. "Fuck me. Please."

He broke through my inner walls with his fingers and rolled his thumb over my clit. "Come for me first."

It didn't take long before I groaned his name, my orgasm ripping through me like a hurricane as I came on his fingers.

Cole slid his fingers out of my pussy and brought them to his mouth to suck my juices. "I love how you taste."

He unbuttoned his pants and lined himself up at my entrance. Once fully inside me, he stilled for a moment, resting his forehead against mine. "You have always been mine. I'll kill Rhys before I let him take you away from me."

Knowing we would be free of Fitzy after tonight changed

Cole. He seemed more relaxed, his guard lowered, and I loved this side of him. From the moment we met, I had dreamed of this moment. I had envisioned us together.

Lifting my feet off the ground, he slammed into me, holding me up in his strong arms, fucking me as if he'd never get to do it again.

"I don't care if you're married to another man," he whispered, "as long you keep squeezing my cock with your pussy."

"Oh God, Cole."

Whenever we were together, the world seemed to fade into the background until there was no one and nothing but us. He took what he wanted from me, so deep inside me that I felt him everywhere.

After we came down from our high, Cole stuffed himself back into his pants and turned to look at the wall so I could pee without an audience. I quickly went about my business. And then he helped me fix my dress so I didn't look like I'd just gotten fucked in the bathroom.

He grabbed my face and kissed me once more. "Your father will come tonight. I'm sure of it. This will all be over once we get the evidence we need from Viktor."

On our way back to the ballroom, someone bumped into me, knocking Cole to the side.

"Sorry," the man muttered. "Pardon me."

I was about to turn around when another man gripped my arm and yanked me backward. I would have crashed to the floor if I hadn't fallen into his chest. He snaked his arm around me and dragged me out of the camera's view. My grandfather had tons of security at his estate.

"It's okay, *kisa*. You don't have to fear me," the man said in a thick Russian accent, one I recognized. "Papa is here."

My heart hammered in my chest, beating so fast I could hardly catch my breath.

I knew his voice.

Papa.

"I can protect you from Fitzgerald," my father said calmly. "You can't trust him. Both of you need to come with me."

Nerves shook through me as my father clutched my hand. His touch felt familiar but possessive as if he were afraid to let me go.

"Where are you taking us?" I asked him, keeping my voice low.

The few people we passed didn't recognize my father, but they tipped their heads at me. I had been the center of attention all night. Cole and my father's friend trailed behind us.

My dad turned a corner, shielding his face from the cameras as we passed them. "We need to hurry, *kisa*. This is time-sensitive. If given a chance, your grandfather will kill you. Just like his daughters."

Fitzy was responsible for Bastian's mother's death. But why? What could he possibly have gained?

"I loved your mother," my father said as we exited a door at the back of the house that led to a paved veranda. "You and she were my entire world and my reason for staying in the United States. I hope you don't believe the Americans' lies about me. I'm not who they say."

"My cousin told me."

"Bastian?" He cut through the backyard and slipped through a row of tall hedges. "Yes, I was accused of his parents' murders."

"My grandfather told me you're a terrorist," I bit out, even though I knew it wasn't true. "That you killed people. He sent me away and changed my name because he feared you finding me."

He shook his dark head of hair, his deep brown eyes meeting mine. "Another lie. I have nothing to do with The Lucaya Group. Never did. I was on the run for years and looking for you. I could never settle down, always watching over my shoulder."

"Then why did The Knights and The Founders believe the lies?"

"Because it's what Fitzgerald told them." Papa's Russian accent was thicker than I remembered. "He's the most powerful man in the country. Everyone fears him. But your mother didn't." He smiled as he tucked a strand of hair behind my ear. "You look just like her. So beautiful. She would have been so proud of you, *kisa*."

"Why did he kill my mom?"

"Because she defied him when she married me. He disapproved of our union. He knew I was lying about my identity, but your mother knew everything. I never hid the truth from her."

"So you were a KGB agent?"

He bobbed his head to confirm. "Your mother was my mark. The Russian government sent me to the United States to get closer to her. They wanted me to learn her father's secrets. The Knights and The Founders have access to valuable information."

"Did she give it to you?"

He raised his broad shoulders, which filled out the black tailored suit. "Some things. But your mother knew little. Her father kept his secrets well guarded."

"So instead of walking away, you stayed. You married her and had me."

He bent down, so we were at eye level, a grin stretching the corners of his mouth. "Every moment of every day for the past thirteen years, I have thought about you." His hand cupped my cheek. "About how you would look. What you would be like. How you would sound. I imagined you with your mother's beauty and my resilience. You're exactly as I had hoped, Katarina."

"I go by Grace now."

"I know." He lowered his hand from my face with a sigh. "But you will always be my Katarina." He tipped his head toward the thick hedges. "We have to get into the neighbor's yard. Your grandfather has too much security on his property."

Viktor made a path for me, parting the bushes. "I worked in intelligence for years," he continued. "I learned things about your grandfather and The Founders. They killed your mother, took you from me, and tried to destroy my life because I knew about your grandfather's plot to kill his eldest daughter."

"Bastian's mom?"

He nodded. "Fitzgerald paid The Lucaya Group to make the plane crash look like an accident."

"So that part is true?" My mouth widened in horror. "Why would he kill Bastian's mom?"

"Because she spent most of her trust fund to start Atlantic Airlines with Marcus Kincaid."

Bastian's father.

"Fitzgerald hated Marcus's family. Your aunt went against your grandfather's wishes when she married him. He considered her a great disappointment."

"What about the Townsends?" Cole asked. "Damian's parents were aboard the plane when it crashed."

"The Townsends would have inherited the shares in the company. But Fitzgerald didn't like them. He thought they weren't good enough to be Founders."

Cole grabbed my hand and pulled me into his chest. "Grace could be his next target."

"We can't leave," I pointed out. "It will only make my grandfather more suspicious."

"You need to come with me," my father insisted. "I can keep you safe until we deal with Fitzgerald."

"No one will go against him without proof," Cole said.

My father handed me a flash drive. "I have evidence of his crimes."

I handed the drive to Cole, and he tucked it into his pocket. After a brief conversation, we exchanged phone numbers, promising to make contact after we read the drive's contents.

My dad bent down to hug me, wrapping me in his strong

embrace as he kissed my head. "I will be watching you, *kisa*. We'll never be apart after Fitzgerald is dead."

Then he disappeared into the darkness with his friend.

Chapter Fifty-Three

COLE

After we entered the house, I handed Drake the flash drive and found another hiding spot for Grace and me. Rhys was looking for his bride, but I didn't give a single fuck. He could look all he wanted because she was mine.

"This way." Grace tugged on my hand and guided me into a dark room. "My grandfather never lets anyone in this part of the house. He never even let me come in here."

We stepped inside a movie theater with enough seating for a hundred guests. It was much larger than the theater we had at Fort Marshall.

The second we were alone, I kissed Grace, capturing her moans. I pushed down the front of her dress and kissed her neck and breasts. Her body quivered with each flick of my tongue on her nipples. The pink buds hardened as I licked, sucked, and nibbled them.

Knowing she was forbidden made me feral. I liked that while Rhys was searching for his wife, I made her scream.

Sweet revenge.

Grace moaned so loud my cock jerked. I pulled my boxers down with one hand and gave my dick a quick stroke. I wanted to take my time and devour every inch of her flawless body, but I couldn't think straight when she made those sexy fucking sounds.

I lowered her onto the leather couch in the front row and hiked up her dress. At least she wasn't still wearing the white gown with a long train. I could have gotten lost under that thing.

Dropping to my knees, I left a trail of kisses down her stomach and spread her legs wider. Each sound of pleasure made my dick so hard that it was agony not being inside her.

She rocked her hips into my mouth, twisting her fingers through my hair. A soft purr escaped her mouth as I licked her clit, her juices dripping onto the chair.

I knew Fitzy would be pissed. So I licked her until she leaked all over the fabric.

"Cole, please." She ran her fingers through my hair. "Fuck me. We don't have a lot of time."

We were going for a marathon tonight. I wanted to fuck the bride as many times as I could while her husband wondered where she was and what she was doing. And I couldn't wait to see Rhys's face when we entered the ballroom together, her lipstick all messed up, her hair looking like she'd been freshly fucked.

I took my time, careful not to fill her right away, lifting her leg over my shoulder as her body relaxed, sliding deeper inside her. With her legs draped over my shoulders, I pounded into her, and Grace's grip on my dick tightened as she screamed my name.

After we both came, my cell phone rang.

"Fuck," I groaned. "I have to get this."

"Answer it," she said with a sexy smile. "I'm not going anywhere."

Still inside her, I raised the phone to my ear. "What's up?"

Drake breathed into the receiver. "Are you sitting down?"

I glanced at Grace and laughed. "Yeah, in a manner of speaking."

"The flash drive has everything we need. Proof Fitzy hired

The Lucaya Group to kill Bash and Damian's parents. Evidence of every crime Fitzy ever committed. It's enough to put the old man away for life."

I pulled out of Grace and dropped to the chair beside her, scrubbing a hand across my jaw. "Why did he do it?"

"If he didn't kill Damian's parents, they would have inherited the shares of Atlantic Airlines stock. Viktor detailed everything in his research. The stock purchase and transfer. Fitzy forged the paperwork to retain a large stake in the company."

"He killed them for shares in the company? Didn't he own part of it?"

"No," Drake said. "Not until after the Kincaids and Townsends died."

I tucked myself back into my pants and hooked my arm around Grace. "What else did you find on the drive?"

"An endless list of Fitzy's crimes. Everything from bank fraud to murder. I'm still going through the files, but I wanted to give you a heads up before Grace hears the news from Bash."

"I'll tell her. Thanks, Drake."

After we hung up, I stuffed my phone in my pocket and looked at Grace. "Your grandfather lied about everything. Viktor is telling the truth. So if you want to see him again, it's safe."

Her eyes widened. "What's next?"

"Bash and Damian are going to confront Fitzy. They'll handle it."

"Good." She pressed her lips to mine. "My grandfather deserves to die."

"Do you know what this means?" I brushed my lips against hers and smiled. "We're free."

"I'm free," she sighed. "Finally."

I raised her hand to my mouth, took Rhys's ring off her finger, and chucked it across the room. "Marry me, Grace. I love you. You're the only woman I have ever and will ever love. So marry me."

She gasped. "Are you serious?"

I nodded. "I want to spend the rest of my life with you."

I reached into my pocket and pulled out my mother's engagement ring. Since her death, I had kept it with me just in case this worked in my favor.

She stared at the massive princess-cut diamond, her eyes as wide as her mouth. "I love you, too, Cole." She giggled. "I can't believe I'm saying this on my wedding day, but yes, I will marry you."

I slid the rock onto her finger and kissed her again. "I hope you're okay with being on the run for a while. We will have a target on our backs until we get rid of your grandfather."

"I don't care," she said, tears streaming down her cheeks. "As long as I'm with you."

Chapter Fifty-Four

GRACE

After I accepted Cole's proposal, we enlisted the help of Bastian and The Devil's Knights to sneak off my grandfather's property. And once we were on the road, I called my father. He gave me an address and said he would be waiting for us.

I knocked on the front door of a brick Colonial with blue shutters. My palm was sweaty, and Cole rubbed it down the side of his pants when he noticed.

A moment later, my father appeared in the entryway with a smile. He wore a black suit, a crisp white shirt, and a red tie. Unlike me, he had dark hair and eyes.

"*Kisa*." He wrapped his arms around me, lifting my feet off the ground. "I'm so glad you're here." He put me down and held me at arm's length to study my face. "You have no idea how much I missed you."

He shook Cole's hand, then ushered us inside the house, steering us down the hallway and into the living room.

"I'd like you to meet Vera, my girlfriend."

I followed his gaze to the beautiful blonde woman perched on the couch with a glass tipped to her lips. She was maybe in her early thirties, much younger than my dad.

She put the glass on the coffee table and approached me

with a closed-mouth smile. A red sundress swayed as she moved her narrow hips, brushing her slender legs.

"Katarina," she said with a thick Russian accent. "Your father has told me so much about you." She pulled me into a hug, her flowery perfume filling my nostrils. "It's so nice to meet you."

Katarina was the name he had given me. So I didn't mind. Grace and Katarina were the same, but they had led different lives.

"This is Cole." I clutched his arm and nodded at my sexy hunk of a man. "My fiancé." I held up the ring he'd given me before he threw Rhys's diamond across the movie theater.

"You're engaged?" My father raised an eyebrow at me. "At least this time, I hope you'll let me walk you down the aisle."

I smiled. "I would like that."

Cole held out his hand, and Vera hugged him, too. She was surprisingly warm and cuddly. I didn't grow up with hugs and random displays of affection, but my dad showed me plenty of love and support. Regardless of paternity, John Hale was still my dad.

Now, I had two of them.

I sat on the couch beside Cole, with my dad and Vera across from us. He drank scotch and offered one to Cole. I sipped from a water bottle and snacked on cookies from the tray in front of me. Vera was a damn good cook and laid out a delicious spread for us.

"You can stay with us until Fitzgerald is put down," my father said as if he were talking about an animal. "I will keep you safe." He rose from the couch and headed over to the flatscreen television on the wall. "I want to show you something. Videos that may help jog your memory. It's been a long time since we were together. You were only eight when I lost you."

He opened the laptop on the table and flipped through the folders on the screen. My dad had worked in intelligence and was ridiculously good with computers. It was funny because I had never owned a computer or a cell phone.

It was too risky.

When he found the correct file, he clicked a few buttons, and a video started playing on the screen. "This was your first birthday party. Your mother was so worried about making everything perfect that nothing went according to plan."

He chuckled as my mom appeared in the video, her blonde hair and blue eyes the mirror image of me.

"Viktor!" Mom pretended to be mad but couldn't help but smile as she looked at him. "Stop filming me. This is a disaster. My father is ruining everything."

Holding the camera in front of them, he hugged my mom from behind and kissed her cheek. "No more fussing, Abigail," he said in a fake American accent. "I won't let your father ruin Katarina's special day."

He was around too many people to let his Russian accent slip. I could see Fitzy in the corner of the frame, glaring at them. He stood against the wall, dressed in an expensive suit, armed with a severe expression.

"What did my grandfather do?" I asked.

"He tried to intimidate me by inviting The Devil's Knights and The Founders to our home." He sat on the couch beside Vera, the remote in his hand. "Your mother knew the truth about me. She accepted it and promised to take my secrets to her grave."

"But Grandfather knew you were lying."

He nodded. "At the time, he didn't have proof. I was good at covering my tracks. It took him seven more years to find a single shred of evidence. And even that wasn't enough to out me the way he did." Dad drank from his glass and sighed. "I was well aware of Skull Island. I knew your grandfather would try to imprison me where The Devil's Knights torture their enemies."

I lifted an eyebrow at Cole, who remained expressionless. Of course, he couldn't tell me every detail about The Knights because of his oath. But having my father explain more about their world didn't break any rules. He seemed to know every-thing about the secret societies.

"So I made friends. Thought ahead." His Adam's apple bobbed as he looked at me. "I knew your grandfather would find a way to send me to Skull Island. And I saw this as an opportunity to learn more about The Devil's Knights. Your mother was well aware of everything I did. I never saw the need to hide from her. She was my partner in every way."

I smiled at his sweet words. Because the man I could see in my mind was protective and fierce, a man who loved his wife and child.

"When the extraction team invaded our home, I planned to go willingly. I never meant for your mother to get hurt. There was no reason for trained men to shoot at me and hit your mother." He downed the contents of his glass and set it on the coffee table. "Your grandfather planned to kill your mother. He'd already murdered his eldest daughter. And with both of them out of the way, he thought he could get rid of me. But I knew too much about him and was already ten steps ahead."

"How did you stay alive all this time? Why didn't he kill you?"

"Because I had help from friends. If anything were to happen to me, they would release the information about Fitzgerald to the world. He knew I would make good on my threat. The information I obtained kept both of us alive. It's also the reason you will inherit his fortune."

Home movies flicked on the screen as he told me more about his life with my mother. Starting with my first birthday party, all the way to the last month we spent together.

In the movies, I could see how much he loved my mom and cherished the ground she walked on. We were his entire world, ripped out from under him.

"You must be tired," he said after we talked some more, and I couldn't stop yawning. "I've prepared a room for you."

I followed my dad and Vera upstairs, latching onto Cole's

arm. My dad pushed open the last door on the left. "I had the designer decorate this bedroom for you, hoping you would one day return to me."

I stepped forward, standing on my tippy toes to hug him. "Thank you, Papa."

He hugged me back, pressing a kiss on my cheek. "Thirteen years," he whispered. "Not a single day went by that I didn't miss you, Katarina. Goodnight. I'll see you in the morning."

After he left with Vera for their bedroom, I closed the door and sat on the bed beside Cole. My mind raced with dozens of questions, one of which I had been wondering all night.

"Why do The Devil's Knights call it Skull Island?"

Cole slipped his fingers between mine and glanced over at me. "Because no one ever leaves the island alive."

"Have you been there?"

He bobbed his head to confirm. "I had to do horrible things to become a Knight on that island. They wouldn't let us pass the initiation without enduring a final challenge permanently imprinted in my mind."

"Like what?"

Eyes on the wall, he breathed through his nose. "Things you're better off not knowing. You have enough nightmares."

Chapter Fifty-Five

GRACE

The following Monday, a judge annulled my marriage to Rhys Vanderbilt. And Fitzgerald Archibald Adams IV died the following night of natural causes.

Rhys got nothing. But we still had to deal with him and his twisted family. They would get what was coming to them soon enough. Every penny that should have gone to Rhys would pass to Cole on our wedding day.

Three billion dollars.

The news anchor announced my grandfather's death, saying the world would miss him because of his contributions.

I wanted to puke.

No one would miss him.

Bastian and Damian had confronted him a few days after I fled my wedding with Cole. And while I was in hiding, the old man told them the truth about their parents. He killed them, ruining their lives, all because he was mad and wanted more money.

So they drugged him.

Watched him die.

They couldn't kill someone as rich and notorious as Fitzy without a major police investigation. So they did it smartly, and now the old man was gone.

I took the top off my coffee cup and threw it at my grandfather's tomb. "Good fucking riddance."

Bastian spit on the mausoleum, right over the top of ADAMS on the stone. "Rot in hell, you bastard."

"You should look away, Grace," Damian said before he whipped out his dick and pissed on the tomb. "Who's a dirty, filthy animal now, you piece of shit?"

I remembered my grandfather calling Damian that when Bastian came to the house years ago. And Bastian defended his brother.

I walked away, laughing, and Alex stumbled into me, holding her baby bump. "Don't mind Damian." She giggled. "He's been the hardest one to train."

I laughed. "No, I get it. My grandfather treated him like shit, too."

Alex smiled. "Come over to the house. I want to get to know you better. And I know Bash does, too. He talks about you all the time."

Three months later, my grandfather's attorney called me. So I drove with Cole to The Hamptons, where we stayed at Cole's house on the beach. It was a short drive to my grandfather's house in Sagaponack.

All of my grandfather's heirs gathered in the ballroom at his house. At least a dozen people sat on elaborate wooden chairs facing the room's front. A man, who I assumed was Mr. Bollinger, my grandfather's attorney, stood in front of a podium.

On Cole's arm, I entered the room a few minutes late. My cousin Bastian was already here. Alex sat between Damian and Bastian, with their newborn daughter on her lap. Sofia was beautiful and had black hair and big blue eyes. I knew without asking she was Damian's little girl.

Bastian turned around as I found my seat a few rows

behind him. I waved, a gesture my cousin returned before Mr. Bollinger tapped the microphone with his finger.

"Thank you all for coming," Mr. Bollinger said. "Before I read the will, Fitzgerald wanted me to give each of his heirs a letter. But he requested you wait to open it until I call your name."

He lifted a stack of envelopes from the podium and handed them out, calling names until everyone had an envelope—a note from my grandfather. The envelope felt like a lead weight in my hand.

We rarely spent time together when he was alive. I couldn't imagine he had much to say. But I followed my grandfather's wishes and waited for his lawyer to read the will. He rambled names of men I didn't know who had inherited shares in my grandfather's companies.

Cole clutched my trembling hand on his knee and gave it a good squeeze. As I waited for him to call my name, my stomach twisted in knots.

Mr. Bollinger cleared his throat, eyes wide as he glanced down at the paper. His cheeks flushed with heat. "To Carl Wellington, I leave my late wife's vibrator so you can go fuck yourself."

It was nearly impossible not to laugh, but I somehow managed.

Cole covered his mouth with his hand to stifle his laughter, shaking his head. "Fucking Fitzy," he whispered. "That old bastard."

Most of the people in the room gasped. In a room full of classy people, no one dared to laugh at my grandfather's final fuck you to Carl Wellington.

Next, Arlo Salvatore inherited shares in Atlantic Airlines, the company Bastian and Damian owned. I wasn't sure how much the shares were worth, and Arlo's face gave nothing away.

"To Damian Salvatore, I leave you the contents of my basement," Mr. Bollinger said with a curious expression.

Damian ripped open his letter, his pale cheeks flushed with heat, and then handed the note to Bastian. I knew what was in the basement and cringed. Shackles he used to chain us to the wall. The cage he put me inside when he didn't feel like wasting his time fastening my ankles to the cold floor.

"To my grandson, Bastian Salvatore," Mr. Bollinger continued, "I leave my home in Sagaponack and its contents."

Bastian scowled at his letter. After Carl got a vibrator and Bastian and Damian looked enraged, I wondered what was inside my envelope.

"To my granddaughter, Grace Hale," Mr. Bollinger announced, and my heart sped abnormally. "I leave the rest of my estate."

I raised my hand. "Excuse me?"

Bastian turned in his chair and glanced over his shoulder at me. And then I realized everyone was staring at me. With so many gazes on me, my skin heated under their careful inspection.

I was the worst dressed in the room. Where everyone wore suits and dresses, I opted for a pair of spandex shorts, a tank top, and sandals. We'd come from the beach, and I didn't think this would be formal.

Besides, I was pregnant, and my clothes no longer fit well. Cole must have knocked me up the first time we didn't use a condom or right afterward because I was almost four months along.

"Yes?" Mr. Bollinger said.

"Exactly how much money is the rest of his estate?" I asked, my voice shaking from all the nerves coursing through my body.

Mr. Bollinger looked down at the podium and flipped through papers. "Including Mr. Adams' real estate, cars, jewelry, stock, bank accounts, and miscellaneous possessions." He looked up at me. "Approximately two hundred and fifty-seven billion dollars."

"No." I shook my head in disbelief. "That's too much money. He didn't even like me. And I don't want it."

"Grace." Bastian raised his hand to gain my attention. "You deserve it. Take the money."

Meeting Bastian's gaze, I nodded.

My cousin turned around and dipped his head down to kiss the baby's head. Alex smiled and rubbed her thumb across his cheek. They looked so in love. And when she looked at each of his brothers, I could see how much she loved them.

Cole hooked his arm around me and whispered, "You deserve this money, Grace. It's your birthright as an Adams."

"But I don't need billions of dollars."

"Of all the people in this room, you're the one who wants the money least. Greed and power motivate us, but not you. After everything Fitzy put you through, you deserve it."

A grin tugged at my mouth. "I'm rich."

He nodded, his expression mirroring mine. "You're wealthy. There's a difference."

"I have to do good with this money."

Cole raised my hand to his mouth and kissed my skin. "This is why I love you, Grace. You always want to do the right thing."

Mr. Bollinger stayed at the front of the room in case we had questions for him. I had tons, but I wasn't even sure where to begin. And then I remembered the letter I nearly crushed in my palm from clenching my fist.

I slid my finger beneath the fold and pulled out the thick notecard that said *From the Desk of Fitzgerald Archibald Adams IV* at the top in fancy script.

I hope the Adams curse finds you, too.

That was all it said.

I showed it to Cole.

He laughed. "Your grandfather had an interesting sense of humor."

After the will reading ended, I left the house with Cole and the Salvatores. They shielded me from a few men and women I assumed were family. Bastian wouldn't let them near me, swatting his hand at them like they were flies.

We stood in the circular driveway and waited for the valet to collect our cars.

Bastian bent down and whispered. "After I torch this place, I'll show you what the Elders key opens."

I smiled so wide my cheeks hurt. And when Bastian pulled me into his arms for a hug, I felt like I was part of his family. Like we had been cousins all these years and no time had passed.

I felt like I belonged.

Chapter Fifty-Six

GRACE

Two months later...

Cole drove us to the Salvatore Estate in his Ferrari with his hand on my thigh. He parked in front of the house 1.5 seconds later, flying down Founders Way in a flash.

Cole turned to look at me and tapped my thigh. "Stay there, Mrs. Marshall. I'll come and get you."

It wasn't my plan to be a mother this young. But I loved Cole and couldn't wait to start a family with him. Cole was so excited about being a dad.

We got married one month after I inherited the money. It was a small ceremony in his backyard. My biological father and the Colonel walked me down the aisle. And then, I stood at the cliff's edge that overlooked the beach with the love of my life. The waves crashed beneath us, and when Cole kissed me, the wind rustled my hair and blew it in my face.

It was perfect.

My sexy husband pulled open my door and helped me out of the car. His hand covered my stomach, moving in a circular motion over my baby bump. "I can't wait to meet him."

"We don't know it's a boy."

"Wishful thinking." Cole led me toward the house with his

hand on my lower back. "But I'll be happy either way. Girl or boy. It doesn't matter to me."

The doors flew open as we approached the entrance guarded by two men in suits. Bastian emerged from the house and welcomed me into his arms. Alex was at his side, carrying a beautiful baby girl on her hip. Sofia was a few months old and looked like Damian.

My cousin held me at arm's length, then his eyes lowered to my stomach. "You're finally showing. I could see the difference in Alex's body when she was six weeks," he said as he ushered us into the house and closed the door.

Alex laughed. "Because you were obsessing over me."

"It's my job to obsess over you." He winked at her. "I notice everything about my sweet cherry."

"I could tell the difference." Cole slipped his fingers between mine as we followed Bastian and Alex down the long tiled hallway. "I noticed Grace was pregnant before she did."

"Because I couldn't stop throwing up." I chuckled. "I turned into the Exorcist. It was disgusting."

"Morning sickness is the worst," Alex said with a sigh. She rubbed her stomach, already pregnant again with twins. "They don't tell you it's all-day sickness. For me, it's worse at night."

"Me, too," I replied. "The smell of fish, coffee, and red meat bothers me."

"Eggs for me," Alex said, her face twisted in disgust. "I can't smell them during the first trimester, or I will vomit."

"She threw up on my Ferragamo's when she was pregnant with Sofia." Bastian hooked his arm through hers and laughed. "We don't eat eggs in this house when Alex is pregnant."

She nodded. "I don't know what it is about eggs, but I can't deal with them when I'm pregnant. The smell of coffee bothers me, too."

"We don't drink coffee around here either," Bastian added. "It's like we're pregnant, too."

"Try living at Fort Marshall," Cole cut in. "We can't have steak or burgers without Grace running out of the dining room."

"I'm sure your dad loves that," Bastian shot back. "I bet he can't wait for you to move out."

"We're looking for somewhere to live in Devil's Creek," Cole told him. "I haven't had much luck."

"Pick a house," Bastian said with a devious expression. "We'll find a way to get it for you."

I didn't even want to know what that meant. The Salvatores had ties to organized crime families. They would probably threaten the homeowners to get us our dream home.

Cole didn't seem bothered by their methods and bobbed his head. "I'll let you know if I find something."

Damian, Marcello, and Luca waited for us on the veranda outback. They sat around a large circular table and drank the amber liquid in their highball glasses. Engaged in a heated conversation, the three went back and forth, speaking in Italian.

Their conversation ceased when they heard our footsteps, and heads snapped toward us. I used to think they were the scariest people I'd ever met. Well, the Salvatore brothers were still pretty damn intimidating. But they were not so bad over the past few months of getting to know Bastian and his brothers.

Luca still hadn't grown on me. He always had an attitude and didn't seem friendly to anyone, not even Cole. I had come to realize that was his personality. He spoke to people like he was more intelligent and better. Everyone in his life had just gotten used to it and didn't bother to put him in his place.

Bastian sat on Alex's right with his hand on her thigh while Damian slid his arm across her neck. Damian kissed Sofia's head and then kissed Alex on the lips.

Marcello smiled at me. I waved since he was the nicest of the brothers. He returned my gesture while Damian nodded.

Luca stared at me.

"What are you drinking, Marshall?" Luca asked Cole.

"Macallan, neat."

Luca poured a glass from the bottle in front of him and slid it across the table. I sat beside Cole, who drank from the glass and moved his arm behind me, resting his fingers on my shoulder.

Then Luca snapped his fingers, and a woman appeared at his side. "Bring my wife and Mrs. Marshall ginger ale. No ice."

Luca was such a control freak. But no one ever seemed to second-guess him. And he was right about what I had been drinking lately. In the middle of the night, I woke Cole up to get me a warm ginger ale to help with my stomach.

I was sipping from the glass a minute later and taking in the breeze blowing off the bay. We had the perfect view from their backyard, the same as Cole, but the Salvatore Estate was at the dead center of Founders Way.

Luca snapped his fingers at Marcello. "Go upstairs and grab my phone. I left it on my desk. The Sicilians are calling within the hour."

Marcello narrowed his eyes at him. "Are your legs broken?"

Before Luca could respond, Alex tilted her head back and laughed. "Luca, stop ordering your brother around like a servant."

He put his elbow on the table and looked over at her. "I *am* the boss of this family."

"You're not my boss," she said with a sweet smile.

He lowered his voice, but it only sounded more menacing. "Keep talking back, and I'll bend you over this table and spank your ass."

Alex tapped her nails against her glass, eyeing up Luca. "We have guests." She winked. "But maybe later."

He shook his head and sank back in his chair, tipping the glass to his lips.

"Cherry," Bastian groaned beside her. "Don't poke the dragon. He's not in a good mood."

"Clearly," Alex deadpanned.

"My mood is not a topic for conversation," Luca said harshly.

Bastian got up from the table, his gaze on Luca. "Take a walk with me to the wine cellar." Then he looked at Marcello, Damian, and Cole. "You too. Let's give the girls some time alone to talk. We got a new shipment of Macallan this morning."

Cole kissed my cheek. "I'll be right back."

I patted his thigh. "Go have some guy time. I'll be fine out here with Alex."

Damian kissed Alex and the baby. Bastian did the same, followed by Marcello, who called her princess. I wasn't sure if he was talking to Alex or the baby.

Then Luca stopped beside Alex and stared at her before he swiped his thumb across her bottom lip. She softly moaned at the sudden gesture. It was clear they had chemistry in the bedroom. A simple touch, and she was practically panting for more.

Once we were alone, Alex let out a deep breath. "Sorry about Luca's behavior. He's not usually this bad."

I almost laughed because she had no idea how rude he was the first time we met. And he hadn't improved all that much since.

"Can I ask you a personal question?"

She shifted Sofia on her lap and nodded. "Sure."

"How did you end up with four husbands?"

"I get that question a lot." Alex chuckled, then sipped from her glass. "I was supposed to marry Luca as part of a deal made by our families. But he made it his mission to ruin my life in high school. So I got to know Bastian better than Luca. Marcello was such a sweetheart, and he made it so easy to fall in love with him. And Damian..." She sighed. "He was so broken when we first met. But so was I. Together, we helped each other heal the wounds from our past."

"How about Luca?"

She smiled with her blue eyes that lit up her face. "I always wanted him. Even in high school when he did horrible things to me. But yeah, he was the last one I fell in love with. He made it so damn hard for me to lower my guard."

"The twins are his, right?"

Alex smoothed a hand over her stomach. She'd recently found out she was pregnant again. "Yeah. We got the paternity test back last week. Luca is the father."

"Any advice for a new mom?" I touched my belly. "I'm kinda freaking out and preparing for the worst."

"I was in labor with Sofia for six hours straight." She rolled her shoulders against the chair. "But it's different for everyone. You could deliver ten minutes after you get to the hospital. Who knows?"

"You delivered Sofia at the house, right?"

She bobbed her head to confirm. "I'm going to have all of my kids at home. My husbands pay my OBGYN a lot of money to be on call. How about you? What are your birth plans?"

"I don't know," I confessed. "I haven't given it much thought."

"You should think about having the baby at Fort Marshall. It took so much stress off me knowing I didn't have to rush to the hospital, eat gross food, and sleep in an uncomfortable bed."

"When you put it that way." I chuckled. "Maybe I should talk to Cole about doing a home birth."

"I would. It was the best decision Luca ever made for me."

"He does that a lot, huh?"

Her lips curled up into a tiny smile. "Yeah, but I like it. I never have to worry about a thing because Luca has already thought about it."

The men reappeared by the French doors, their conversation carrying across the backyard.

Cole dropped into the chair beside me. "What did we miss?"

"Nothing. Just talking shit about all of you."

He snickered. "Not about me. I'm the perfect husband."

I kissed his lips. "So true."

Luca and his brothers resumed their places at the table. He opened a new bottle of Macallan and passed around glasses.

"I think a toast is in order." Alex raised her glass of ginger ale that had one sip left. "To Cole and Grace having their first child."

"And to Grace becoming the next Elder of The Founders Society," Bastian added.

Everyone lifted their glasses.

"*Salute*," Luca said.

Chapter Fifty-Seven

GRACE

I sat at the head of a table large enough to seat fifty men. All of them stared at me, eying the Elders key in my hand. Now that I possessed the Adams fortune, it made me the wealthiest woman in the world.

I didn't want the money.

Or the power.

"Women are not allowed to become members of The Founders Society." Carl Wellington was the highest-ranking Elder now that my grandfather was gone and spoke for the group. "But it seems Fitzy has left us with a bit of a predicament." His gaze moved to the other three Elders. "However, The Devil's Knights made an exception to allow my granddaughter to become their queen. And with that precedent set, I don't see any reason we can't allow Grace to maintain control of the Adams' right to a seat at this table."

A few of The Founders stiffened. Some shook their heads or cleared their throats to disagree. They didn't like the idea of me joining their elite society. This was a rich boy's club, and I didn't fit their ideal of being a Founder.

The Elders made up the top five spots on the Forbes Billionaires list. I would never go back to being an Adams. Now, I was Grace Marshall.

"All in favor?" Carl asked the Elders.

Archibald glanced at me, one eyebrow raised. "Do you understand the power that key holds, young lady?"

Cole's grandfather looked at me like I was a little girl. In his eyes, I was just a kid. The same as his grandson.

"Yes, I do." My eyes drifted to Bastian, who sat at the opposite end of the table beside the Salvatore brothers and his adoptive father. "That's why I want Bastian to take my place. He's an Adams, too, and risked his life to steal this key from our grandfather. I'm only alive because of him. If not for his selflessness, I wouldn't be sitting here."

An echo of shock rang out among the men at the table.

Gasps.

Whispers.

They couldn't believe anyone would give away this much power. Even Bastian looked surprised, his mouth hanging open.

Luca Salvatore smirked as if he'd won. His family had just been admitted into The Founders Society because he married Alex. She was the only reason they were allowed to be members.

But now?

If Bastian were allowed to take my place, it would give the Salvatores the freedom they needed. The other Founders would no longer look down on them for not being descendants of the Founding Fathers. I understood what it was like not fitting into this world, even though I was born into it.

"I just want to know one thing," I said to Bastian. "Why did you take the key and give it to me? You didn't even know me."

He leaned back in the leather chair and studied my face before saying, "A man approached me outside my high school. I was a kid and didn't know any better. He said he would give me information about my parents' deaths if I stole the key from Fitzy and gave it to you."

I nodded. "I would have done the same thing to know more about my parents."

"I also did it because he said it would save your life. Viktor's information against Fitzy kept you alive." He tipped his head at the key cradled between my fingers. "An Elders key is power, Grace. I hope you understand what you're giving up."

"I understand." I opened my palm and held out the key. "You deserve it more than I do. It's yours if you want it."

"Don't be an idiot. Take it," Luca hissed under his breath, tapping Bastian on the back when he didn't immediately respond.

Bastian leaned over and muttered something to Luca, his voice so low I couldn't hear him. Then he rose from the chair and strolled toward me, passing two dozen men as he approached. Some men reached out and touched his arm, but he didn't look at them. He kept his eyes on me.

"I'll tell you what." Bastian lifted the key from my hand and tucked it into the inner pocket of his suit jacket. "We'll share it."

"That's not allowed," Jonathan Jay interjected. "Five Elders. Five keys. Not six."

"I can be Grace's proxy, can I not?" Bastian stared at the older man with black hair streaked gray. "It's in The Founders Society Charter that an Elder can appoint a family member to serve as proxy if otherwise incapacitated."

Jonathan wrinkled his nose. "She looks healthy to me."

Bastian shook his head. "Grace is pregnant. She needs to focus on her family."

Cole smiled at me as I rubbed my stomach. The doctor pinpointed my conception date to the week of my wedding to Rhys. So even if I stayed married to that miserable bastard, I would have carried a part of Cole inside me. Thankfully, my drama with Rhys was about to be over soon.

"This is precisely why we don't allow women into The

Founders Society," Henry Jefferson said with an attitude. "Their job is at home. Not in the boardroom."

"No offense, Henry," Bastian shot back. "But I respectfully disagree with you. Alex is pregnant again, this time with twins, and I can assure you, my wife is just as formidable as the men sitting at this table. And so is Grace."

"Let's take a vote, gentleman," Carl said to the Elders. "All in favor of Bastian serving as Grace's proxy?"

Carl raised his hand.

So did Archibald.

Henry Jefferson glared at Carl, who raised an eyebrow, giving him a menacing look. Jonathan Jay also hesitated. His eyes moved between the two Elders who voted in favor.

Jonathan snapped his head to me. "You better not make me regret this."

"You won't," I promised.

I knew Bastian would do an excellent job on my behalf. He was tough and could handle these old bastards.

Jonathan raised his hand, leaving Henry to decide my fate. He didn't seem to like me all that much. None of them did. I could only imagine what this must have been like for them. They went from having my grandfather telling them what to do to a young girl with no real-life experience.

"Fine," Henry hissed. "But Bastian is to speak for the Adams family."

"He will," I agreed. "I don't want any part of what goes on here."

We were at a secure location inside Independence Hall in Philadelphia, where our ancestors signed the Declaration of Independence in 1776. Like Fort Marshall, this place had hidden doors and secret passages, so we could access the building without being seen.

It was close to midnight, many hours after the guided tours ended for the day. The walls were soundproof, anyway. But once we stepped outside these four walls, we'd be greeted with the familiar sounds of the city. I was staying in Philly with

Cole for a few more days before heading back to Devil's Creek to finalize the plans for our son's birth.

"The vote is unanimous," Carl announced to the room. "Bastian Salvatore will serve as the fifth Elder on behalf of Grace."

Bastian smiled down at me before gazing at his brothers and adoptive father. They were grinning like maniacs.

My cousin bent down to my height, clutching my shoulder. "After we deal with the Vanderbilts, I'll show you what the key opens."

Rhys strolled into the room with Remington, wearing suits and smug expressions.

"Remington," Carl said in a stern tone. "You know why you're here."

He nodded. "I do."

Carl shoved a stack of papers across the table and chucked a pen at Remington's chest. "Sign and get out of my sight. You're a disgrace to our society."

Rhys could barely look at anyone as his father scribbled his name on the pages. But his eyes found mine for a moment. A look of sadness washed over his dark features. He was so beautiful, and now that I knew him better, I could see he was sorry. But only because he lost.

"What is Remington signing?" I whispered to Bastian.

"He's forfeiting the Vanderbilts' right to the common equity. All of The Founders are given an equal share, except the Elders. They have a lot more."

"So I get more than what our grandfather left us?"

He nodded. "Billions more."

After Remington signed the last paper, he set the pen on the table, a look of defeat on his handsome face. He couldn't have been much older than his early fifties. Not an ounce of gray hair. No wrinkles. I could see what Rhys would look like in twenty-five years.

"The Vanderbilts are exiled from The Founders Society," Carl told Remington and Rhys. "You are to have no contact with any member of The Devil's Knights or The Founders Society. I would suggest fleeing the country. You're finished here."

Cole said exile from The Founders Society was worse than death. Overnight, the Vanderbilts went from one of the wealthiest families in the world to bankrupt and connectionless. No one would go near them out of fear of angering The Founders.

"Understood," Remington said with a nod.

He turned to leave, grabbing his son by the shoulder to steer him out of the room.

I got out of the chair and strolled toward them. "Rhys, wait."

Before he reached the door, he spun around to look at me.

"You could have gotten further if you weren't such a dick to me. I would have helped you." I shook my head, hating the sight of him, but I had to get this off my chest. "We could have been friends. Using me to get ahead backfired. I hope this is a lesson you never forget."

"I was only trying to save my family," he said in a hushed tone, head hung low. "I never meant for you to get hurt."

"Well, I did. And God only knows what you would have done to me if Cole hadn't contacted my father and saved me from our wicked union."

"If it's any consolation," he said as his eyes met mine, blowing out a deep breath. "I'm sorry for everything. I like you. It was never personal."

"I said yes to marrying Cole at our wedding." I wanted to piss him off, hoping it would sting a little. "And when I took my vows, I was pregnant with Cole's child. So even when you thought you won, you didn't. I just let you believe you did."

His eyebrows furrowed at my confession. "It was always going to be Marshall, anyway. I could see you two were in love with each other. But I couldn't help myself. I had to have you. And my family needed the dowry."

I wasn't the same girl who arrived at Fort Marshall months

ago. That version of Grace Hale didn't exist. I was tainted by Rhys and loved by Cole. Between the two, I found the perfect balance of who I wanted to become.

"I feel sorry for you, Rhys. I even wanted to give you the benefit of the doubt because horrible people raised you." My eyes darted to Remington, who stood in the entryway, before returning my gaze to Rhys. "But then I thought about how I was raised. By an abusive grandfather who made me think I was the daughter of a terrorist who killed my mother. You can use your family as an excuse for why you do horrible things to people, but if that's true, then so could I. I could have been like you. But I chose to see the good in people. That's why I gave you a chance, even when Cole warned me about you."

He bobbed his head, swiping a longer strand of black hair away from his face. "You're right. I fucked up. And I'm sorry."

Pressing my lips together, I nodded. "Goodbye, Rhys."

He winked. "Bye, princess."

Chapter Fifty-Eight

After Carl adjourned the meeting, Bastian guided me beneath the building. No one was allowed to come with us. Only the Elders could use the key to access the secret door.

In typical Founder fashion, we moved through hidden passages until we were directly beneath the ground level. It smelled like dirt and sewage down here, and with me being pregnant, I wanted to puke. Even the slightest smells turned my inside to mush.

Bastian stopped in front of an ancient door and removed the skeleton key. He turned it in the old lock and smiled when it clicked into place. "Are you ready to see what kind of power this key holds?"

I nodded. "Open it."

He pushed on the door. But as I had expected, we needed more than the key to access what was behind it. Before Carl left, he transferred the security access to Bastian. I would only have to intervene if he was unavailable.

My cousin put his hand on the scanner on the wall, then leaned forward to let the computer take a retinal scan.

I laughed. "Why even use the key if no one can get past this door?"

He chuckled, giving me a light shrug. "The Elders keys are

symbolic. You have to possess the key to access what lies behind this door." He tipped his head. "After you."

"But how did our grandfather get in here without the key?"

He shrugged. "I think that's why he wanted Carl Wellington's Black Book."

I entered a massive room with dozens of bookshelves and turned to look at Bastian, one eyebrow raised. "Seriously? All of this secrecy for a library?"

"It's not what you think." He tapped on my back and followed me inside, shutting the door behind us. "Take a look at the names on the shelves. See if you recognize any of them."

Despite the age of the exterior, the room looked as if it had been updated in the past ten years. The decor was simple but modern, with paintings and art that looked priceless donning the walls and tables. Of course, The Founders did nothing half-assed. Only the best for the five wealthiest families in the world.

There was a lounge area on the right side of the room. I imagined Carl and the other Elders sitting in the leather armchairs, smoking cigars and drinking scotch from the bar. It looked like an old saloon, reminding me of Fitzy's office at his home.

After Bastian inherited the mansion, he and Damian burnt it to the ground. I was glad that place was nothing but ash. It held nothing but nightmares for the three of us.

I took my time inspecting each shelf as Bastian did the same. He seemed to know what he would find here, yet he looked equally surprised.

"Hmmm…" Bastian removed a box from the shelf and set it on a round table to dig through its contents. The exterior said *JFK Assassination*. He lifted a few photos and showed them to me. "This is interesting."

I nodded. "How did The Founders get this stuff?"

"Secrets keep us in power," he explained. "The Founders

have collected information on every major event over centuries. They have dirt on every politician in the world. There's no one they can't bribe."

My eyes traced over a few boxes on the shelf, widening at one with the name of the President of the United States. And as I walked each aisle, I saw the names of people I recognized throughout history. No wonder why my grandfather had so much money and control. He only needed to use this information to get ahead.

"Do the other Founders ever get access to this room?" I asked Bastian.

He shook his head. "No, but my dad would kill to see what's in here. We have a saying in Devil's Creek that originated from the Salvatores."

"Secrets are commodities?" I asked him since I'd heard it plenty of times before.

He bobbed his head to confirm. "If you collect enough secrets, you have more power than money." A sly grin tugged at his mouth. "Was this what you expected when I handed you the key?"

I shook my head. "Not even close."

Bastian dumped the photos and papers into the box and returned them to the shelf. "Ready to go? I promised Alex dinner at Del Frisco's. We're eating downstairs in the vault. You and Cole should come with us."

I smiled. "Yeah, we would love that."

None of this would have been possible if my father hadn't sent that man to Bastian's school. And my grandfather probably would have found a way to get rid of me.

At least the good guys won.

About fucking time.

Chapter Fifty-Nine

COLE

Five months later…

My cell phone rang with a call from Grace. She was ready to have Hale any day, and I counted the days until I could meet my son.

I raised the phone to my ear. "Hey, baby. Did your water break yet?"

"No," Grace groaned into the phone. "I wish. I've been having cramps. And he's been moving around like crazy. I can't wait to get Hale out of my belly. Your son is possessed."

Resting my shoe on my knee, I leaned back in the chair and laughed. "Hang in there. He'll be here soon."

"Easy for you to say." She laughed. "You got to have fun making the baby, but you didn't have to carry him. Try having aches, pains, heartburn, and a million other symptoms for nine months. I will lose my mind if he doesn't come soon."

My assistant entered my office, and I raised my hand, telling her to give me a minute. Despite my request, she shook her head and entered the room.

I moved the phone away from my mouth and raised an eyebrow, suggesting she speak.

"Mr. Battle just called for you. It's urgent. He said to get to the lab."

I nodded. "Okay, I'll be there in a minute."

"No, he said now." She bit her lip as if she feared for her job by telling me what to do. "He sounded upset before the line disconnected."

"Thanks, Cindy."

I shot up from the chair and rushed out of my office. "Hey, Grace. I hate to cut our call short, but Drake needs me."

"Okay," she cooed. "I'll call if my water breaks or anything eventful happens with Hale."

"Sounds good."

Before I could hang up, an explosion above me echoed throughout the building. It sounded like a nuclear weapon detonated, and the structure was about to crack in half.

Grace gasped in my ear. "What was that?"

"I don't know." I power walked past the elevator bank and went straight to the end of the hall, toward Drake's private elevator. I hit the button on the wall. "I have to go, baby."

"Cole," she whimpered. "Tell me the truth."

"I think we're under attack."

A second later, a woman's voice floated through the loudspeakers. "Activating Battle King Protocol."

No!

"If anything happens to me, I will activate the Battle King protocol," Drake had told me on the day I started working for him. "Lovelace will lock down all of my company's buildings and homes. You're the only person, other than Tate, with access to override the system."

If Drake activated that protocol, it means he could be… No, don't think about the worst-case scenario.

Even though Viktor wasn't the leader of The Lucaya Group, it didn't take the target off our backs. They wanted Drake's tech. In the wrong hands, Lovelace was a weapon of mass destruction.

"Fuck," I groaned, hitting the button on the wall repeatedly, but nothing was happening. It didn't even light up. "Fuck, fuck, fuck."

"Cole, you're scaring me."

"Initiating sequence in five, four," Lovelace said over the speaker.

I abandoned the elevator and headed for the stairwell, rushing down the hallway.

"Three, two, one," Lovelace continued.

Metal bars inched down from the ceiling, caging the employees into their offices and conference rooms. People screamed and begged to let them out. Those in the hallway with me halted in place, unsure what to do. Then, a thick layer of bulletproof glass slid out from the walls, locking us inside.

"Grace, I have to hang up now," I said calmly. "I need to deactivate the protocol. If you don't hear from me within the hour, I want you to call Sonny."

Bastian would have been my first choice, but he was in Italy with Alex and his brothers.

"Cole, what's going on?"

"Baby, I don't know. I heard an explosion."

Grace breathed heavily in the receiver.

The elevators were on lockdown, and when this protocol was activated, only my keycard would work. So I jammed it into the slot on the wall to open the elevator doors. Once inside, I repeated the same process, and a panel opened, allowing me to enter my passcode.

"One hour," I said as the doors closed, and the car shot upward toward the fifty-first floor. "Do you understand me, Grace? I'm fine. Don't worry about me. But if you don't hear from me, call Sonny. He knows what to do."

"Is Drake okay?"

Before Drake left this morning, he said he had a bad feeling. He was in New Mexico with Tate doing a demo of

Lovelace because the military wanted to use the AI to deploy weapons.

"I'll find out." Running as fast as I could up the stairs, I climbed to the fifty-first floor in record time, scanned my palm again, and opened the door. "I'm hanging up now. I love you."

"I love you, too, Cole."

I shoved the phone into my pocket and covered my mouth and nose with my jacket. The floor smelled of lingering smoke, most of which had been sucked up by the ventilation system.

I took a deep breath and raced down the corridor. Drake's lab didn't have a door. It was completely blown off the hinges and lying on the floor.

I poked my head inside the room. Nothing looked out of the ordinary. The supercomputer was untouched, surrounded by floor-to-ceiling glass with an independent power source and cooling system.

I took off in the opposite direction and marched into Drake's office. Again, everything looked in order. None of this made any sense. Why didn't they take the computers if they wanted Drake's AI software?

Because they wanted Drake. They needed his brain.

His access and knowledge.

I dialed Drake, and no surprise, the call went straight to voicemail. Then, I tried Tate Maxwell since he was the head of security and got the same result. Only two people knew all of Lovelace's storage locations. Drake and Tate. Even I wasn't privy to that information.

Fuck.

Lovelace wasn't the target.

It was Drake.

And Tate.

My stomach clenched at the thought of what my cousin would endure at the hands of The Lucaya Group. All Knights went through months of hell during initiation. It bonded The Knights in the same pledge class.

Tate was a Marine before he left to join Drake at Battle Industries. He could handle the torture and beatings they would go through at the hands of terrorists. But I wondered if I would ever see them again. And if they didn't survive, what would I tell Olivia?

Fuck. No.

Don't think about it.

I entered the lab and went straight for the glass-paneled room at the back of the space. Whoever attacked this floor couldn't get past the layer of security.

I let the scanner read my handprint and retinas. Once inside the room, I typed the passcodes into the computer. I was then prompted for my handprint again, holding my palm to the device on the desk. A popup on the screen prompted me to stare directly at the red dot.

"Cole Marshall accepted," the female voice said. "Initiating deactivation sequence in five, four, three, two, one."

***

After a thirty-minute drive from the office, I pulled up to my house and didn't even bother to turn off the Ferrari before I raced inside. Grace called on my way home to tell me her water had broken.

Running upstairs to the birthing suite, I didn't stop until I was inside the room, breathless. My wife was in bed with her thighs spread, cradling her baby bump.

A pained expression crossed her beautiful face as our eyes met. "Cole," she groaned. "You made it."

"Of course I did." I got on the bed beside her and kissed her forehead, wiping the sweaty strands away. "Nothing could stop me from watching you deliver Hale." I squeezed her hand. "I'll be here every step of the way. It's okay, baby."

"Did The Knights find Drake?" Grace choked out, wincing with each contraction.

I shook my head. "They're out looking for him. The Salvatores are on their way home from Italy. Marcello has a lead on Drake."

She screamed when she had another contraction. "Oh God, Cole. It hurts."

"The doctor is on his way. Any minute now, baby." I placed my hand over hers on her stomach. "Hang in there."

Seven hours later, Grace delivered our beautiful baby boy. She lay back on the pillows, eyes half-closed, holding our son. His tiny fingers wrapped around one of hers, and she smiled.

Hale Colton Marshall.

Grace's adoptive father moved on to his next duty station after our wedding. And since he was the reason she stayed alive for all these years, we wanted to honor him. If we had a girl, we would have named her Willow, after my mother.

"He's perfect." I bent down to kiss him and brushed my fingers over Hale's white-blond hair, the same color as mine. "We make good-looking kids. We should have another one."

She giggled. "He ripped apart my vagina coming into this world. Let me heal before we think about having another kid."

I turned onto my side and kissed her lips. "I love you, Grace. I knew you were the one from the moment we met. And I can't wait to have more kids with you. I want to give you everything you never had growing up."

"I love you more." A smile tugged at her delicious mouth. "I knew the second your fingers brushed against mine while we watched Captain America that you would be in my life forever."

"Speaking of Cap." I grabbed the remote from the night-stand, turned on the television, and hit Play. "How about a Marvel marathon? I have a feeling Hale will be a fan of The Avengers."

Grace trailed her fingers down my arm as she held a sleeping Hale between her breasts. She was always so petite until her body changed from having Hale. And I loved the extra weight on her.

"I think Hale is going to be on Team Stark." A smile tipped up the corners of her mouth. "He's going to be a troublemaker like Tony."

My cell phone dinged, interrupting our perfect moment. Before I glanced at the screen, I knew it would be Marcello Salvatore and dreaded telling Grace the bad news.

MARCELLO

We leave at 2200 with Alpha Command.

COLE

I'll be there. Grace just delivered Hale.

MARCELLO

Congrats.

Sorry to do this to you. But Drake needs you.

I typed a quick reply and stuffed the phone into my pocket.

Grace glanced at me. "You have to go, don't you?"

I nodded. "I'm sorry, baby. I've trained with Marcello and his team. And I have insider knowledge about Drake and his tech. They need my expertise."

"You're my hero, Cole." She clutched my hand and grinned. "One day, I will tell our son stories about his father's bravery. Find Drake. We'll be waiting for you when you return."

Epilogue

GRACE

One year later

Cole moved behind me and slipped his tie over my eyes, pulling it tight. He pressed his lips to the shell of my ear, his breath sending chills down my arms. "I have a surprise for you, Mrs. Marshall."

"Are we playing a game?"

I touched the silky fabric, and Cole grabbed my hand, leading me down the hallway.

"No peeking."

"Where are we going?"

"Shh… Don't ruin the surprise. I want you to hear and smell everything."

Excitement bubbled in my chest as we walked out of the house. Cole guided me into the passenger seat of his car and drove off the estate with the top down, the wind blowing through my hair.

He didn't speak a word.

Even when I asked where we were going, he shushed me. But after a few minutes, the car slowed to a stop.

I reached up to touch the tie covering my eyes. "Am I allowed to look yet?"

"Not yet, brat. Be patient."

My nose perked up at the scent of the bay. A distinct smell I would know anywhere after living in Devil's Creek.

Cole opened my door and scooped me into his arms, removing the tie from my eyes. "Surprise."

I glanced around at our new scenery, shocked to be standing in front of a mansion not as large as Fort Marshall but equally imposing.

"What are we doing here?"

He bent down to kiss my lips. "It's time for us to move out of Fort Marshall. We're married." His hand dropped to my stomach. "We're having our second child and need a place to raise our kids."

We named Hale after my adoptive father because of his sacrifices to keep me safe. Without him, I wouldn't be alive. I wouldn't have the life I had always envisioned with Cole. And I wouldn't be carrying our daughter, who we planned to name Willow after Cole's mom.

"I love it." I pressed my lips to his. "And I love you."

He caressed my cheek with his hand, and I leaned into his touch. "I love you, too."

Cole clutched my shoulders and steered me toward the backyard. We stared at the bay from the large veranda as the waves crashed on the beach.

"This place is incredible," I muttered. "Hale is going to love it."

Our son enjoyed sitting on the beach on my lap and watching the waves crash. And for the next few hours, he was with Alex and Bastian having a playdate with Sofia and the twins. I could already see Hale being best friends with Michelangelo and Leonardo Salvatore. They were only a few months apart and seemed to gravitate toward each other.

Our new house had balconies overlooking the water and an infinity pool. I envisioned our children running through the yard and playing on the beach.

It was perfect.

Neither of us wanted to move out of Devil's Creek. The Knights were here. And Bastian lived down the block from us. Alex had become my best friend over the past year, and I couldn't imagine not having her close by.

For most of my life, I had no family or friends. Only the Colonel. Now I had Cole and the Marshalls. I had my biological father and Vera. And the Salvatores, the Battles, and The Knights.

I was happy and content.

"How about we go inside and christen the house?" Cole slid his arm across my back and tapped his fingers on my hip. "We have a lot of surfaces to break in."

I laughed at his suggestion and let him lead the way. Cole lifted me onto the granite counter in the kitchen. He shoved up my dress and pushed my panties to the side, dragging his finger down my wet slit. And then he buried himself inside me, claiming me on the counter of our new home.

I winced when Willow kicked.

Cole thrust harder, not realizing my eyes snapped shut from the baby and not his big cock. But then his eyes lowered, his pace slowing as he moved his hand in a circle.

"She kicked me. Am I hurting her?"

I shook my head. "No, we're perfect." I dug my heel into his backside. "Don't stop. Willow likes the sound of our voices."

His lips brushed mine as they curled up into a smile. "Then I guess I better give you something to scream about."

Dirty Heirs Sneak Peek

Get to know Sonny and find out what happens the day Drake is taken…

Read a Sneak Peek of Dirty Heirs

The Frost Society

Welcome to The Frost Society!

You have been chosen to join an elite secret society for readers who love dark romance books.

When you join The Frost Society, you will get instant access to all of my novels, bonus scenes, and digital content like new-release eBooks and serialized stories. You can also get discounts for my book and merch shop, exclusive book boxes, and so much more.

Learn more at JillianFrost.com/The-Frost-Society

Also by Jillian Frost

Princes of Devil's Creek

Cruel Princes

Vicious Queen

Savage Knights

Battle King

Boardwalk Mafia

Boardwalk Kings

Boardwalk Queen

Boardwalk Reign

Devil's Creek Standalone Novels

Wicked Union

The Darkest Prince

For a complete list of books, visit JillianFrost.com.

Get to know Jillian Frost

Watch Jillian's latest videos on TikTok
@jillianfrostbooks

Become part of a reader community when you join Jillian's
private Facebook group called Frost's Fangirls

Check out the latest teasers and updates on Jillian's Instagram
@jillianfrostbooks

About the Author

Jillian Frost is a dark romance author who believes even the villain deserves a happily ever after. When she's not plotting all the ways to disrupt the lives of her characters, you can usually find Jillian by the pool, soaking up the Florida sunshine.

Learn more about Jillian's books at JillianFrost.com